A rodeo cowboy could distract her family from the tough announcement about her next career move…

"Are you any good?" Georgie asked.

"Top ten calf roping and bronc riding in the country." The cowboy shrugged.

"It's like a full-time job."

"You don't have to sound so surprised."

"That's impressive." And exactly the thing that would impress Georgie's newly found grandfather and her ranch-loving cousins. That wild, stupid idea took hold again, stronger than ever. "So, I take it you've never been anyone's pretend date before?"

"When I date, I make sure it's for real." There was a vow in his voice and a guarantee in his gaze.

What would a real date with Mr. Green Eyes entail?

He was a stranger. Yet he made her want to take a dare.

And Georgie never felt daring…until now.

Dear Reader,

I have a large extended family that doesn't live close, but we share a special bond that when we do see each other, it's as if we were together just last week, not months or years ago. It's something I treasure.

My daughter is currently researching colleges. One is located in the same city where my cousin lives. I suggested that would be a good choice. My daughter wanted to know how my cousin is related to her. I told her: *she's family*. It's that simple. If my daughter will be a plane ride away, I'd like her to be near family. And I know without asking that my cousin would be there if my daughter ever needed anything. That's what family does.

Montana Wedding brings family, new and old, together for a Christmas wedding. Georgie Harrison and Zach Evans learn to trust each other and the people surrounding them. After all, sometimes family does know what's best for us, if only we open our hearts and listen.

Connect with me on Facebook (carilynnwebb) or Twitter (@carilynnwebb) or via my website.

Hope you have many special moments this holiday season with your family. And all the best for a wonderful New Year.

Cari

HEARTWARMING

Montana Wedding

—

Cari Lynn Webb

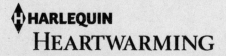

HARLEQUIN®
HEARTWARMING™

ISBN-13: 978-1-335-88997-3

Montana Wedding

This edition published by arrangement with Harlequin Books S.A.

For questions and comments about the quality of this book, please contact us at CustomerService@Harlequin.com.

Harlequin Enterprises ULC
22 Adelaide St. West, 40th Floor
Toronto, Ontario M5H 4E3, Canada
www.Harlequin.com

Printed in U.S.A.

Cari Lynn Webb lives in South Carolina with her husband, daughters and assorted four-legged family members. She's been blessed to see the power of true love in her grandparents' seventy-year marriage and her parents' marriage of over fifty years. She knows love isn't always sweet and perfect—it can be challenging, complicated and risky. But she believes happily-ever-afters are worth fighting for. She loves to connect with readers.

Books by Cari Lynn Webb

Harlequin Heartwarming

City by the Bay Stories

The Charm Offensive
The Doctor's Recovery
Ava's Prize
Single Dad to the Rescue
In Love by Christmas
Her Surprise Engagement

A Heartwarming Thanksgiving
"Wedding of His Dreams"

Make Me a Match
"The Matchmaker Wore Skates"

Visit the Author Profile page
at Harlequin.com for more titles.

To my cousins. With love.

Special thanks to Kathryn Lye, my editor,
for continuing to challenge me to become a
better writer. To my writing tribe: Amy Vastine,
Anna J. Stewart, Carol Ross and
Melinda Curtis—I'm so blessed to call you
friends and to be writing with you again.
To my family—there aren't enough words to say
how much I love you all.

PROLOGUE

EXCITEMENT SWIRLED THROUGH Georgie Harrison like stripes on a candy cane.

Christmas Eve, one of the best days, according to her and other eight-year-olds everywhere, had finally arrived.

Georgie surveyed the kitchen island. Flour covered the marble countertop like snow. Cookie cutters rested on a large cutting board. The sweet scent of sugar and cinnamon filled the air.

And caution wrapped around Georgie's joy like the plastic cover protecting that candy cane. After all, accidents could happen, even on special days. Watching over her four sisters was especially important and a duty Georgie willingly accepted.

She checked the cookie sheets cooling on the stove top. The hot trays were far enough away from the decorating station and her sisters' fingers. No one would get burned. Georgie picked up the rolling pin and set it back in its holder.

"Mrs. Claus needs her own cookies, too." Fiona, the youngest of the five Harrison sisters, set a star-shaped cookie on a paper plate. "These are for her."

"We're making cookies for Santa." Georgie nudged Fee, adjusting her sister until both her bare feet were centered on the stool she stood on. Fee might be steadier on her feet now that she was six years old, but falls happened at any age. Lily was proof of that. And Georgie had to be alert and prepared. "Mrs. Claus has to stay home."

"That's not fair." Fiona frowned.

"Yes, it is." Georgie sat on her stool at the island and dipped a thin spatula into the bowl of bright green frosting. "Mrs. Claus is the one who takes care of the elves and Santa. If an elf gets sick or hurt, she has to be there to help them."

"What if Santa is hurt dropping off presents tonight?" Amanda, one-third of the Harrison triplet trio that included Georgie, tossed a handful of glittery silver sugar across a row of frosted cookies.

"Then the reindeers will fly him back home." Georgie slathered a thick layer of green frosting over her tree-shaped cookie and grinned. Everyone got better at home.

Georgie had cared for Lily, the final triplet, after Lily returned home from her accident, and her sister had improved. Georgie added, "That way, Mrs. Claus can make Santa feel better."

"Santa can't be sick." Lily walked into the kitchen and washed her hands. She had skipped cookie making to play soccer with her best friend, Danny Belmonte. One of the things you could still do in San Diego even though it was December.

Lily and Danny had already built snowmen out of sand and decorated palm trees in the front yard with Christmas lights. All thanks to the girls' dad, Rudy Harrison, who had explained snow wasn't necessary to get into the California Christmas spirit. What they needed, he'd said, was a little imagination.

"We won't get any presents if Santa is sick." Bits of grass stuck to Lily's shirt, and mud smeared both her cheeks and forehead.

Georgie concentrated on Lily's face, searching for scratches underneath the dirt, making certain her sister didn't need her care.

"No presents?" Fiona pressed her sprinkle- and frosting-coated fingers against her pale cheeks. Her bottom lip trembled. "But we gotta have those. I've been very good."

"Mom!" Peyton shouted from the family room. The oldest Harrison sister stood in front of the Christmas tree, where she'd been organizing the gifts from family by size and name.

Peyton scowled at Georgie and yelled again. "Mom! Georgie is messing up Christmas Eve."

"Aunt Pru will be here in an hour." Susan Harrison rushed into the kitchen and hung up the cordless phone on the wall. Her gaze darted around the kitchen. "We need to finish the cookies, clean up and be ready for family pictures. We can do this."

The Harrison sisters ignored their mother's instructions and instead launched their complaints like rapid-fire snowballs.

"Santa is sick," Fee cried.

"Georgie said so," Amanda added.

"I did not," Georgie hollered.

Lily steamrolled over Georgie's denial. "Santa had to go home for the night. And it's Christmas Eve. The most important night of the year."

Fee threw her hands over her head. "We don't get no presents."

Amanda rounded on Georgie. "It's all Georgie's fault."

"It is not." Georgie jumped from her stool and straightened. Still she failed to look Amanda in the eyes. Her mother promised Georgie every night that she would grow taller soon, the same as Lily and Amanda, who were identical twins in their triplet trio with Georgie.

Lily and Amanda had sprouted like sunflowers, according to Great-Aunt Pru. Georgie might lack her sprout, but Pru had told her to always face the sun. Then Pru would hand Georgie a book from her private collection to nourish her mind, of course. After all, the tallest sunflower wasn't always the one with the strongest roots. But Georgie liked the endless supply of books and simply wanted to be as tall as her sisters, to face them eye to eye.

"Santa is only going home *if* he gets sick." Georgie set her hands on her hips and tipped her chin up. She might be short, but she was still a Harrison. "I never said he was sick."

Amanda opened her mouth.

"Girls." Their mother raised her voice above the beep of the timer on the oven. Her tone was firm. "Girls! That's enough. No one is sick."

"Told you so." Georgie handed her mom the pair of oven mitts. None of the sisters, even Peyton, the fourth grader, could take out the cookies. Their mother had declared they had to be twelve years old to reach into a hot oven.

Amanda narrowed her eyes at Georgie, a small hint that Georgie hadn't won yet, and returned to her cookie decorating.

"Peyton, find the cookie containers in the pantry. Fiona and Lily, you two go get cleaned up." Their mother tugged on the oven mitts and continued issuing her orders. "Amanda and Georgie, you are on dish duty. One washes and one dries."

A collection of sighs shifted through the kitchen.

"Move. Faster!" Their mother clapped her mitts together. The timer blared again, signaling the cookies were more than finished. "Aunt Pru is coming and we can't have our guests think we live in such a mess. And what will Santa think?"

That got the girls' full attention. Suddenly five sisters scrambled into action.

Peyton raced into the pantry. Lily guided Fee off the stool. Amanda sprinted to the sink and Georgie grabbed a clean towel from the drawer for drying. Their mother opened the oven door at the same time Lily and Fee squeezed behind her.

Georgie watched the oven mitt slip off and her mom's bare forearm press against the inside of the oven door, then heard her mom's loud gasp. Georgie dropped her drying towel and lunged forward. "Mom, are you okay?"

The oven door slammed shut. Her mom shook off her mitts and studied her arm. "It's nothing."

Georgie rushed into the pantry and grabbed the first-aid kit. She'd convinced her parents to put first-aid kits on both floors of their house, as well as inside the garage and on the screened-in porch, for easy access after Lily's accident.

"But you're hurt." Fee wrapped her arms around their mom's waist.

"She's burned." Amanda gaped. "Look how red her arm is."

"It's fine." Their mom rubbed her forehead. Her voice shook.

"Mom, you need to put your arm under cold water." Georgie guided her mom and Fee toward the kitchen sink and motioned for Amanda to turn the faucet on.

Peyton and Lily crowded closer. Worry worked across their faces. Georgie tested the water. "It's not supposed to be too cold."

"How do you know that?" Amanda asked.

"I read it in the safety book for kids that Dad got me on our birthday." Georgie made sure the water flowed over her mom's arm.

"What else does your book say?" her mother asked.

Georgie chewed on her bottom lip. "You can't pop the blisters. That's bad."

Peyton leaned closer. "Does she have blisters?"

"Bad burns get bad blisters," Georgie stated.

Fee buried her head in their mom's waist and held on.

"Does she need to go to the hospital?" Fear speared through Lily's whisper.

Lily had gone to the hospital in an ambulance

after her bad fall. Lily didn't remember much from that afternoon, but Georgie remembered every detail. The worst part had been when the paramedics told Georgie she wasn't allowed to ride in the ambulance with her sister. Georgie hadn't been there to hold Lily's hand. To promise her everything would be all right.

Georgie grabbed her mom's free hand and squeezed. "It's okay to cry, Mom. You don't have to be brave for us."

"I don't need to cry." Her mom pressed a kiss on Georgie's forehead. "I'm being so very well taken care of that all my tears are gone now."

"I promise, Mom," Georgie vowed. "I will always be here to take care of you."

CHAPTER ONE

GEORGIE HARRISON SKIDDED around a stroller, swiped at the coffee splattered on her shirt and kept up her manic sprint through Chicago's international airport. She had to make her connection. It was the last flight to Bozeman, Montana, that day. And flights were already being canceled and delayed because of a weather system that was expected to drop well over a foot of snow around greater Chicago.

Panic pushed her to move faster.

Georgie couldn't be stuck in Illinois. Her sisters would accuse her of conjuring the weather gods to avoid Lily's wedding.

But it wasn't Lily's wedding Georgie wanted to avoid. It was her new family—the one she hadn't known of until several months ago. An extended family of over a dozen relatives they'd only recently discovered they had, all with the last name of Blackwell, who would no doubt team up with her father and four sisters in pointing out the joys of life outside the research lab.

And by joys, her family meant boys. Or, more

accurately, available single men who were ready to exchange rings and read their handwritten vows, and welcome kids into their lives. Men who'd expect Georgie to be home in time for family dinner and math homework instead of staying late into the night at her soon-to-be-occupied research lab in England.

But if Georgie had to immerse herself in meddlesome family at her sister's wedding, she was going in wearing full body armor—namely, a fake date.

Her colleague, Colin Townsend, had agreed to join her for the week. Colin would prove she could have work–life balance and help convince her family her new job in England was the best career move for her. She was pursuing a treatment to help save aneurysm patients. An aneurysm had stolen her mom too soon. No one should have to suffer such anguish.

Colin was also heading to the same medical research lab in England. She wouldn't be alone. How could her family, the Harrisons or the Blackwells, disapprove?

Her boot slipped on the moving walkway, scuffing her confidence that this fake-date scenario would succeed.

No. Her strategy was foolproof.

She had briefed Colin on every contingency. He'd reluctantly memorized the Harrison family spreadsheet she'd created. She'd scripted a schematic chart, specifying the body language and interaction between a couple at their supposed stage in their relationship. Then, last week, they'd spent every lunch hour at a café, where she'd picked up the tab, and they'd rehearsed the big London reveal.

She glanced at her phone. Colin hadn't answered her texts. Or returned her phone call. Grilling him about her family over takeout in the lab last night might have been overkill.

Maybe. But it'd also been necessary. Georgie never left anything to chance.

She rushed on, stomping on her worry. Colin was a rule follower. He was probably already seated in row 12, seat B, his seat belt buckled, and his cell phone stashed inside his carry-on, which was secured safely in the overhead compartment.

Georgie boarded the plane last and alone. Her gaze skipped to row 12 and the empty middle seat. Unease skimmed along the back of her neck. A cowboy sat in the window seat of row 12, his worn hat pulled down low. Where was Colin?

Georgie dropped into the aisle seat, slid her laptop bag under the seat in front of her and set her purse on the empty one between herself and the cowboy. She craned her neck to see if Colin had chosen an aisle or window seat elsewhere. He'd probably already guessed she intended to fill the flight with pop quizzes and color-coded family flash cards.

The cowboy next to the window shifted, making her wonder how he'd wedged into the row. His legs were splayed, his right knee edged in front of the middle seat. His elbows rested on both armrests, spread wide, as if he wanted to claim as much space as possible.

The scratch of the intercom disrupted Georgie, pulling her thoughts away from the cowboy. The pilot cheerfully introduced himself and requested that the cabin be prepared for takeoff.

Georgie stopped the nearest flight attendant. "Can you wait to shut the door? I just need to text my companion. He's not here. I'm sure he's coming. It'll only take a minute."

"All mobile devices and laptops must be turned off and stowed for takeoff." The flight attendant's smile tightened into an implacable don't-mess-with-me-on-my-last-flight-of-the-day expression while she coolly waited for compliance.

"Right." Georgie powered off her phone and flipped the blank screen toward the flight attendant. How would Colin get in touch with her now?

The woman patted Georgie's shoulder, her

voice thawing. "Maybe your friend got an earlier flight."

"There are no earlier flights to Bozeman." Georgie knew. She'd booked their trip. Colin wasn't here. Colin wasn't going to Montana. "And there are no direct flights to Falcon Creek."

Panic cinched around her, tighter than the seat belt. Now she'd arrive in Falcon Creek and get dropped into the petri dish of family without a buffer to convince her family to give her their London blessings. Her strategy had been solid. Foolproof.

Georgie loosened the belt across her lap. She hadn't panicked when she'd overslept the morning of her medical board exam and missed her bus. She'd flagged down a cab and given the driver the fastest route to the testing facility. She just needed to devise a new approach. Quickly.

Her apartment was packed into boxes, her one-way flight to London booked. All that remained was telling her family in a way that wouldn't cause concern or undue worry. Since her mom's death, Dad had become overly anxious about his daughters. Now Lily had walked away from one fiancé and into the arms of another, and her other sisters had succumbed to love, too. But Georgie had no intention of joining their lovesick bandwagon.

"You're going to Falcon Creek, too?" The cowboy shifted, tipped his black hat up, revealing deep green eyes.

Sixteen different genes had contributed to his vivid yet rare eye color. Georgie took in the small scar paralleling his tanned, defined jawline. He could be one of her long-lost relatives in Falcon Creek. He looked similar to the cowboys in the pictures her sisters had texted her. Maybe it was the jeans, worn in the right places, or the gray plaid flannel shirt that looked oddly perfect on him. "Do you live in Falcon Creek?"

"Headed there for business," he said.

His reply indicated he wasn't a Blackwell. Her shoulders relaxed.

"What about you?" he asked.

"Wedding."

"Cold feet." He tipped his chin at the seat between them. His voice was sympathetic. "Sorry you lost your groom."

"My groom?" Georgie sputtered. "It's not my wedding. It's my sister's wedding. And he was my date."

"Wow. Even worse to get cold feet on a date." He pushed his cowboy hat up even farther, revealing thick chestnut hair. His gaze zeroed in on her. "What did you do?"

"Me? I did nothing." Irritated, Georgie yanked on her seat belt, tightening the strap across her hips. His arched brow broke her more easily than her four sisters ganging up on her. No one deserved to have perfectly shaped eyebrows and rare green eyes, especially a charmingly aggravating cowboy like him. She blurted, "I might have been too intense last night."

"He didn't roll his clothes to prevent wrinkles and you criticized him. Or you refused to share a suitcase with him because that's another rung on the relationship ladder." He shook his head. The playful note in his voice interrupted his thoughtful expression. "You have to face it. You two just weren't ready for the next level."

"You're completely wrong. He's only a colleague who agreed to come with me," Georgie argued, pointing at him like her genetics professor used to when a student dared to challenge his theories. "He didn't bail on me either."

"But he isn't here." The cowboy removed his hat and ran his hand through his hair. The chestnut strands weren't even crimped or dented, which was entirely too unfair.

He placed his hat on top of her purse, effectively hiding it from the passing flight attendant and saving Georgie from another flight attendant reprimand. *All carry-ons have to be stowed for takeoff.* In that instant, they were accomplices the same way she'd wanted Colin to be her partner in what she'd dubbed her London Project.

Her cowboy could take Colin's place.

She squelched the thought, slipping her purse from beneath the soft felt of his black hat and placing it underneath the seat in front of her.

"Why do you need a pretend date, anyway? He was pretend—you can admit it." He studied her. One corner of his mouth tipped up, as if igniting the tinder in his gaze. "You want to upstage the bride. It's a battle of the sisters. It's sister wars. I'm right, aren't I?"

"No." Clearly, he'd watched too much reality TV. She'd watched too little. Still, she couldn't shake the notion of him stepping into Colin's shoes. "It's nothing like that. Our family loves each other even when we disagree."

"How does it work?" His curious voice tumbled through her.

"What?" Georgie tugged the in-flight magazine from the seat pocket in front of her, flipped it open and studied an ad for the perfect neck pillow. She could've used it on the plane and feigned sleep. That would have politely ended all conversation with the cowboy, but not the radical theory that he could be her plus-one.

"Getting a pretend date," he said, as persistent as she was when testing one of her theories in the lab. "What makes a person want to pretend in the first place?"

"Why are we talking about this?" Georgie closed the magazine and flattened her hands on the cover.

Why was she considering this cowboy—a basic stranger—as her alternative strategy? No one would believe she'd fallen for a cowboy. She would've had to leave her research lab in Raleigh, North Carolina, and ventured out of the city. Her family knew she lacked a car and preferred to walk the two blocks to the research facility every day.

"We have three hours together, a previous passenger already completed the crossword puzzle in the in-flight magazine and there's no in-flight movie," he said. "Talking passes the time."

Georgie stuffed the magazine back into the seat pocket. She had to invalidate him as a potential alternative. Observation and facts had to be recorded. She noted his well-worn boots, from scuffed heels to dirt-coated toes. He appeared to be a cowboy from head to toe, and appealing, if you liked dust and the outdoors. Which she didn't. "Ranch business must be taking you to Falcon Creek."

"Rodeo," he said.

"You're bringing the rodeo to Falcon Creek?"

she asked. His shoulders looked capable of pulling it off.

He grinned at her. "I'm in the rodeo."

"Really?" She'd never been to a rodeo. She'd seen the bulls bucking on TV while flipping through the channels. But a rodeo cowboy could distract her family from her next career move. *Stop right there, Georgiana Marie.* Her mother's inflexible tone had always halted Georgie's unapproved science projects, rendering her theories unproved. "Are you any good?"

"Top ten calf roping and bronc riding in the country." He shrugged as if being modest about the accomplishment.

"It's like a full-time job."

"You don't have to sound so surprised."

"That's impressive." And exactly the thing that would impress Big E—her newly found grandfather—and her ranch-loving cousins. As for her dad, he couldn't argue that the man wasn't driven to succeed. That crazy, stupid idea took hold again, stronger than ever. "So, I take it you've never been anyone's pretend date before?"

"When I date, I make sure it's for real." There was a vow in his voice and a guarantee in his gaze.

What would a real date with Mr. Green-Eyes entail? Picnic basket and a tailgate, most likely.

Not her style. Or at least, she'd never been asked on a picnic. Disappointment sat down beside her. Which was about as outrageous as the idea she couldn't quite toss away—him as her replacement date. He made her want to take a dare. She never felt daring. The wildest thing she'd done in a long time was arrange for a fake wedding date, and look how that had turned out. "So, if the rodeo isn't in town, what rodeo business do you have in Falcon Creek?"

"Horses." He rubbed his chin.

"My cousins own several of the largest ranches in the county," Georgie said.

He dropped his hand and stilled. "Who are your cousins?"

"The Blackwells," she said. "My sister's wedding is going to be out at the Blackwell Family Guest Ranch. I would show you pictures of the ranch, but my cell phone is off."

"It's fine." His fingers tapped against his leg. "The Blackwell family has a reputation."

"Is that a good or bad thing?" Was it good or bad that he was a perfect fit for her family, but all wrong for her? She'd always dated the buttoned-up and bookish types, like herself. Men who understood that her mind might wander sometimes as she pondered new theories and possible outcomes. And she had to accept that she would need another script for her

London announcement. One that didn't include her green-eyed cowboy.

"It depends." His gaze narrowed on her as if he'd devised his own plan B. "Would you consider a different person as your fake wedding date?"

"Someone like you?" she asked.

He ran his hand through his hair and frowned at her as if she'd bruised his pride. "Yes."

"Why?" She was instantly hot and cold, wanting to shiver and break out in a sweat. This was simultaneously horrifying and fantastic.

"I haven't been able to reach Ethan Blackwell by phone or email," he said. "I was hoping to meet him in person. Talk to him face-to-face about my horse."

"You want to be my pretend wedding date to get access to my cousin," she clarified. Warning bells rang in her head.

"Yes." He winced. Apprehension creased the corners of his eyes while concern lowered his voice. "It's important."

And she believed that, to him, it was very important. "Give me your name and number. I'll pass it on to Ethan and personally vouch for you."

"Right. That's the logical option." He took her in-flight magazine, tore a page out and asked the flight attendant walking by for a pen. He wrote in bold script across the ad and handed it to her. "I really appreciate it."

Georgie did not appreciate the defeat in his gaze, as if he'd lost something precious. Nor did she appreciate the sense that she'd somehow let him down. They were two strangers, with only a destination in common. That they were both headed for Falcon Creek wasn't enough of a connection to bring someone she'd just met to her family's home as her fake wedding date. She folded the paper without reading his name.

Colin and she had been classmates in medical school and colleagues for close to a decade. And she'd spent more than a week convincing him to be her pretend wedding date.

She glanced at the cowboy. He'd settled back into his seat and dropped his hat back over his eyes. His shoulders slumped slightly.

An apology rolled into her throat, although she had nothing to apologize for. She opened the in-flight magazine to an article extolling the virtues of island living. That she wanted to help make him feel better was only natural. She might prefer to work in a research lab, but she'd earned her medical degree and the right to be called Dr. Georgiana Harrison. At heart, she was a nurturer.

If only her family would believe that working in a lab was enough to give her a fulfilling life, she wouldn't have ever concocted a fake wedding date. She wouldn't have convinced Colin to take part. And she never would've considered her cowboy for the role.

But that was the thing about strategies. She could always devise a new one.

CHAPTER TWO

I'M NOT GIVING UP, Cody. Zach leaned against the stainless-steel bar in the Last Call Cavern at Bozeman Airport and swirled his unfinished beer around the mug.

I'm sorry, Zach. There's nothing more I can do for Rain Dancer but keep him comfortable. Dr. Morrow had gripped Zach's shoulder, held on for one beat, then left Zach to collect himself alone in his horse's stall.

Bad news was always delivered in three go-rounds.

An apology. Always the first. Always the lead-in. *I'm sorry to have to tell you...*

A gut punch. Always second. Always breath stealing. World tilting. *But your brother's cancer has returned. Your horse's condition is terminal. Your father never woke up from surgery.*

A hand on the shoulder. Always last. As if the messenger intended to hold him together long enough to escape the office, the stable or the waiting room.

Anguish thrashed through Zach like a bucking bronc without a rhythm. If only his misery faded in eight seconds like a bronc ride. Still, he allowed his sadness so many seconds to consume him before stepping back into the moment. The way he preferred to live his life: one moment at a time.

For one brief instant on the airplane, Zach had believed fate had finally granted him a miracle by seating him next to Ethan Blackwell's cousin. Ethan Blackwell was the one veterinarian in the country who could save Rain Dancer. Ethan Blackwell was known for his outside-the-box thinking and innovative treatments when other vets and conventional medicine had failed. Ethan had to treat Rain Dancer. The quarter horse was Zach's last connection to his brother.

Zach dropped a tip on the bar, left his beer unfinished and tightened his grip on the handle of his rolling carry-on. He had a rental car to pick up and a two-and-a-half-hour drive to Falcon Creek, as long as the weather held.

The woman on the plane hadn't been his miracle. He still couldn't quite believe he'd offered to be her pretend date. He'd learned as a child the danger of pretending. The truth always came out eventually, and the longer it'd been concealed the harder it struck.

Fortunately, the woman on the plane wasn't

reckless and she'd turned down Zach's offer. He'd find his own way to Ethan Blackwell.

Speak of the devil. His *in* with the Blackwells stood with her focus fixed on the baggage claim carousel circling in front of her. She clutched a cell phone in one hand, her purse and a laptop bag in the other. The tilt of her chin toward the scuffed floor and the slouch in her shoulders gave away her distress.

Zach slowed and veered toward her. "Everything okay?"

"My bag isn't here." The woman lifted her head, pushed her honey-streaked hair off her face and blinked at him.

But the lost look in her gaze never faded. And that lost look tugged at places inside him. Places he'd shut down after Cody had passed. Still, he heard his brother's laughter. *Can't resist trying to fix things, can you?* He wasn't fixing anything for her. He was simply checking in on his way out of the airport. "Guess you don't have a change of clothes and the essentials tucked in with your laptop, right?"

She patted the very slim laptop bag. "Does a pack of gum count as essential?"

Zach winced.

"All my Christmas gifts were in my suitcase." She scanned the baggage claim as if expecting her suitcase to appear. "And outfits for every different wedding event, of which there are many."

"That's impressive." He'd folded his clothes only to ensure everything fit inside his carry-on. Good thing she hadn't accepted his offer to be her pretend date. Their differences started at their suitcases and most likely extended to living habits. He had no roots. With a family like the Blackwells, her roots probably extended past county lines and ran deeper than still waters.

"What's worse is my sister's something old for her wedding is in my bag, too," she said.

"Can you get another gift as a replacement?"

"It's a charm bracelet that belonged to our mother." She paused and bit into her bottom lip. "We gave her a new charm every year on her birthday."

He reached forward to grab her hand, then pulled back. Not his place to offer her comfort. Not his place to guarantee her suitcase would be returned in time for her sister's wedding. "That's definitely hard to replicate."

"Tell me about it." Her sigh deepened her frown. "And now I have to tell my sisters I lost another piece of Mom."

She had no Christmas presents, no date for the wedding and no clothes. Those she would most likely resolve soon. She was too self-contained and lacked any melodramatic tendencies not to solve her own problems.

What tugged inside him was the loss of her mother's bracelet. That he understood all too well.

The conveyor belt slowed to a stutter, then stopped. An airline employee rolled the handful of unclaimed bags against the far wall. Right next to a room labeled Lost Luggage. Zach pointed to the Lost Luggage sign, likely hoping to make his exit. "They should be able to find your bag."

And he should be able to wish her luck and leave.

Except his long legs easily matched her pace. He strolled, she rushed, straight into the Lost Luggage office and right up to the customer service counter as if it'd been their suitcase that had gone missing, not hers.

Carla, the airline's customer service manager, according to her badge, took the claim ticket from his plane mate and tapped on her keyboard. "I apologize for your troubles, Ms. Harrison. I'm sure it's on another flight here."

Ms. Harrison nudged her elbow into Zach's side. "What are you doing?"

Zach was picking through the candy bowl on the counter, leaving the chocolate candy and stashing extra mints in his shirt pocket. "Never know when I might need to combat bad breath." Then he grinned. "Last name Harrison. I bet I can guess your first name."

"You'll never get it." The smallest of smiles rippled across Ms. Harrison's face, disrupting her frustration.

He accepted the victory, as Cody had liked to call it. His brother and he had relied on laughter to keep from sinking beneath the continuous stress and hard times his brother's disease had dragged him through. Zach depended on laughter lately to balance the loss. "Katherine? Alexandra? Eleanor? Victoria?"

She grimaced.

"Right. Way too formal." He considered her. No extra jewelry or glitter nail polish weighed down her fingers. He liked her less-is-more natural appearance. "Definitely something more simple. Sarah? Jane? Ellen? Diana?"

She arched an eyebrow. "That's what you came up with?"

"Those are good names," he argued. "Famous people have those first names."

Carla studied her computer screen, reread the numbers on the claim ticket. Her face pinched, from her penciled-in eyebrows to her shimmery lip-gloss-covered mouth. The keyboard tapping resumed.

Zach leaned forward. "Is there a problem?"

Other than the fact that all his first-name choices offended his companion.

"There's no problem for your suitcase." The woman's stiff smile never brightened her wide eyes. "It's gone tropical."

"Tropical," Ms. Harrison repeated.

"Your bag is on a flight to Belize City." Carla adjusted her name badge as if considering taking it off and leaving for the day.

His companion rested her forehead on the counter and groaned as if he'd suggested Florence or Hettie or Myrtle for her first name.

"At least your bag isn't lost. And here, chocolate makes everything better." Zach pushed the candy bowl toward her. That bit of wisdom he'd heard from his ex-girlfriend. He selected a chocolate from the bowl, unwrapped the candy, popped it into his mouth and tested the theory.

She turned her head and peered at him. Her words were dry. "Feeling better?"

"Not as good as your suitcase, likely enjoying the tropical heat." He shrugged. "Although Belize City isn't exactly the beach I'd pick."

She straightened and gaped at him. "You like the ocean?"

"Would it surprise you if I said yes?" He smiled. "Give me a surfboard and beach towel any day."

Her gaze tracked from his hat to his boots

and back, as if she was trying to picture him in swim trunks, holding a surfboard. He would've reacted the same way, surprised and unconvinced, if she'd told him she liked mud bogging and four-wheel off-roading.

She shook her head, opened her mouth as if she wanted to verify his surfer claim, then abruptly turned to face Carla. "When is my suitcase expected to return from its vacation in Belize?"

That was for the better. This wasn't a get-to-know-you meeting. Her first name hardly mattered to him. He'd walked with her to Lost Luggage, which was enough. *Goodbye, Ms. Harrison* would suffice as a parting line.

Cody would remind him that not everyone wanted help or needed fixing. Ms. Harrison appeared more than capable of taking care of herself.

Cody would also tell Zach that he should concentrate on fixing himself first.

You can't fix what's not broken, Cody. How many times had Zach launched that statement at his brother?

The truth will catch up with you one day, Zach. How many times had his brother recited that same prediction?

Zach popped another chocolate into his mouth and rubbed his hands over his jeans. He kept on moving—always moving—for a reason. He'd wait until Ms. Harrison finished with Carla and then get moving again. Alone like always. Just how he preferred it. After all, he couldn't be abandoned if he was already alone.

"I've put rerouting instructions into the system." Carla slipped a piece of paper and pen across the counter. "If you could fill this form out, we'll contact you as soon as your bag arrives here in Bozeman."

"Can't it just return on the flight back from Belize tonight?" She filled out the form.

"Flights have already been delayed into Chicago due to the inclement weather and won't arrive until late tonight at the earliest." The apology in Carla's voice dipped her mouth into a small frown. "Your bag has to travel through Chicago to get here."

"Of course." Georgie handed Carla the form.

"There's a toll-free phone number on this card to inquire about your bag." Carla held out a business card and plastic-wrapped amenity kit. "We apologize for your trouble."

His companion sank her hand into the bowl on the counter and clutched a fistful of assorted candy.

Zach accepted the airline's consolation gift and thanked Carla for her help. Outside in baggage claim, he turned to wish Ms. Harrison good luck with her bag and the wedding.

Her phone buzzed in her pocket. She reached out, dumped her candy into his hand and tugged her phone from her jacket. She glanced at her screen and grimaced.

"Something else wrong?" he asked. Other than his standing there, holding her candy and not walking away.

"The rental car is listed under my colleague's name. They won't rent the car to me and they don't have another snow-ready vehicle available." She dropped her arms to her sides. "I cannot believe this."

"I have a rental car." He couldn't believe the words tumbling out of his mouth. "You can ride with me."

She slowly raised her head. "Seriously?"

"I'm only offering you a ride." He gave her the candy and the amenity kit. "You already have my cell number. If you decide a cowboy fits your wedding-date criteria, you can always call me. I'll check my availability."

"I'd be grateful for the lift." She dropped the candy and overnight kit into her laptop bag. "And I promise, I'll give your number to my cousin like I said."

"If we're going to be carpooling, we should

probably know each other's first names." He reached out. "Zach Evans."

"Georgiana Harrison." Her grip on his hand was brief, as if she didn't quite believe his offer. "Everyone calls me Georgie."

"Pleasure to meet you, Georgie." Zach liked her name and holding her hand. He stopped himself there. That was more than enough to like about her. "Ready to get on the road?"

CHAPTER THREE

GEORGIE'S SUITCASE HADN'T ARRIVED. Lily likely would not have her something old on her wedding day. The one wedding task Georgie had been assigned and she'd failed. The dread in her gut expanded, refusing to be dismissed.

Her phone buzzed on her lap. A group text from Lily and Fiona flashed on the screen.

Are you on your way? This from Lily.

Fiona added: Can't wait to see you.

Georgie swallowed around the lump in her throat and replied: Lost bag. Driving now. Making a stop at the store. Be there soon.

You can borrow my clothes. Lily offered.

But Georgie couldn't borrow Lily's confidence or her sister's pants. Lily and Amanda were several inches taller than Georgie. Hopefully my suitcase will be here tomorrow. Just need pajamas.

Lily answered: I've got you covered. No need to stop. You can get here faster now.

I need to pick something else up. A replacement gift for their mother's charm bracelet. An impossible task.

She always hated letting down her sisters. And now she faced a week that she feared would be one massive letdown.

Are you picking up something for me? Lily's text was followed by several smiling emojis. Lily added: I love presents. And my sisters. And Conner.

Georgie squeezed her phone. Lily believed she loved Conner. How could she really know in such a short time? There was a protocol to falling in love. A schedule and specific steps that ensured the love between two people was real. Both Lily and Fiona had ignored love's guidelines, along with Peyton and Amanda, too. Georgie, on the other hand, had graduated from medical school and passed her medical board exam precisely because she had adhered to a strict timetable and regime that had ensured success.

We know you're in love. Now go find your groom, Lily. Fiona responded. See you soon, Georgie! Can't wait to meet this new man in your life. Several heart emojis followed to reveal her younger sister's excitement.

Concern, not excitement, sifted through Georgie. She didn't have a new man in her life. She had a carpool with a green-eyed cowboy who wanted to use her to get to her cousin Ethan Blackwell.

Zach spoke horses and most likely understood ranch life. He'd relate to Conner and probably support Lily's decision to embrace both—horses and ranch life. Cowboys looked out for each other. Georgie understood hypotheses and validated data, research and key findings.

Georgie knew nothing about the man her sister intended to marry. Nothing more than that her other sisters liked him. But Georgie wanted details, specifics about Conner Hannah to prove his and Lily's love was the kind that would last.

She glanced at Zach. He radiated confidence, from his calm grip on the steering wheel to his casual posture. He was seemingly undisturbed by the falling snow continually swept aside by the windshield wipers and the silence stretching inside the car.

Try as she might, there was something she couldn't ignore about the cowboy. Something that kept her thoughts and gaze circling back to him. Something that made her curious about him. And that was not good.

Georgie made a living asking questions and testing theories inside her lab. But her cowboy wasn't another one of her experiments. He was simply her ride to Falcon Creek. She tapped on her phone screen and broke the silence. If only her interest in the man beside her was as easily fractured. "There's an antiques mall up ahead at exit fifty-two. Can we make a quick stop?"

"You can't want to stop there." Zach's voice was bland and uninspired. "At a mall."

"I need to replace that something old." And inhale several bracing breaths of the brisk, ice-chilled air and determine her next steps to prove to her family that they didn't need to be concerned about her choices. That a move to London was the best thing for her, even if she would be alone.

"Why not get something from your Blackwell relatives?" Zach drummed his fingers on the steering wheel and glanced over at her. "They're certain to have a lot of old things on their ranches. And it'll mean more than buying something that was once owned by a stranger."

The Harrison sisters had only learned about their Blackwell connection four months prior. The Blackwells were strangers to Georgie. No more than faces in photographs her sisters had texted her. Today would be the first time she met her new relatives in person. Asking for an heirloom from her new relations to give to Lily for her wedding was as inappropriate as walking into a sanitized lab in street clothes. "I'd like to look. Can we just please stop?"

He pulled off at the exit. "What's your definition of *quick*?"

"Less than thirty minutes." She only needed enough time to collect herself.

Signs pointed to the antiques mall. A handful of local restaurants and gas stations were clumped together like an oasis in the snow-covered pastures. Christmas lights blinked in the frosted store windows and garland hung from the doors.

Zach parked in front of the large antiques mall and checked his phone. "You get twenty minutes. We have to stay ahead of the incoming storm."

"I'll be done in fifteen." She opened her door and glanced back at him. "What are you doing?"

"Joining you. I need to stretch my legs." He set his hat on his head. "I'm not built for airplane seats and confined spaces. I prefer trucks and open country roads."

"Where do those country roads take you?" She smashed her lips together.

"Anywhere you want to go." An invitation wove through his words, and his smile settled someplace deep inside her. Someplace that defied logic and common sense. Georgie was never flustered, especially by a man. And she wouldn't let one cowboy, however adorable, rattle her.

Or make her reconsider replacing Colin with a cowboy.

She hurried toward the mall entrance, intending to leave her bad judgment outside for the wind to sweep into a snowdrift.

Zach moved in front of her to hold the door open. She was perfectly capable of opening a door for herself. But she appreciated his consideration.

Inside, Georgie's gaze skipped over the massive area. A gold-edged, ivory-colored china set filled a cherrywood dining-room table in the front window. Gold flatware and smoky, etched wineglasses completed the table setting. Knickknacks from every time period stood crammed inside curio cabinets and old hutches. No shelf, no part of the store, was empty, from the ceiling with its old-fashioned chandeliers and lights to the floor covered in tasseled area rugs. What had she been thinking?

Georgie headed down the first aisle, which was crammed on every side. Her gaze refused to settle.

And the panic took hold. Nothing could replace her mom's charm bracelet. *Nothing*.

Just as no one could replace their mom. Their mom, who should've been there on Lily's wedding day. Should've been the one to give Lily her bracelet and her unconditional support.

Not Georgie, who'd remembered to put a research journal in her laptop bag but not the bracelet. As if the research journal was more precious than her mom's jewelry. Georgie rubbed her chest and the ache pressing into her ribs.

As for unconditional support, Georgie always wanted proof. The only time she'd never questioned the world was inside her mom's embrace. There, in her mom's arms, she'd known love, acceptance and strength. She wanted her mom now. Wanted her mom to tell her to fly, like she used to. *Fly, Georgie. Spread your wings and never be scared to look down and see how far you've gone.*

"Are you okay?" Zach's hand settled against her lower back. Concern deepened his voice.

His touch was steady. Solid. Grounding. And gave her the strength to pull herself together. "Just a bit overwhelmed. There's so much of everything."

"Never would've guessed from looking at the outside." He laughed. "It's all a bit unexpected, isn't it?"

The same as her entire day. And like him, too.

He moved around her, farther into the jumbled array of antiques. Georgie remained where she was.

"Here. These are old. They come in a pair.

A perfect gift for a new couple." Zach waved his hand over a display of vintage salt and pepper shakers that filled an ornate side table. He picked up a pair shaped like nutcrackers. "They can be the start of a collection. You can give them a set every year."

"I'm not sure Lily wants to collect those." Georgie welcomed the laughter building inside her, nudging the sadness aside. Great-Aunt Pru would've added the shakers to her collection of all things holiday, calling them tacky but cute. "My sister always liked wind chimes, but I'm not sure her soon-to-be husband will want wind chimes dangling all around their house."

Zach shrugged. "A man in love will agree to a lot of things, even a wind-chime collection."

"Sounds like you speak from experience." Georgie faced Zach, seeking a reprieve from scouring the antiques shop and her grief. "What did an in-love Zach Evans agree to?"

"I agreed to enter a rodeo." Zach rearranged the salt and pepper shakers on the table.

"Doesn't seem like such a bad decision." Georgie added elf shakers to Zach's growing Christmas shaker gathering. "You're one of the best in the country in your events."

"I am now." Zach glanced at her. "I entered my first rodeo after I'd been working on a ranch for exactly five days."

"But you grew up around horses." Or so she'd assumed. His cowboy boots were too worn. His jeans too relaxed. His cowboy hat too much a natural extension of him. His wasn't a look anyone could simply purchase in the Western store they'd passed on the way to the antiques mall.

"I grew up in the suburbs in Cincinnati." Zach crammed his hands in his front jean pockets and avoided looking at her. "We lived on a cul-de-sac in a two-story house with a basketball hoop in the driveway and a sandbox in the backyard."

His words sounded over-rehearsed. His voice too automatic, like a prerecorded message informing you of a past-due bill, then inviting you to have a good day. There was nothing good about a bill-collection phone call. She sensed pain, not happiness, in Zach's childhood memory, and that pulled at her. And made her instantly want to know more. "How did you get to a ranch?"

"Met a girl in college, followed her home to her family's ranch in Colorado the summer after our freshman year," Zach said.

That answered the love part. "How did you do in your first-ever rodeo?"

"Failed spectacularly on both the bull ride and with the girl." A small smile softened across his face. "But I found a home on the ranch with the horses."

"And you've been riding ever since," she said.

"Something like that. Everything just clicked. The boots, hat and my love for horses." Zach adjusted a pair of penguin salt and pepper shakers, then wiped his hands together as if the display was finished along with the conversation about his past. "How about you? What extreme thing have you done for love?"

Georgie had gone to extremes to avoid love. Love hadn't been part of her medical degree requirements. She wanted nothing to distract her from her career. Besides, she loved her work. Her work fulfilled her. "I'm not really an extreme person."

"That's the thing about love." Zach stepped closer and considered her. "Love makes you believe every risk is worth it."

Or it made you believe you could leave the California beach town you were born and raised in to live on a ranch in zero-degree weather with acres of land and cattle as your only neighbors. At least that was what her sister Lily believed. Now that Lily had fallen in love with Conner. There was the problem with love. Once you fell, love made the decisions, not logic and common sense. Then the chances of failure multiplied exponentially.

"I don't see any jewelry cases and there's no one to guide us through this maze." Georgie turned toward the entrance. "This was a bad idea. We should get back on the road."

Zach followed her to the parking lot, started the car and buckled his seat belt.

Her cell phone buzzed. Her dad's face filled the screen, signaling the incoming call. Georgie pushed her voice into upbeat. "Hey, Dad."

"Your sisters texted that you're on your way to the ranch." Her dad's enthusiasm never paused. "I've been really looking forward to this. It's good to have you home for the holidays and with someone special, too. I can't wait to meet Colin."

"You mean…" Dread collapsed Georgie's voice into a wheeze. "Zach."

"Who's Zach?" Her dad's tone instantly shifted into alert mode.

And Georgie free-fell into instant panic. "Dad? You're breaking up. I can't really hear you."

"Georgie?" he shouted.

"I'll call you when we get to the ranch." Georgie disconnected the call. She'd never hung up on her own dad. Never been so abrupt with him. Even when he'd called during her most intense work sessions in the lab.

"Everything okay?" Zach asked.

"Bad connection." Bad decisions. She had a father who expected her to have a date. Expected to meet her "someone special." She dropped her head back on the seat. Her cowboy could not be...

She had no bracelet. No clothes. No date. None of the armor she'd intended to use to support herself the entire week. Everything had been so carefully planned and then it had all started falling apart in spectacular fashion.

She needed something. Something to bolster her confidence and put her back in charge. All strategies started with a good plan. Good plans required detailed lists. She opened the notes app on her phone and began a list. "I know I said only one stop, but I need to make another one."

"I don't think I can handle another antiques store." He pulled out onto the road.

"I need a clothing store. I can't meet my family in a stained, wrinkled shirt." Georgie crossed her arms over her chest, covering the dried coffee stain on her sweater. That would be like arriving for the first day of her new job without her ironed lab coat and personal protective gear.

"But they know you've been traveling all day," he argued.

But the Blackwells did not know Georgie. First impressions mattered. Everything from her appearance to her manner would set the tone and ensure the next ten days proceeded as she intended. "It won't take long. There's a mall two miles away."

Zach followed her directions and parked the car outside the department store.

"Tell me you have a shopping strategy." He rubbed his hands together. His gaze was fixed on the snow quickly covering the windshield. "So we can be in and out really fast."

"I made a list of clothes I need for tonight and tomorrow."

Zach leaned over the console. "'Black fleece-lined leggings. Charcoal boot socks. Oatmeal fleece pullover. Thick infinity scarf, gray with red or purple undertones.'"

She tipped her phone away before he read her undergarment requirements. "I like lists."

"That's a rather specific clothing list," he said.

"I know what I want." And she certainly didn't want to edge closer to him or explain that was the exact outfit she'd planned to wear to meet her sisters and her new Blackwell family. Nothing too bold but coordinated and very weather appropriate. An outfit that proved she could make smart choices outside of the lab, too.

Zach touched her arm, stopping her from getting out of the car, and pointed at a Western goods store. "You know, there's nothing wrong with a pair of jeans and good flannel shirt."

There was everything wrong with jeans and flannel for Georgie. She was not a cowgirl, a future rancher or an impostor. She was a doctor, more comfortable in a lab coat than a dress. More at ease surrounded by microscopes and petri dishes than on a date. "I never find jeans warm enough."

"Maybe you're wearing the wrong kind." A tease shifted through his voice.

Maybe if she stopped noticing his charm, she'd stop considering him as her Colin replacement. She seemed to have lost more than her luggage on the flight. Her common sense still floated thirty-five thousand feet in the air. Her feet were firmly back on the ground, yet she was less sensible now.

"Feels like we should set a time limit." Zach tapped his wrist, then tipped his chin toward the café inside the main shopping area and the large easel announcing the day's dessert specials. "I'm heading to the café for the Peppermint Brownie Ice Cream Cake."

"I'll be done before you finish the last bite," she said.

"Care to bet on that?" he asked.

She set her hand in his. "Loser has to buy the second piece of cake."

CHAPTER FOUR

ZACH PEERED OVER at Georgie. She polished off the last bite of the to-go Peppermint Brownie Ice Cream Cake he'd purchased for her. Shopping bags in hand and a wide smile on her face, she'd located him in the café, eyed his unfinished piece of cake and declared herself the winner.

Georgie waved her plastic fork toward the car window. "It feels like we've gone one hundred miles already."

"Thirty-five," he said.

"Miles," she clarified. "That's all?"

"Now it's thirty-six since we left the mall."

"There is nothing productive about sitting in a car that's crawling through the snow." Georgie leaned her head back against the seat and groaned. "Tell me something about yourself, Zach."

Perhaps if he told her something about himself, she'd open up about her family. He really only wanted information on one person in particular: Ethan Blackwell. Specifically, on the best way to approach the veterinarian who had refused to take Zach's calls or answer his emails about his horse. "I can give you my sixty-second short."

"What's that?" She closed the to-go container and set it on the floor.

"A quick summary of everything you need to know about me in sixty seconds or less. Sort of like a sound bite." One he'd often relied on during interviews over the years. He'd never liked probing inquiries and never divulged too much personal information.

"And if I still have questions?"

"You won't."

"You don't know me." She tapped her fitness tracker. "Time starts now."

"My parents are both gone. I'm the last branch on the Evans family tree." He cleared his throat, dislodging a knot of grief. He was completely alone. Nothing he hadn't been able to handle. "I live for the rodeo and the moment. In that order."

"Always?" She arched one eyebrow.

"Always."

"It's good to love what you do," she said.

"And do you love what you do?" He leaned his elbow on the console, shifting the focus to Georgie rather than himself.

"I do," she said. "I'm a doctor."

Being a doctor suited her quiet reserve and understated appearance.

"The doctor and the cowboy." She nodded. "Sounds like we're characters from a movie."

"Who met in the ER." He grinned. "That sounds more realistic than a chance meeting on an airplane."

"Except I don't do patient care." She frowned. "I do clinical research."

Now he frowned. He thought of Cody then, always upbeat and agreeing to clinical trials. Zach loosened his grip on the steering wheel, but not the ache inside him.

Her job didn't matter. After all, he was only driving Georgie to Falcon Creek. She wasn't his fake girlfriend and he didn't have to pretend to support her career. He did have to gather more information about her cousin. "How many sisters do you have?"

"Four," she said. "They live in California, except Lily. She lives in Falcon Creek now and is getting married to Conner."

"And you don't like him," Zach guessed.

"I haven't met Conner," Georgie said. "I haven't met my other sisters' significant others either. They'll all be coming in for the wedding later in the week."

"But you're convinced you won't like them."

"I never said I wouldn't like them." She stretched out her words. "I said I haven't met them."

"It's the way you're saying it," Zach said. "You already don't like them."

"How am I saying that exactly?"

"There's dread in your voice, not excitement," he said. "If you were looking forward to meeting them, you would have said just that."

"I'm not dreading meeting them." Georgie crossed her arms over her chest. "I don't know them, so I can't decide whether I like them or not."

"That's the polite answer." Zach tapped the navigation screen. "We have one hundred and fifty-three miles to go at a slow pace thanks to the snow falling. You can tell me the truth. I don't have anyone else to tell. What would you tell me if we were dating?"

His family confidences would be much more complicated. For years, the rules had included a mask and latex gloves to protect his brother from infection. Not ever visiting their childhood home after dusk. Dusk was the time when his mother had always declared she'd endured another day, and had rewarded herself by camping out beside the liquor cabinet for the rest of the night.

Zach accelerated, pushing the SUV and himself away from his past.

"That's just it." Georgie shifted in the seat,

facing toward him. "If we were in a real relationship, we'd follow a certain structure."

"You mean like a schedule," he said.

"No, I mean a blueprint." She waved a hand around in front of her. "You know, like a relationship guideline."

Zach changed his grip on the steering wheel and focused on Georgie, not his own broken family memories. Only pain hovered in his past. He'd told Georgie he lived for the moment. For the present. And the present belonged to the entirely too intriguing woman beside him.

"You better give me the details." He offered a teasing grin. "I'm not sure I've seen a relationship blueprint before."

"Maybe that's why you're single." Irritation clipped her voice. "You obviously missed several steps."

Her concise matter-of-fact tone released his laughter. What was it about her that made him smile? Made him feel lighter? "I could say the same for you."

"Not really," she said. "I'm single by choice."

If that was all it took not to have failed the relationship guidelines, then he passed. "I choose to be single, too."

"You followed a girl to a ranch and entered the rodeo for her." Doubt layered through her words like the snow piling up on the side of the interstate.

"That was years and too many bad decisions ago."

"Still, if she had said yes to your proposal, you'd be married now," she argued.

"Well, there was that minor inconvenience of the other guy she fell in love with," he admitted. He'd only ever revealed that detail to Cody. No one else. He wasn't a secret-sharing kind of person. He'd spent most of his life putting a spin on his home life and burying the truth so deep that he could barely recognize it.

"Sorry." She reached over and squeezed his arm. "You're better alone than with someone like that."

And there it was—sincerity and frank honesty. Add a dash of confident optimism and that was Georgie. Exactly what he already really liked about her. He shrugged. "Lessons learned and all that."

"So, we're both single by choice." She released him and ran her hands over her leggings. "But there is still a relationship road map."

"So you've claimed." He left his past in the snowdrift and ignored the urge to grab her hand to keep them connected. Connected right there in the present. He genuinely liked her. That would be good if they crossed paths at the Blackwell ranch in the next few days. Nothing wrong with getting along with her. It wasn't like he'd suddenly acquired relationship goals. "If I follow this relationship road map, where does it get me? To a penthouse suite at the True Love Hotel?"

"You end up with a partner for life." She pulled off the wool hat she'd purchased at the store on their way out. "That was how it was with my parents." But she winced when she said it.

"What about love?" He ground his teeth together. *Love.* Really? He wanted to talk about the best means to approach Ethan Blackwell, not about love. Not again. He'd tiptoed into the romance conversation earlier in the antiques store. And only because something like misery seemed to have gripped her and he'd wanted to take it away. It wasn't a conversation that needed to be revisited.

"Sure, love's part of it." She pulled her hair back into a ponytail. No mirror or hairbrush required, her movements as casual as her position on lasting relationships. She added, "But there are other factors."

"Like what?" he asked. "Love is supposed to conquer all."

She skimmed over that claim as smoothly as her fingers went over her hair. "Other factors like friendship, mutual respect, shared values. Common interests."

For reasons Zach could only blame on the relentless snow falling on the windshield, obscuring his clear view and common sense, he continued their banter about love. "Let's pretend that you and I fall madly in love." *Key word: pretend.* Zach loved the rodeo and his rootless life on the road.

"Okay." Her disbelief stretched her one word like a lasso hurled toward a calf.

Did she not believe in mad love or falling for him? Zach switched the windshield wipers to move faster. "Because we don't share the same interests or values, we fail. Is that what your relationship guidelines state?"

"If we had followed the road map, we wouldn't have ever fallen in love in the first place," she said.

Simple. Blunt. Matter-of-fact. Had that been his problem all these years? The love he knew— the love he'd seen—was complicated. Messy. Made a man weak and vulnerable. It exposed and abandoned. And was best avoided.

She continued, "We would have known early on it'd never work out between us."

He glanced at her. "You follow this road map?"

Georgie nodded.

"And your sisters?" He returned his attention to the road.

"Have not," she said.

He heard the deep frown in her voice. "Then you believe their relationships are going to fail?"

"How could they not?" Her voice lowered into a gruff whisper.

The defeat in her tone bothered him. He avoided love, but that hardly meant he didn't believe in it for other people. "You haven't been in Falcon Creek. Maybe your sisters have followed the road map, and everything lines up."

"How could they?" She clutched her hands together. "It's only been four months since Lily met Conner and several weeks since Fiona met Simon. Not to mention Peyton and Matteo."

Zach rubbed his eyes. "There's a timeline, too."

"Why are we talking about this?" Georgie turned the heat down to cold, as if it had been set to sweltering.

"Because of your dread about meeting Conner and the others," he reminded her.

"Tell me you don't have any standards or dating rules." A bold defiance was wrapped around her words, daring him to deny her.

"I don't kiss and tell." He winked at her.

She scowled. The irritation tacked between her bunched eyebrows and the frustration tightening her sweet mouth made him want to kiss her. Truly, once and for all, fluster her like she'd never been. Now he'd flustered himself.

"That's not original." She pushed on his shoulder, a light, playful nudge. "Tell me something serious."

I seriously think I want to kiss you. He cleared his throat, spilled a different truth. "Loyalty matters. A lot." Despite everything, the all-night binges and his mother's addictions, his dad had been loyal to his mom their entire marriage. "Actions are always stronger than words."

"Words are simple," she said. "But how do you measure the other person's loyalty?"

"You don't need to. At some point the person you're dating faces a decision, and their true loyalty surfaces." How many times could his dad have walked away? His dad could've headed out on one of his jobs in his 18-wheeler and never returned to his family. But his father had always come back to them, and those had been the times that Zach had lived for. He'd endured until then, marking the days off on a stained calendar.

"What if the other person never faces a big decision?" she asked. "How do you really know they'll be loyal to you?"

Georgie liked proof. He'd picked up on that much already. He smiled. "People are challenged every single day to make a choice. Could be as complicated as defending a friend's character or as simple as choosing omelets for dinner."

"How does choosing omelets for dinner prove a person's loyalty?" She laughed.

The lighthearted, carefree sound filled the car and Zach. He wanted to make her laugh more. "Choosing breakfast for dinner proves you're loyal to the most important meal of the day."

"Or it proves you need to go to the grocery store."

"That, too." He chuckled. "Still, you can learn a lot about someone if you pay attention to the small details."

"What details have you noticed about me?" She bit into her bottom lip on the same side, in the same corner, as she'd done before.

The tiniest of actions cornered Zach's attention, drew him in and made him consider her even more. Was she nervous? Shy? Perhaps rattled. Zach fastened his gaze back on the road. She bit her lip. Nothing unusual about it. Nothing very interesting about such a common quirk. Yet there was something entirely too intriguing about Georgiana Harrison.

He might have wanted to learn more about her, but their time together ended soon.

Fortunately, her phone vibrated in the console where she'd put it and rescued him from answering her question.

She lifted her phone and looked at him. "It's my sister Amanda."

Within minutes, Georgie's conversation turned into a conference call and then a video chat among the five Harrison sisters. Georgie slipped on a pair of headphones and left Zach decoding a one-sided conversation about Lily's upcoming wedding.

He turned up the radio and concentrated on keeping the car at a reasonable speed.

The next hundred miles included more phone calls, a distinct fidgeting from Georgie until she finally fell asleep and only one wrong turn for Zach. Finally, he drove under the Black-well Family Guest Ranch sign. Beside him, Georgie woke and became more and more restless, touching her hair, her face, tugging on her sweater, then repeating the process. He parked the car in a wide parking lot.

Two women bundled from head to boots in snow gear cheered from the sidewalk outside an impressive two-story lodge with a wide wrap-around porch. The women rushed the car.

"These are my sisters Lily and Fiona." Georgie jumped out and embraced the two women.

The excited trio hugged and talked at the same time. Words tumbled over each other, making it hard for Zach to follow their conversation. He waited inside the car, unsure of the proper protocol. Did he introduce himself? Give Georgie her shopping bags and leave without an introduction? He waited for guidance from Georgie. This was her family.

The sisters spun around as if joined and peered at him inside the car. Zach lifted his hand and waved.

Seconds later, Georgie climbed back into the car and slammed the door. Her words sputtered out like steam from a blown radiator. "Sorry. I didn't mean to. I mean, I considered it earlier. But not for long. It's all kinds of wrong. We'd already agreed on that."

Zach rubbed his chin. Her face was pale. From the windchill or something else, he wasn't quite certain. He turned up the heat, aimed the air vent in her direction.

"Then Lily called you Colin and I laughed." She clutched her computer bag on her lap and rambled on, "You two would never be confused for each other. Never. But they never met Colin, so how would they know?"

Zach remained quiet. He'd learned the value of silence as a kid.

Georgie's sisters climbed into an ATV and shut the doors of the hard cab enclosure. The

ATV reversed and the sisters gave them the thumbs-up sign.

Nothing inside their rental car was thumbs-up worthy. "Your sisters are signaling to us."

"Follow them." The tension in Georgie's voice matched her grip on her bag. "I'm sorry."

"You mentioned that." Zach nodded.

"I told them you were my wedding date." Her voice climbed an octave higher. "It just came out. I blurted out—that's not Colin, that's Zach, my date."

Zach searched for air in the suddenly too-warm car. And everything seemed blurrier than being caught at midnight in snow fog. Everything...except the fact he'd be able to use the leverage of being Georgie's boyfriend to get full access to Ethan. His horse wouldn't survive without Ethan's care. He'd lose Rain Dancer and his rodeo career. But not now, thanks to Georgie's slipup.

"What are we supposed to do? We have to tell them the truth." Her aggravated voice nudged the sudden quiet aside. "This is what happens to people who take shortcuts. I never take shortcuts."

He only wanted an introduction to Ethan. The opportunity to plead for his horse in person. Zach followed the sisters' ATV around the main lodge and down another road, past the stables, several barns and a white farmhouse. He wanted to take the shortcut to Ethan Blackwell. Was that so wrong? "What happens when shortcuts are taken?"

"Failure happens, that's what." Georgie's fingers drummed a silent, angry beat against her leg. "Then your family really believes you can't function outside of your research lab. And when you tell them you're moving to London, they'll worry and become even more anxious."

He followed the ATV into a circular driveway in front of a two-story log home. He parked beside a silver truck and shifted toward Georgie. He'd take it one thing at a time. "We can keep up the pretense."

"You can't be serious," she said. "I worked with Colin for over a month so he could get all the details straight."

"You don't leave anything to chance, do you?"

"No, especially not with a risk this big." She clutched the dashboard and gaped out the window. "This cannot be happening. I cannot stay here."

Zach tracked her gaze. An older woman wrapped in a long sweater coat and fur-lined boots stepped off a wide porch framing the log house. She hugged each of Georgie's sisters, touching their cheeks, her smile kind and gentle. "Who is that?"

"I think it's my grandmother."

Zach had never met his grandparents. Georgie's grandmother looked like the kind he'd always wanted as a kid. He scratched his cheek. "What do you want to do?"

"I'll give you my sixty-second short." She inhaled, held her breath. Her words streamed out on her long exhalation. "None of my four sisters will believe we're dating. We lost our mother earlier this year. Now my father is on a mission to have each of his daughters blissfully settled into married life."

"Sorry about your mom." Zach set his hand on her arm.

He had no college degree and no family. He lived on the road with his horse, chasing the next eight-second ride. Georgie had a medical degree, a tight-knit family and everything going for her. Of course her sisters would not believe they were together. The doctor and the cowboy. Maybe on TV. But in the real world… "You're right. We should tell them."

She blinked at him. "They won't believe we're dating because they know I don't believe in insta-love, like they do."

"It's your guidelines, isn't it?" he asked.

"We don't have time for this. They're waiting for us." She clung to the door handle. "Colin and I practiced how we'd fake the relationship. We've known each other for years."

"Right." He opened his door. "I'll tell them I'm just dropping you off. As we agreed."

"Fine." Georgie nodded. "That's what we should do."

A sense of foreboding washed over Zach. "One last question. Is there a problem with your grandparents?"

"Just one."

"Is it a big problem?" Zach pressed.

"It depends on your definition of *big*. If you consider the fact that I've never met my Blackwell grandparents big, then yes. It's a very big problem." Georgie scrambled out of the car. "I only wanted to make a good impression." She looked away.

But not before he saw the terror on her face and heard the alarm in her voice. Zach joined Georgie on the shoveled path and took her gloved hand. "It's going to be okay."

The three women huddled together on the sidewalk, each one grinning wider than the next. Plump snowflakes drifted around them, but their attention remained fixed on Zach and Georgie. More exactly, Georgie and Zach's joined hands. One of her sisters bounced in her snow boots. The other pressed her hands over her mouth as if sighing out her excitement.

Dorothy Blackwell introduced herself. She embraced Georgie, then Zach, in a warm, welcoming hug. "Please call me Grandma Dot like the rest of the family. The whole family can't wait to meet you both."

Georgie had never met any of her Blackwell family. *None of them.* Zach searched for air. A bull had kicked him in the ribs twice years ago and he hadn't been as winded as he was now. The only clear thing he knew was that he didn't want to leave Georgie alone, but he'd given his word. He opened his mouth.

Georgie twisted and set her hand on his chest, stalling his confession. "Grandmother. Dorothy, this is Zach Evans, my boyfriend."

CHAPTER FIVE

MY BOYFRIEND. GEORGIE just jumped in with both feet. Never mind that the last time she'd jumped in with both feet had been at summer camp in seventh grade. And she had ended up with a concussion and a broken arm. She strained to find her most convincing smile.

Beside her, Zach wheezed as if he choked on air. "Pleasure to meet you all."

She was going to owe him. Big-time.

"We're pleased to welcome you to our home." Dorothy clasped her hands together. "Let's get your things inside and get you two settled."

"Zach, I'm not sure if Georgie explained that the guest cabins and the main guest lodge have been winterized," Lily said, unaware that Georgie hadn't explained anything. "Hadley and Ty Blackwell manage the guest ranch. They like to save on electric and utilities by closing down the guest cabins and rooms while it's only our family at the ranch."

"Simon and I are in Lily's former one-bedroom cabin. It's the only one not closed for the winter."

Fiona's words tumbled out in an excited rush. "But you two will have your own suite, with a bathroom and sitting room, here at Grandma Dot and Big E's private home."

"That's generous." Again, Zach sounded winded, like he still hadn't recovered from his air hiccup. Or Georgie's outburst.

Georgie wrapped her arm around Zach's waist and searched for balance.

"I'll show you to your room. Zach can get your things later." Dorothy led the way into her house. "Then I have to get my sewing supplies together. Georgie, we need to get you fitted for your bridesmaid dress before dinner."

"Grandma Dot is our seamstress." Lily beamed from the entryway. "Fee and I need to run to Hadley's to pick up the faux fur stoles she found for all of you. We'll be right back for Georgie's fitting."

"Be careful, you two." Dorothy closed the thick oak door. "Come in. Come in. Help yourself to anything in the kitchen."

Georgie would race in there right now if she thought the pantry held the answers to what she should do next. The truth wound around her, ready to be spilled. *Grandmother. Dorothy. It's not what...*

"We want you to feel right at home." Dorothy led them into the great room.

A stone fireplace dominated one wall. Monogrammed stockings hung from the mantel, while lights twinkled in the lush holly-berry garland and wreath above it. Windows extended from the first floor up into the second story toward the vaulted ceiling and framed the snow-covered forest and frozen creek outside.

A Christmas tree joined the kitchen and great room. A pie and holiday cookies waited on the granite countertops. Candles burned on the island. Vanilla and cinnamon scented the air. Fleece blankets and throw pillows, announcing joy and glad tidings, covered the oversized couch and love seat. The padded bar stools around the island invited guests to sit and stay for a while.

Georgie felt instantly warm and welcomed inside Dorothy's home. And ready now to confess. "Thank you for letting us stay here."

"You're family and will always have a place here," Dorothy said.

Maybe not. Not once her grandmother learned the truth about their deception. *Speak now or forever hold your peace.* Zach wasn't Georgie's groom, only a fake wedding date.

"Your room is upstairs." Dorothy motioned to the curved staircase. "I've added extra blankets, pillows and more firewood."

Georgie followed Zach into the upstairs guest

suite. A smaller stone fireplace, thick plush carpets and a king-sized four-poster bed accented the space.

Dorothy finished the tour, pointing out the bathroom and attached reading nook. "I'm off to gather my sewing basket. I'll let you two get situated."

A soft click of the bedroom door and Georgie was alone with Zach.

Zach scrubbed his hands over his face. "What just happened?"

"I met my grandmother for the first time." Georgie flopped back on the center of the bed and dropped her arm over her face. "And introduced you as my boyfriend."

"I got that part," he said. "How is it that you only just met your grandmother?"

"We don't have time for that story now." She lifted her arm and eyed him. "But the short version is my sister Lily found her birth certificate with Thomas Blackwell listed as her father, not Rudy Harrison. Our dad confirmed the truth and here we are."

Currently the man Georgie called Dad, Rudy Harrison, and Georgie's new Blackwell grandfather, Big E, were on a road trip to locate the girls' biological father, Thomas Blackwell. An impossible mission.

If Thomas Blackwell had wanted to be found,

he'd have returned to his family long before now. If a wife and five young daughters hadn't been enough for Thomas to stay, what could Rudy and Big E offer Thomas now to come back to the family he'd abandoned?

He set his hands on his hips and stared down at her. "What now?"

She worked her voice into optimistic. "I get to introduce you to my cousin Ethan."

His eyebrows lowered and his gaze narrowed. "What do you get?"

A reprieve from her father's disappointment. *Georgiana, I promised your mother. Georgiana, you can't marry your job. Georgiana, you'll never find a partner inside the lab, so let me introduce you to...* "A wedding date." And a potential supporter of her London Project.

"If we're going to do this, you have to tell me everything," he said. "Colin was more than a simple wedding date, wasn't he?"

"Colin was my security." She sat up, crossed her legs on the bed and hugged one of the fluffy pillows. "I've accepted a new job in the UK at a medical research lab. Colin is a colleague and longtime friend. He'll also be working at the same lab."

Zach rested his arm on the wooden fireplace mantel and watched her, his face unreadable.

"Colin was going to help convince my fam-

ily that London was a good career move," she
continued.

"You can't convince your family of that yourself?" he asked.

"They think I get lost in the lab and forget to
enjoy life," she said. "My dad constantly lec-
tures me on work–life balance, specifically that
I don't have any. It's work, work, work, all the
time. If they thought I was going to London
with my boyfriend, then…"

"They wouldn't worry so much," he filled in.

"Exactly," she said. "After the year we've had,
losing our mom and Lily canceling one wedding and planning another, I don't want them
to worry."

"So, you need me to reassure them you're
perfectly capable, so they won't be concerned,"
he said.

"It won't work now," she said.

"Why not?" he asked. "I can be persuasive
if I need to."

"They won't believe you," she said. "You're
a cowboy, nationally ranked in the rodeo. They
won't believe you'd give all that up to move to
London with me."

"Maybe I want a change," he suggested.

She arched an eyebrow at him. "Are you re-
tiring from the rodeo sometime soon?"

"It's not in my immediate plans." He paused.

His gaze narrowed as if he were looking into a future he didn't want to see. "Not unless…"

"Unless…" she said. He'd wanted her to tell him everything. She wanted the same.

"I have a sick horse." He wiped his palm over his mouth as if he'd like to retract his confession.

"And your horse is the reason you need Ethan's help." Her cousin was a veterinarian and well-known for not turning his back when other veterinarians walked away. She'd heard stories about Ethan and his animal healing skills. Georgie didn't know much about those kinds of skills and patients, opting to spend most of her time in the lab.

Zach moved to the window, set his hands on his hips and kept his back to her. If she was good with people, she'd know the right thing to do right now. The right thing to do for Zach. "Do you ride your own horse in your events?"

"Only in the calf roping," he said. "The broncs are drawn from the stock."

"Then you could continue in the rodeo, even if your horse can't," she said.

"It's complicated." He turned toward her. Distress tightened across his jaw. "Rain Dancer has been with me since I started competing. We never missed a rodeo together. Not one."

She nodded, although she didn't quite under-

stand his connection to his horse. She understood connections to people. Her sister Amanda
would recognize and value Zach's relationship
with Rain Dancer. All Georgie really understood was that everything seemed complicated.

And the only way to handle complications
was to deal with them head-on. Formulate an
approach and dismantle the obstacle piece by
piece.

"Are we fessing up, then?" Zach asked.

"We just misled my grandmother and my sisters, then accepted Dorothy's hospitality." Georgie tossed the pillow against the headboard.
"We have to play this out."

Zach stilled and eyed her.

"No one knows you're a rodeo star except
me." Georgie turned over possible strategies and
outcomes in her mind. "It could work. I just
need you to be less cowboy."

"Less cowboy," he repeated.

"You know. Leave your hat off." She glanced
at his feet. "Do you have any other shoes besides boots?"

He shook his head.

"We'll figure something out." She recited one
of her pages from Colin's spreadsheet. "I need
to know your favorite food. Favorite color. Important things about you."

"That's not necessary."

"Yes. It is." Georgie reached for her laptop bag. She had copies of Colin's material for the London Project on her computer.

"If I told you my favorite food was deep-dish pizza, does it make you like me more?" He interrupted her search for her paperwork.

Georgie glanced at him.

He continued, "Or what if I claimed forty-clove garlic chicken and pasta was my favorite dish ever?"

"That makes me like your breath less." She unzipped her laptop bag.

"Fair enough." He smiled and relaxed against the window frame. "But those details don't really matter."

"If you're allergic to peanuts or shellfish or milk products, those details matter very much." She pulled out her laptop and power cord.

"No allergies, food or otherwise." He tipped his head toward her. "What about you?"

"No allergies either."

"Look, I think too many specifics give us too many chances to slip up and get things completely wrong." He sat on the bed, blocking her access to the electrical outlet. "Then our pretend relationship will be blown for sure."

Her fingers curled around her laptop. She had a strategy already outlined on her computer. "What do you propose we do?"

"Make things up as we go." He stretched out until his back rested against the headboard and stacked his hands behind his head. "It's all fake anyway. The particulars don't have to be real either."

"But it's the details that ensure the ruse will be believable." She'd spent her life immersed in details. The small things mattered.

"We don't have a month to prepare like you and Colin," he said. "We can have a signal."

"A signal like touching our noses." Her voice and tone were drier than desert dust.

"Not that obvious. When we get asked a personal question about our relationship and I don't know what to say, I'll say, *Georgie tells this story better than me*. And then you tell whatever story you want."

"What about when we aren't together?" She was doubtful his scheme would work.

"We make it up." He lifted his hand and added a warning to his words. "But keep it succinct and short."

"Sixty seconds short," she said.

"Exactly." He sat up and leaned toward her. "So, to be clear. It's an introduction and good word to your cousin from you in exchange for London backing from me."

"That's our deal." She patted the mattress.

"But nothing in our arrangement includes sharing this bed."

"We'll trade off," he said. "Tonight, you sleep here. Tomorrow night it's mine. I'm not as young as I used to be."

He looked more than fine stretched out on the bed. Hardly worn down at all.

"It's only fair," he said. "You never really gave me a chance to agree to this ruse. You sort of owe me."

He was right. She'd been the one to continue the lie, even after they'd decided to come clean. She'd been as surprised as he must have been. Truly, she'd been desperate, and her mouth determined to continue the hoax. "Fine. We trade off nights in the bed."

He grinned. "Your sisters are calling you."

"I need to go." She searched his face. "We're really doing this?"

"Appears so."

"They're going to ask me questions about you," she said. "Like, what do you do?"

"I'm good with my hands," he said.

Not the answer she'd been looking for. "I'll come up with something. Are you going to be okay?"

He took off his hat and set it on the nightstand. "I'm going to try out the bed. See how it works. I could use a nap."

She crossed her arms over her chest. "We never discussed napping terms."

"I think naps are optional." He tugged off his boots and grinned at her.

"Optional," she repeated.

"You can join me if you want, but you have to stay on your side of the bed." He fluffed a pillow. "Your sisters are calling you again. Do you want me to tell them we're busy discussing napping conditions?"

Georgie spun around and hurried out of the bedroom. Zach's deep chuckle trailed after her.

Join me. Georgie stumbled and sprinted down the stairs.

Her sisters and Dorothy had gathered in the enclosed sunroom. Late-afternoon light streamed in the oversized windows, the better to highlight Georgie's deception.

"Good. You're here." Lily held a deep red gown. "Put this on."

Dorothy pulled a pincushion from a vintage sewing basket. "There's a powder room down the hall, toward our bedroom."

Georgie padded across the hardwood floors in her fleece socks and clutched the top of the strapless floor-length gown to her chest.

It didn't take very long for her to wiggle into the dress, which Fee zipped closed. "It's not fair. The dress fits you perfectly."

Georgie stepped onto the small riser in the sunroom and tugged at the material dragging behind her. "It does not."

"That's nothing but extra yardage." Fee adjusted the drop shoulder on Georgie's arm. "The dress fits where it counts."

"It certainly does. You're making my job easier." Dorothy stood back and eyed Georgie. "You look lovely, dear."

Georgie smoothed her hands down her stomach. The gown was cut to accentuate a woman's figure without displaying too much. Still, Georgie felt exposed in the fitted gown. Her shoulders were bare. There were no pockets to bury her hands in. And the bold, deep crimson color demanded notice. Promised she would be hard to miss, like the scheme she'd orchestrated.

"Okay, don't be mad." Lily clapped her hands together.

Alarm clapped around Georgie.

Fee picked up a shoebox and took off the lid to display the contents. "We picked out shoes, too."

Faux fur trim covered the tops of the gray ankle-high boots. The *heeled* ankle-high boots. "We know you like flats."

Because she could walk in flats. Because she wouldn't wobble or trip or face-plant in flats.

Because outrunning bad decisions was easier in flats.

"But these are adorable." Fee picked up the matching gray faux fur wrap. "And we coordinated the colors."

"At least put them on," Lily urged. "You can wear them around the house this week and practice."

While she practiced reciting all the things she made up about her relationship with Zach. Georgie took the boots from her sister and slipped them on.

Fee and Lily sighed at the same time.

"They do look rather fetching. I admit I was worried about the fur." Dorothy knelt in front of Georgie and tugged the gown around Georgie's feet. "But it all comes together rather well, doesn't it?"

"Now we have nothing to do but talk about Zach." Fee quickly chose a seat and folded her hands in her lap.

Georgie swayed on the wedge heels and locked her knees. "I want to hear about Conner and Simon."

Lily swept up the pile of faux fur wraps and made a place for herself on the sofa. "We've told you all about the men in our lives on our phone calls."

But Georgie had been avoiding everything

related to Falcon Creek, including her sisters. She'd buried herself in her lab, finalizing the last of her research paper to submit for possible publication in a well-respected medical journal. And had been more concerned about coaching Colin on how to be a flawless partner in her ruse than really listening to her sisters.

Guilt splashed through Georgie. How she'd often heard the refrain *family first* from her dad.

Rudy Harrison had always put his wife and daughters first. He wasn't the girls' biological father, as they'd believed all their lives. Yet Rudy was and would always be Georgie's dad. As for her family, she had the next ten days to put her sisters first.

"It's all we seem to talk about it, isn't it?" Fee grinned. "We should find a new topic, I suppose."

"Talking about the people who mean the most to you isn't a conversation that ever goes stale." Dorothy stuck several pins in the hem of Georgie's dress.

"There." Georgie motioned to Dorothy and tried not to wobble like the pincushion on her grandmother's wrist. "You've been given permission to keep on talking about Conner and Simon."

"But it's your turn. You have the floor and our

undivided attention." Lily sorted the silver faux fur wraps on the sofa. "Tell us all about Zach."

She had a cowboy who'd agreed to be her pretend date. A cowboy she'd met on an airplane. If he'd only remained a superficial charmer, she could've dismissed him. But pain and angst shadowed him, and Georgie wanted to know all about him, too. That was only her inquisitive nature stepping forward. "He's really tall."

"We saw that for ourselves." Fee stretched out as if to get even more ready for a long tale.

"I don't know what to say." Finally, the first truth she'd spilled. Still, she flinched, fought to keep her shoulders from sagging forward.

"Start at the beginning," Lily said. "How you met. Where your first date was. Your second date."

There hadn't been any dates. Not a first or a last. She scrambled to recall the details of her most recent date. Nothing came to mind. How long had it been since she'd gone on a date? Her sisters accused her of losing herself inside her research lab. That wasn't true. Couldn't be true. Uncertainty arced through her guilt.

"What does he do for a living? Have you met his family?" Fee joined in. "Why have you never mentioned him to us?"

She hadn't known Zach had existed until today. Her shoulders drooped. Deception weighed more than the weight of the world. "I told you I was bringing someone to the wedding."

Fee glowered at her. "You know what I mean."

"He's a good guy. He likes horses, plaid and peppermint brownie ice cream cake." And that was all she really knew. Except he concealed his pain beneath his charm. Had secrets—the kind she sensed hurt—and his claim that he liked being alone sounded more like a shield than the truth. If she probed into his past and the painful parts, she'd move their relationship into something more than fake. Fake was all it could ever be.

"We know he's a good guy or you wouldn't have brought him home to meet us," Fee countered.

"You definitely wouldn't have included him in our Christmas," Lily added. "This is our special time to spend together as a family."

That weight of deception rolled against her, the force rocking Georgie in her heels and shoving her off-kilter. She'd brought Zach home to further her own cause, not for him to become part of the family. What had she done?

"Almost finished." Dorothy reached up, set her hand on Georgie's waist and helped steady her. The older woman's perceptive gaze lifted to Georgie. "Once you put your other clothes and boots back on, you'll find your balance again."

If only that was true. Not only did she not have the right clothes for the week, they were lost in Central America. She didn't have the right plus-one either. He'd never made the connecting flight. She didn't even have the right words. Georgie pressed her heels into the platform, willed herself to stand tall and accept the weight of her deception. Silently, she urged Dorothy to hurry before she buckled.

Finally, Dorothy rose and smiled. "Fiona, help your sister out of the dress and be careful of all the pins. I'll meet you in my room. The sewing machine is in the alcove and I could use an extra set of hands."

Georgie did another quick change and headed for the sunroom. Her feet were back inside her suede booties. Her fleece leggings were back on, too. And she'd put on the new sweater she'd purchased earlier at the store. Any minute now, she'd surely start feeling like herself. She stepped through the archway and Lily stood up from the sofa.

"You know what's weird? I could have sworn that you told me the name of your plus-one was Colin...not Zach. Is something going on?"

"You misheard." Georgie cringed and tugged on the high collar of her new sweater. It hadn't been so tight or so scratchy in the dressing room at the store.

"I hate to say it, sis, but Zach is no more a research doctor than I am."

Georgie lifted her chin. "Mom always told us we could be anything we wanted. Cowboys can be doctors, too."

"I know that." Exasperation saturated Lily's words. "Is that what you're telling me? Zach is your colleague?"

Georgie spread her arms wide, as if the more space she occupied, the more credible she'd sound. "I'm telling you Zach is my boyfriend."

Lily tilted her head to the side. Her gaze searched Georgie's face as if scanning for proof of Georgie's deceit.

Georgie held her ground. Refused to wince at the sunlight reflecting off the windows. Her heart raced. She had to convince Lily. Otherwise her sisters, not to mention her dad, would send Zach packing. Then they'd argue Georgie shouldn't be left alone, especially in another country, and would plead with her to move closer to them. They'd offer friends, neighbors and coworkers as potential love interests for her. All because they loved and cared about her.

She loved and cared about them, too. But it would be the hurt from her deception that would bring Georgie to her knees. She'd never wanted to upset her family. *Ever.* The truth couldn't come out.

"You're serious?"

The surprise on Lily's face sparked inside Georgie, kindling her irritation. She chose not to date. It wasn't that she couldn't date. "Why does it sound like, despite what you said, you'd have an easier time believing Zach is my colleague, rather than my boyfriend?"

"Because you don't date." Lily lifted her eyebrows, challenging Georgie to debate that fact.

"I do now." As of an hour earlier. As of this moment. If only she knew what that meant exactly. She'd outlined the parameters for Colin. When to hold hands. When to hug. Emphasized the no-kissing rule. But Zach was definitely not Colin. *You can join me.* Georgie wiped her hand over her mouth. The no-kissing rule would remain in effect. She ignored the twinge of regret and faced her sister.

She curled her toes inside her boots, prepping for that growing ball of deception to slam into her. How many lies could she shoulder and not crumble? She was about to find out. "I'm dating Zach."

"Are you trying to convince me or you?" Lily asked.

"Cut me some slack, will you?" Outbursts weren't her thing. *Ever.* Neither was kissing cowboys. She steadied her tone to be calm and practical. "You're right. I don't date a lot. And

I never bring guys home to meet my family. But I just did."

"Does this mean you've been converted?" Lily grinned. "That you believe in things like the heart knows what it wants and love at first sight?"

"Love." Georgie's voice cracked. Her knees unlocked and wavered.

"Yes, love. It's the thing Conner and I are in."

"I know what love is." She'd just never wanted it for herself.

"Oh, Georgie." Lily laughed and wrapped her in a strong hug.

The heartfelt sincerity made her sister's joy all the more distressing. Georgie hung on to Lily. But all she wanted to do was collapse on the guest-room bed and have her cowboy hold her.

Lily added, "I'm really happy for you, Dr. Harrison."

CHAPTER SIX

FAMILY DINNER ON the Blackwell ranch was no simple occasion. It was an experience. The twenty-plus gathering included all five Blackwell brothers, their wives and kids. Then extended to Frank and Alice Gardner, Grace's parents and Ethan's in-laws. As well as Conner Hannah's mom, Karen, who was Lily's future mother-in-law. Everyone arrived in a steady stream at the main dining hall. The smell of fresh-baked bread and barbecue permeated the air. A fire crackled in the stone fireplace, transforming the massive space into something quaint and intimate.

Seven towering Christmas trees, all individually decorated, twinkled on one side of the room. Festive decorations extended from the thick pine branch garland and red candles on the fireplace mantel to the assortment of over twenty stockings fastened to the opposite wall in an explosion of holiday cheer. Christmas on the Blackwell Family Guest Ranch exceeded anything Zach and his brother had ever dreamed of.

Lily and Fiona flanked Georgie and Zach, making the introductions to every family member. Hugs were offered and accepted as if standard greeting behavior. Zach couldn't recall another time he'd embraced so many people. Or that so many people had embraced him. Heady and addicting, if he allowed himself to believe he really belonged.

The family-style, help-yourself dinner only escalated the lively and spirited conversations. Ben and Ethan Blackwell, brothers and identical twins, tossed dinner rolls to their other brothers, Jon and Chance, across several tables, earning cheers from the kids and scoldings from Dorothy. The brothers happily changed to underhand bun tosses until Katie, Chance's wife, seized the bun basket. Undeterred, the brothers plucked candy canes from one of the Christmas trees and rewarded the kids for their support.

Georgie's sisters joined the conversations easily, doled out and received their own ribbings as if they'd always been a part of the Blackwell clan. Georgie and Zach sat on the fringes, at the end of one table. As the evening progressed, Georgie had retreated more and more into herself, her hugs awkward, her greetings simple and quick. Zach hadn't left her side.

Dinner concluded and the kids shouted for s'mores outside. Cleanup became another family affair. Everyone knew their role and responsibility in the process. Within minutes the dining hall was put back to rights and prepped for breakfast the following morning.

S'mores supplies ready and the kids bundled up for the cold weather, the group drifted outside to the firepit area. Before Zach could catch her, Georgie escaped to the firepit the farthest away from the others and sat on a river-rock bench.

Zach carried over the s'mores ingredients and set them on the tree-stump table beside Georgie.

"There are too many marshmallows and too many Blackwells." Georgie's shoulders slumped inside her heavy coat. "I don't belong here."

"This is your family." Zach unwrapped a chocolate bar, broke it and handed her half.

"My family is my four sisters and my dad." She snapped off a corner of the chocolate bar and nibbled it.

Once again, Lily and Fiona wove through the Blackwells, laughing and teasing the others. The Blackwells were the kind of family he'd wished for growing up. The kind of family he'd thought his ex-girlfriend had invited him into. The kind of family that had always been out of his reach.

That fact he had to remember. "They all seem like very nice people."

"That's not helpful." Georgie dropped the piece of chocolate back onto the plate. "We're deceiving them, remember?"

"We can come clean," he suggested.

"And tell them that I picked up a virtual stranger on an airplane to deceive them?" She gaped at him. "They really won't like me then."

"You want them to like you?" He handed her one of the extra-long stainless-steel roasting forks.

"No. Yes." Georgie stabbed a marshmallow onto one prong and waved it in and out of the flames. "Maybe. I don't know."

"What do you want?" he asked.

"To at least know who is who," she blurted out. "I know all their names on paper. But now, in person, my mind keeps skipping. I should at least know who my family is, shouldn't I?"

Zach watched the flames scorch his marshmallows. He'd spent years altering the truth of his family. Years not wanting to admit what his family really was: broken and damaged. Money had been tight after his father passed. Zach's mother had been cremated without a memorial—Zach had chosen his brother's treatments and care over his mother's funeral.

He'd spent more nights than he cared to remember watching the moon rise and wishing for some unknown relatives to enter his life. Anyone to lessen the relentless loneliness. Georgie Harrison had been given a gift, and rather than embracing it, she wanted to run.

"I mean, I know the entire periodic table by heart. I can recite every bone, muscle and tendon in the entire body," Georgie continued. "Names to faces shouldn't be difficult. Not for me."

But fear scattered common sense. And Zach sensed Georgie's fear. Yet he wasn't quite sure how to help her. Knew only that he wanted to.

"You have to put the marshmallow in the fire if you want to roast it." A young girl, her big blue eyes wide and her pink snow boots even brighter, circled the firepit and tapped a glittery pink fingernail against her cheek. "Unless you like to eat them out of the bag like Uncle Ethan and Mama K."

Mama K was Katie Blackwell, and she managed the ranch. Zach searched for the girl's name. Summer or a flower or something from nature. He'd been associating names and characteristics since he was a kid to help himself remember first names. The neighbors had always responded better to his partial truths about his mom if he recalled their first names. The twin red spots on the young girl's cheeks clued Zach in. The adorable bundle of pink cheer was Rosie Blackwell.

Zach knocked his burned marshmallows into the fire. Then he doubled up with fresh marshmallows on his roasting fork, gripped the wooden handle and set it over the fire. "I'm Zach and this is…"

"Auntie Georgie." Rosie climbed onto the bench and scooted over until she bumped right into Georgie's side. "I know. Auntie Georgie is a doctor and she cures people."

"That's right." Georgie smiled and zipped Rosie's coat under her chin. She handed Rosie a marshmallow for her stick.

"What do I do for a job, Rosie?" Zach grinned. Rosie had flipped off the tops of her mittens and left them to dangle near her wrists. Cute mitts for a cute kid.

"The grown-ups aren't sure." Rosie rolled her marshmallow through the flames. "Auntie Georgie never really talked at dinner."

Georgie had seemed to lose her voice and her place amid the happy chaos of the group dinner. Zach said, "I like to ride broncs in the rodeo."

Rosie nodded and pulled her stick from the fire. "I like horses a lot. Just like my mama K."

Zach liked friendly, easy-to-talk-to kids like Rosie. "Do you like games, Rosie?"

"Definitely." Rosie built a s'more quickly and

handed the finished sandwich to Georgie. "Want to play one?"

"We do." Zach slid his slightly toasted marshmallows onto a graham cracker and eyed Georgie. "We want to play the name game."

Georgie took a bite of Rosie's s'more. "You definitely have the magic touch. This is the best one I've ever tasted."

Rosie beamed. "What's the name game?"

Zach lowered his voice into confession soft. "Georgie and I need practice learning everyone's names."

"There's a lot of new people here." Georgie wiped a napkin over her mouth and nodded at him as if acknowledging his plan. "We don't want to get a name wrong and hurt someone's feelings."

Rosie nodded. "Want to know a secret?"

Zach and Georgie leaned in.

"Even Uncle Ethan mixes up the cousins' names all the time." Rosie licked chocolate from her finger. "He's always calling us by the names Aunt Grace gives to the petting-zoo animals."

"Let's start with the Blackwell family." Georgie set her unfinished s'more on a napkin on her lap. "We can move to the animals tomorrow."

"I'll test you to see who you don't know." Rosie snatched a plain marshmallow from the supply plate. "Mama K tests me on my spelling words and then I'm not scared to take my spelling tests."

Leave it to a child to point out the obvious. But Zach wasn't sure what scared Georgie more: the Blackwells' acceptance or rejection.

Between Zach and Georgie, they knew most of the family. The game paused and Rosie added, "Auntie Rachel—remember, she's married to Uncle Ben. Well, she won't eat any s'mores. She didn't eat anything at dinner either."

"Why not?" Georgie frowned.

"Aunt Rachel says the babies are making her stomach angry every day." Rosie patted her own stomach. "And she hasn't found any food the babies like."

"That's not good." Georgie wiped her hands on another napkin. Her focus remained on Rachel, who sat between Katie and Hadley. The three pregnant women had propped their feet on the rim of a firepit.

Zach recognized Georgie's distracted tone. The assessing, deep-in-thought voice every one of his brother's doctors had lapsed into during their first appointments with Cody. Zach wasn't certain if Georgie—the patient-care doctor or the research doctor—had stepped forward.

His brother's early doctors had only ever wanted to qualify Cody for their trials. To turn him into a statistic. After the last failed trial, Cody had ordered a cease and desist and finally located a doctor who treated Cody, the person, first. Zach would be forever grateful to Dr. Holloway and his team for the care they'd given his brother in his last year.

Zach searched Georgie's profile and wanted to believe she was interested in more than the research data and clinical trials.

"I got sick once after my friend's birthday party." Rosie swung her booted feet back and forth. "Mama K said I ate too much cake. I asked for extra icing."

"Stomachaches are no fun." Georgie rubbed Rosie's back. "What did you do?"

Zach watched Georgie's hand move in circles on Rosie's back. She didn't lean away from Rosie or dismiss her past experience. If anything, Georgie edged closer to listen better. Bedside manner could be taught, he supposed. But the medical professionals with the best bedside manner possessed a quality Zach couldn't name, but that he recognized. Like now, between Georgie and Rosie.

"I only eat cupcakes at birthday parties now." Rosie slipped the tops of her mittens back over her fingers. "And I only eat half the frosting. Do you think Aunt Rachel has to stop eating food now, too?"

"I think the babies would be really upset then," Georgie said. "We just need to find foods Aunt Rachel and the babies like."

"You can do that?" Rosie asked.

"I can try," Georgie said.

And Zach would try to show Georgie why she belonged in the Blackwell family.

"Can you try to find something for Grandma Dot's knee, too?" Rosie clutched her hands together even though the worry lifted from her voice. "She won't rock in her favorite chair in the dining hall anymore 'cause of her knee."

Zach watched Dorothy massage her right knee. Lily and Fiona sat on either side of the older woman. Their significant others, Conner and Simon, stood on the other side of the firepit and handed the women toasted marshmallows. "Did she hurt her knee?"

Rosie shrugged. "Grandma Dot says when you get to be her age, every bone inside your body seems to have a complaint."

Zach was only a few years into his thirties and most mornings he woke to his whole body complaining. The rodeo lifestyle wasn't kind to the bones. But those eight seconds on a bucking bronc provided a thrill that life never could. A thrill he didn't think he could live without.

"Grandma Dot also says she tells herself

every morning that the complaint department is closed." Rosie giggled and lifted her legs straight out. "I tell my toes that when we have to walk really far and they get really tired."

Zach grinned at Georgie over Rosie's curly blond head. "So, we shouldn't complain to Grandma Dot. Good tip. Anything else we need to know?"

"Aunt Hadley and Mama K are about to pop with their babies and that means they're the only ones who get to complain out loud," Rosie added. "Everyone says so."

"Any tips for telling Uncle Ethan and Uncle Ben apart?" Zach asked.

"That's easy." Rosie smashed her hat over her curls. "Uncle Ethan smells like animals. He makes them feel better. Uncle Ben smells like a new book. He's a lawyer and studies books all the time."

Zach could not rely on a sniff test to tell Ethan and Ben Blackwell apart.

"That's very helpful," Georgie said. "I think I'm ready to run through the name game one last time."

Now that final identifications had been made, Zach only needed the evening to practice what would be his conversation with Ethan Blackwell. A conversation that would not include coming clean. If he confessed now, Ethan would definitely refuse to talk to him. That wasn't an option.

Tomorrow, he saved his horse and his rodeo lifestyle.

CHAPTER SEVEN

ZACH PROMISED DOROTHY he'd return for her homemade bourbon French toast, so ten minutes after sunrise he slipped out of the house. He'd dropped an extra blanket on Georgie and dressed without disturbing her.

He'd overheard several of the Blackwells discussing the morning chores the previous night. They'd been dividing and conquering, since the ranch staff had been given time off to spend Christmas with their families. With luck, Zach would catch Ethan at the stables.

Zach knew Rain Dancer wouldn't survive without Ethan's treatment. He wanted to ask Ethan for his assistance before the truth came out.

Zach rubbed his hands together, but the chill and fear lingered. He just had to find Ethan and talk to him alone. Face-to-face. He tugged open the stable door and stepped inside.

Ethan wasn't the Blackwell twisting around to scowl at him.

Rather, Katie Blackwell—Chance's very pregnant wife and the Blackwell ranch manager—pointed at Zach. "Do not tell me I should be in bed. Or resting. Or sitting down."

Zach took off his hat and rubbed his head. His experience with pregnant women was limited to sows, cows and mares. "I was going to ask if you've seen Ethan."

"Emergency with one of the mares out at Shadow Ridge Ranch." She crumpled a piece of paper in her hand. "You and I both missed him by about fifteen minutes."

Fifteen minutes. He'd lingered too long over his cup of coffee. The one Dorothy had already poured before he reached the kitchen. Now he faced another morning without obtaining help for Rain Dancer. Frustration knocked against his fear. The only outlet he'd ever relied on was work. "Is there anything you need help with?"

"I don't suppose you can help me see my ankles, can you?" Katie rubbed her lower back.

"That I can't do." Zach tugged off his gloves and moved to the first stall. A paint peered out, assessing the early morning disruption. He stroked the horse between its ears. "But anything equine and ranch related, I'm your guy."

"How do you feel about retirees?" Katie asked. "We call them our Blackwell Ambassadors."

"I like horses, all ages, any temperament, working or retired." Horses he understood. And they understood him. No words required. Besides, he needed time alone to revise his approach to Ethan.

Even more, to rework his feelings for Georgie. He had to stop confessing truths to her. He had to stop before he started wanting more than a temporary relationship. Before it became harder to convince himself that what he felt for Georgie was pretend and far from real.

"The Ambassadors are at the end of the stables." Katie motioned in their direction. "They've more than earned their free time, but Ethan likes to make sure they get plenty of attention and daily exercise."

"Turnout is essential for all horses," Zach said. "Too much time indoors can weaken the Ambassadors' health."

"Exactly." Katie's eyebrows hitched higher. "Are you a fan of the Ethan Blackwell school of equine medicine and therapy?"

Most definitely. And he was desperate for Ethan Blackwell to apply his own equine treatments to Rain Dancer. "Ethan is quite well-known in the equestrian world and for good reason."

"He does have a gift with animals," Katie said. "Now he has Grace to help polish his people skills."

Georgie came instantly to mind. She'd wanted

him to be less cowboy, as if that was possible. Perhaps his boots could use a good polish. His cynical nature a good smoothing out. Georgie could... No. Zach's people skills were fine. And he didn't need a woman, or specifically Georgie, to improve his life. He was okay as he was.

He walked toward the back stalls. "Anything special I should know about the Blackwell Ambassadors?"

Katie grinned and moved to a stable. A cream-colored draft horse popped his head out. "Elmer here is our resident chairman of the Ambassadors. He likes a longer, slower stroll and extra hay cubes for his effort. I'd take him last."

Zach stroked the large horse's neck. "I bet Elmer also likes a good rubdown."

"He'll follow you anywhere for the reward of a rubdown." Katie laughed and indicated the two stalls across from Elmer. "Misty Day and Ms. Aggie prefer their stalls heated and their mash wet and warmed. They can be stubborn. We listen, but eventually get our way."

Zach glanced at the two mares. "The ladies will go first."

"Good choice." Katie pointed to the next stalls. "Monty suffers from cataracts and likes his fly mask to block the sun's glare off the snow. Add salt to Lumber Jack's warm water to encourage him to drink more. They'll both enjoy a walk through the pasture."

Zach studied the names on the stalls. "Does Ethan stable Butterscotch in another barn? I read about her on the Blackwell ranch website." Butterscotch was listed as the honorary ranch mascot. He'd heard about Butterscotch's condition—the same one as Rain Dancer's—and Ethan's experimental treatment from a vet in Colorado.

Katie inhaled. Her eyebrows pulled together and her voice cracked. "Butterscotch passed away earlier this fall."

"I'm really sorry." More than he could express. More than he could put into words. Dread clenched the back of his neck like sharp talons. No wonder Ethan had refused to take his calls about Rain Dancer. What was he supposed to do now?

"Everyone took it hard, but Ethan the worst. Butterscotch had been their mother's horse. After their mom died, Ethan became even more attached to Butterscotch." Katie reached for Elmer, as if she wanted to hug the older horse. But her stomach stopped her. She wrapped her arms around her belly, clearly drawing comfort from her baby. "Please don't mention Butterscotch to Ethan. He hasn't talked about her since she passed."

"I won't mention anything." Except he had to tell Ethan his horse suffered from the same condition as Butterscotch. That he wanted Ethan to give Rain Dancer the same experimental treatment as Butterscotch. Maybe Rain Dancer's outcome would be different. Either way, Zach had to try.

He reached for the mare's stable door and gripped the thick wood. Still, his world tipped and slanted. "I think I'll get started with Ms. Aggie."

"I really appreciate your help." Katie pulled a knit hat from her jacket pocket and yanked it over her head. "I'm going to head to the dining hall and pretend I've been sitting there all morning before my husband wakes up."

"Too late." Chance stood in the doorway, hands on his hips, a grimace on his face.

"Zach can vouch for me." Katie waved toward Zach, the motion frantic. "I haven't lifted anything heavy or climbed any ladders or even sat on a saddle."

Chance arched an eyebrow at his wife.

"She introduced me to the Blackwell Ambassadors," Zach offered. "And she's letting me handle their morning exercise."

Katie gave Zach a grateful glance.

Just like that, he'd gained a Blackwell supporter and a possible favor owed. The corrupt piece of him, honed by a childhood spent conning people for food and money, grasped on to an idea. Could he earn enough Blackwell supporters and favors to convince Ethan to treat Rain Dancer?

Selfish. His mother had hurled that word at him often growing up. Past girlfriends, too.

Selfish. Ruthless. That and desperate. Desperate to keep his one last connection to his brother alive. As long as he had Rain Dancer, he hadn't really lost everything—and everyone— that had ever meant something to him.

He'd help where he was needed. When he was needed. He wouldn't insert himself where he wasn't wanted. Man had to keep some boundaries uncrossed. If he tallied favors owed in the process, all the better. He had to try. He couldn't give up.

"Thanks for the help, Zach." Chance wrapped his arm around Katie's waist. "If you do see my wife doing anything that appears to be against doctor's orders, feel free to tell on her."

Katie curved her arm around Chance's back. "Once our baby is born, I'm getting back to my usual life, along with our child."

Chance kissed her cheek. "Never too early to learn the family trade."

Katie and Chance walked toward the stable entrance, their heads touching and their low

voices swirling together. If Zach had a pregnant wife, he'd be as protective as Chance. Zach
checked the mare's water bucket and considered
dunking his head inside. A wife had never been
on his radar. And a pregnant one, at that... He
needed to work extra in the stables to remind
himself where he truly belonged.

"Hey, Zach," Chance called out. "Don't forget to eat and enjoy yourself. You're a guest,
not an employee."

"Working with the horses is the best kind of
enjoyment." And the best escape.

Wade McKee, the manager at his ex-girlfriend's
family ranch in Colorado, had hired Zach on as a
hand that first summer. His mother's death two
years later had forced Zach to drop out of college and care for his brother full-time. Wade had
hired Zach permanently and had given Zach and
Cody a cabin to live in on the property. The free
room and board had allowed Zach to pay for his
brother's treatments. The ranch work had taught
him how to survive.

"We sure could use someone with your experience." Katie tucked her arm around Chance.

He'd always worked alone. His mentors, Wade
and Marshall Yates, the horse trainer, had both
been steadfast bachelors. Yet now, watching
Chance and Katie together, Zach considered the
appeal of a partner. He shook off that thought

like a horse scattering the flies from its face. He was dishonest and selfish and better on his own.

"Katie is really a good boss to work for." Chance laughed. "Don't let her gruff, know-it-all manner fool you."

"Don't listen to him." Katie pushed on her husband's chest. "But please remember to get something to eat."

"I promised to head back to Dorothy's place for bourbon cinnamon French toast." Zach touched his stomach. He planned to work up an appetite and work off his guilt. "I tasted the bourbon vanilla syrup and spiked whipped cream before I left, and that was incredible."

"Grandma Dot's made her homemade bourbon cinnamon French toast?" Accusation echoed around the stables. Katie added, "This morning."

Zach paused and considered Katie's frown, then glanced at Chance. "Is that a problem?"

Chance rocked back on his boot heels. He shook his head and his burst of laughter slipped free. "Katie has been requesting Grandma Dot's special French toast for a while now."

"Grandma Dot has been refusing to make her specialty, claiming the bourbon isn't good for the baby." Katie's frown slipped into a pout.

Zach refrained from mentioning he already planned to have two helpings. "It will probably be just okay."

Katie glared at him. "You're lying."

"Of course he is." Chance released another gust of laughter. "Everyone knows Grandma Dot's bourbon cinnamon French toast is the best in the state. She has a first-place ribbon from the state fair proving that very thing."

"I can't believe she made it." Katie rounded on her husband. "Did you get invited over there, too?"

"First I've heard that she made it." Chance touched his chin. "But now that I know..."

"If I can't have the French toast, neither can you." Katie grabbed Chance's hand.

Zach had done the same thing with his brother. Zach had never eaten anything Cody couldn't during his brother's treatments. He'd never wanted his brother to feel left out.

"That hardly seems fair." Chance kissed Katie's cheek. "But for you, I'll wait."

Zach had stood by his brother the same way Chance backed his wife. Zach and Cody had been at Rain Dancer's birth. During Cody's remission, they'd trained the colt together. Later, on his good days, Cody had ridden Rain Dancer around the small pasture. The joy on his brother's face had surpassed Zach's. Zach and Cody had been a team. The only team Zach had ever known and ever trusted.

Zach swallowed back his grief. He knew what

he had to do. "I won't mention the French toast again either."

"Did she make anything else?" Katie asked.

Chance shook his head at Zach, a warning on his face.

"Not that I can recall." Zach opened the stall door and slipped inside.

Katie and Chance walked outside, Chance promising all the French toast and bourbon whipped cream his wife could eat after the baby arrived.

Babies. Weddings. Family celebrations. Traditions. The Blackwells embraced life and had opened their world to Zach. Now he planned to use their compassion and kindness for his own gain.

Guilt filtered into him. He lived his life without regret. Without apologies.

And already he wanted this family to forgive him.

Perhaps if Grandma Dot's morning hugs weren't the kind that lingered.

Perhaps if he liked Georgie a level below a stranger.

Perhaps then he'd walk away without remorse. He only wanted to walk away with a chance to save Rain Dancer. With hope again. Was that so wrong?

But this was Georgie's family. People she loved.

Yet Zach had given his word to Georgie to be her pretend boyfriend.

A man is worth nothing if his word can't be relied on. Zach's dad had always kept his word. Taught his son to do the same. He'd continue the ruse.

Maybe if he helped Georgie get to know her Blackwell family, that would be the positive to balance the negative. Balance made the difference between lasting the full eight seconds on a bucking bronc or dropping off in two seconds. There was value in balance, whether on a bronc or in life.

He'd give Georgie her family and save his own in the process.

CHAPTER EIGHT

*PLEASE, LET THE dining hall be empty. No Black-
wells. No more new family members.* Georgie
quickened her pace across the gravel path leading from Dorothy's house to the guest building.

Okay. Not empty. Even Georgie recognized
that would be impossible with a ranch the size of
the Blackwells'. Georgie hunched her shoulders
against the cold wind and hoped only her sisters
would be waiting for her inside the dining hall.

Thanks to Zach, she'd survived her first night
at the Blackwell ranch. He'd remained by her
side the entire evening, from dinner to dessert,
absorbed the overwhelming presence of her new
and extended family gathered together in one
place and maintained his humor. She'd fallen
asleep listening to his even breathing on the
floor in front of the fireplace. She'd woken alone
and disoriented. A note on her pillow requested
her presence in the dining hall at nine o'clock.

Georgie was five minutes early. She wore a
snowflake-and-reindeer-patterned sweater she'd
borrowed from Lily. The thick-knit sweater

peeked out from beneath her coat, giving away its too-large size. Her scarf clashed with the ice-blue color and her socks did not match.

Georgie tapped the snow from her boots and lingered outside the dining-hall doors. Too many voices and too much laughter swooshed around for the occupants to be her sisters only. She gripped the iron door handle and searched for her backbone. This was her family, after all.

A blast of welcome heat surrounded her. She eased inside, seeking more of the warmth, and plotted how to slip unnoticed to the coffee station on the other side of the hall. Then she could quickly down a cup for a bit of caffeinated courage and finally face her cousins, their spouses and kids...

The doors had barely eased shut behind her before her sisters spotted her. Plan interrupted.

"Georgie, come and see." Lily waved to Georgie, ending Georgie's chance at remaining unnoticed in the massive hall.

Several Blackwells called out good-morning greetings. Georgie smiled and nodded, then joined her sisters at the Christmas tree collection. Closer to the coffee station, but not close enough.

"Conner found the perfect tree topper for our Harrison family tree," Lily explained. "I was telling him how I couldn't find one anywhere."

Georgie lifted her gaze to the top of the ten-foot Christmas tree. A double starfish had been placed on top. Burlap and aqua tulle surrounded the two starfishes, one white, one orange, to transform the topper into something elegant and Christmassy. Conner couldn't have picked a better topper for the Harrison tree. He'd understood Lily's vision for the tree. Even more, Conner understood her sister and put her happiness first.

Georgie massaged her neck. That was something couples who'd been together, dating seriously for more than a year, did. Couples who'd taken the time to get to know each other on a deeper level and learned to listen to each other. Listening wasn't a relationship skill picked up and perfected in only a few months.

"Peyton sent these beautiful ornaments." Fiona held up a small globe. A palm tree decorated in colored Christmas lights had been painted over the glass, and the bottom had been dipped in real beach sand. "There's one for each of us with our name on it."

Their oldest sister, Peyton, would be arriving from California in a few days. Clearly, Peyton had lost focus, too, now that she'd fallen in love with Matteo Santos and his son, Gino. The old, single Peyton would not have been wandering through boutique shops and picking out beautifully handmade Christmas ornaments. Peyton would've been concentrating on closing deals for the Fortune 500 tech company she worked at. Georgie and Peyton loved their work and their jobs. Neither had ever apologized for that.

Now Peyton loved Matteo. And Georgie resisted the urge to apologize for her outfit and for not being like the others.

"Isn't it all perfect?" Lily stepped back, linked her arm through Georgie's and sighed.

It really was quite perfect. The Harrison family tree—beach themed to represent their childhood home in San Diego—was nestled in among the six Blackwell family trees. Turquoise ribbon extended like waves from the top tree branch to the bottom tree branch. The seahorse and coral ornaments and the soft blue lights should have made the tree stand out among the others. But the unconventional Harrison tree looked as if it belonged between Katie and Chance's Whimsical Candyland tree and Ben and Rachel's Winter Wonderland tree. How was that possible so soon?

"Next year, Conner and I get our own tree." Lily pressed her hand over her heart. "Then Fiona and Simon."

"Peyton and Amanda, too, if they want one." Fiona wrapped her arm around Georgie's waist and squeezed. "You and Zach."

Georgie swallowed to reset her dry throat. "Zach and me."

"Of course, you and Zach," Lily said.

"Wait. Yesterday you didn't believe we were dating." Georgie discovered her voice despite her sudden confusion. "Now we get the honor of our own family tree at Blackwell."

She'd learned last night that the Blackwell family tree tradition had started after Big E and Dorothy remarried two years ago. Now, when a Blackwell married, they were given their own ten-foot tree to decorate. It was an honor and a tradition. But tradition did not extend to those who deceived their own families. Georgie swallowed again. This time to push the guilt away.

"You wouldn't have brought a guy home if you didn't have really strong feelings." Fee squeezed Georgie again.

Each hug from her sister only pressed against Georgie's guilt, shoving it to the surface.

Georgie had strong feelings about keeping the peace in the family. About them not worrying about her. She also had very strong feelings about her work and her career path. Such strong feelings that she was willing to deceive her own sisters. Unfortunately, the deception was leading to even stronger feelings of remorse. And strong feelings for Zach...

"Zach told us this morning how you two

met." Lily smiled and rubbed Georgie's arm. "So sweet."

There'd been nothing sweet about it. Georgie had backed him into her scheme with one outburst. She shifted to search the dining hall for Zach. Where was he? She'd never excelled at making up stories. He'd made one up, but she didn't know the details. Where was he?

Lily tugged on her arm, pulling Georgie's attention back to her. "I still can't believe you started going to rodeos."

Was that how they'd supposedly met? *At a rodeo?* He couldn't have mentioned a coffee shop or a grocery store? Someplace Georgie went often. Someplace her sisters would believe. "There was a rodeo in town. I went with friends."

"You always claim your lab is your friend." Lily laughed.

"And that your colleagues work longer hours than you," Fee added.

"You can't believe everything I say," Georgie said. *There. I warned you. Don't say I didn't warn you guys.*

"It's refreshing that we've all stepped out of our comfort zones lately." Lily set her head against Georgie's and grinned. "And we're better for it."

"Who would have thought we'd find our happy places?" Fee added.

Georgie would be truly happy stepping into her new lab in London. Georgie knew where she belonged. Where she fit in.

She touched the glass ornament from Peyton, traced her finger over the cheerful lights on the palm tree. She'd loved to read, propped against a palm tree on the beach. In the North Carolina mountains, she'd traded palm trees for tall oak trees in the park. But never forgot her book. Surely in England she'd find a new favorite place to read.

Doubt flickered through her, chasing her sudden uncertainty like the colored Christmas lights on Katie and Chance's tree. She shoved aside her doubt, blaming it on her lack of caffeine, and grabbed her sisters' hands. "You both are happy? Truly happy, right?"

A wide smile blossomed across Fee's face. "Yes. Very much."

"I didn't know it was possible to be this happy." Lily's smile highlighted the spark in her gaze.

Georgie wanted to be happy for her sisters, yet she worried about their getting hurt. It was so sudden. So soon. Yet a part of her believed them. That was only her heart inserting itself. She'd relied on reason and common sense too long to listen to her heart now. Besides, the practical side of her knew that her sisters being in blissful moods when she delivered her job news would better serve Georgie. She wrapped her sisters in a group hug. "I really missed you guys."

Lily wiped at her eyes. "Come on. Let's get back to Georgie's new man and the fun stuff."

He's not my new man. Georgie forced herself to smile. There was nothing fun about the guilt pulsing inside her.

"Zach is really funny and kind." Fee smiled. "He even adjusted Grandma Dot's rocking chair this morning to make it more comfortable for her. Then he put together a breakfast plate for you, Georgie, of foods that wouldn't need to be reheated."

"He mentioned how you don't like rewarmed eggs or cold toast." Lily laughed. "Clearly he's been paying attention to your quirks. He's good for you, Georgie."

Zach was good for her now. For one week. "I don't have quirks. I have preferences. Nothing wrong with preferring my food hot." And her men as friends only.

"We can see why you like him," Lily said.

Because Zach agreed to be her pretend date. Because he agreed to be a placeholder to stall all the matchmaking madness. All her sisters were in love. Georgie was the last holdout and she intended to remain that way.

"It's so sad about his brother." Fee frowned, then found her smile. Optimism wound through her words. "But now he has you and all of us to make sure this Christmas is extra special."

Zach had a brother. Zach had told her sisters about his brother and not Georgie. Granted, she hadn't asked. Still, she should've known, shouldn't she? He'd stopped Georgie at his sixty-second short. Apparently, the same rule hadn't applied to her family. He was a stranger and seemingly fit in with her family better than she did. Something close to jealousy curved around her spine, tapping her guilt aside.

"We're so happy for you." Fee hugged Georgie.

Georgie embraced her sister and searched for the catch. One conversation with Zach and they suddenly believed Georgie and Zach were a real couple. How could that even be possible? Georgie pulled away and studied her sisters. Was that the catch? Were they calling Georgie's bluff? She should confess. End it all.

Her gaze landed on Zach, surrounded by her Blackwell cousins and Conner. The group laughed and shared high fives. Zach received several slaps on the back. She heard the words: *bull. Eight seconds. Intense. One time only.* Then more laughter ensued, and more stories dropped between the men.

Zach grinned at her and she felt the warm intensity of his gaze all the way to her toes. He'd lost his brother and his parents. He was completely alone. She'd promised to help him with Ethan. His horse had to be extremely sick for him to fly to Falcon Creek the week before Christmas.

If she confessed, Zach would be expected to leave. She knew nothing about horses. She needed her family to help Zach. And she wanted to give him something. She held her silence and her secret.

"Let's get settled. It's almost time to begin." Lily guided the sisters toward a table near the fireplace. Conner was already seated there, holding a large cup of coffee.

"I can't wait for the team scavenger hunt." Fiona slid onto a wide bench.

"Team?" Georgie said. "Then we can be Team Harrison."

"You're already on a team," Lily said. "With Zach."

Lily drew out Zach's name in several extended syllables, as if emphasizing the obvious. But Zach wasn't Georgie's person. Not the one Georgie automatically reached for. Georgie relied on herself and she'd been doing quite well. Besides, she hadn't been part of a couple in years. It wasn't her fault she didn't think like one.

Zach rose as if Lily had called him and moved from the table with the Blackwell brothers to theirs. He set a napkin-covered plate in front of Georgie and sat in the empty chair beside her. "Thought you might be hungry."

Zach had no problem thinking about Georgie, his supposed other half. Her sisters' approval swept across the square table. Georgie's stomach cramped and not from hunger. Her overly enthusiastic thank-you overtook her cringe.

"It's a couple's scavenger hunt." Fiona jumped up and greeted her boyfriend with a long, tight embrace.

Fiona's hug surrounded Simon and his enveloped her. The power in the affection between the pair radiated joy around them. Georgie searched for the name of that particular hug. It had to have a name. If she could name it, she'd know if she'd ever experienced an embrace like that.

Simon and Fee settled on the bench across from Georgie. The embrace had ended, but the joy lingered, as if powered by the pair's connection.

Lily drew Georgie's focus back to her. "The winning team gets an all-expenses-paid four-day and three-night trip to an adult-only spa and resort in Sedona."

"The losing couples babysit and step in to run things while the winners enjoy their leisure time away." Fiona leaned across the table and peered under the napkin at Georgie's food.

There it was again. That word and thing that Zach and Georgie were not—*a couple*. And they wouldn't be there to help. Georgie glanced at Zach. "We should sit this one out."

"Zach, I need to tell you something." Lily sighed as if she'd expected Georgie's statement. "I know you've learned a lot about our sister, but you should be aware she's averse to fun."

"I am not." Georgie pulled the napkin off the plate and nudged the plate into the center of the table for everyone to share. Her own appetite dwindled.

"Yes, you are." Fee snatched a cranberry-orange muffin from the plate and handed half to Simon. "You stopped playing pretend with us in the fourth grade. Then in eighth grade you declared board games interfered with your studies. Don't get me started on high school."

Fiona's mouth dipped as if she'd been hurt by Georgie's decisions. She'd had a goal to achieve and a medical degree to receive. Besides, Amanda, Lily and Fiona had their own interests and they'd stopped including her. Georgie acknowledged her own twinge of pain and tucked it away.

"I believe your exact words to us were *winning at cards isn't going to get me to the next level, you guys. This is serious.*" Lily leaned into Conner. His arm curved around her waist, as if comforting her.

As if Georgie had hurt Lily, too. But Georgie had been the outsider. The one not included in Amanda and Lily's private jokes. The one not asked on the double date with the Harrison sisters. Georgie straightened her shoulders, resisting the urge to tilt toward Zach.

"Georgie, the only team you joined was the soccer team." Fee frowned. "And that was to round out your college application profile."

Her sisters made her sound like a bad person. A bad sister. A sour taste coated her throat. "Getting into medical school was cutthroat."

"Georgie was the MVP of the high school varsity soccer team all four years," Lily added.

Why was that such an awful thing? "I worked hard."

"That's all you do." Fee tipped her head and considered Georgie. Worry was etched in her face and clear in her words. "You work hard and harder still. Always focused on work and that next level."

She had goals to reach. That required focus

and dedication. But had she missed out on the fun and games over the years? She shook her head. She wasn't the carefree type. Never had been. Her sisters knew that. Yet she set her hand flat on the table as if she'd been knocked off balance.

"Please don't turn the scavenger hunt into work." Lily set her hand on top of Georgie's on the table. "Just have fun with it."

How was she supposed to do that? What if she ruined it for Zach? Georgie pulled her hand away from Lily and turned to Zach. "They're right. Maybe you should find another partner."

"Not happening." Zach reached over, grabbed her hand and looked her in the eyes. "I choose you."

I choose you. Georgie locked onto Zach's gaze—serious and intense. He meant it. And three simple words gave her the courage and the permission to participate. Three simple words gave her a place to belong: on Zach's team. Too bad it was only for a scavenger hunt. Georgie tugged on her hand. Zach tightened his grip. Georgie gave in. She liked holding Zach's hand. Liked how they fit together. She firmed her hold and settled in beside him. She'd remind herself to let go tomorrow.

Zach bumped his shoulder against hers.

"Georgie and I had fun shopping for Lily and Conner's wedding present."

"Time out." Lily made a letter T with her hands. "Georgie shopped for our wedding gift."

"Yes," Georgie hedged.

"With Zach," Fee clarified.

"It's not a big deal." Georgie massaged her temple. A headache pulsed. Nothing coffee and caffeine wouldn't cure. "Can we get back to the hunting game?"

"I'm stuck on you shopping," Lily said.

"Me too," Fee said. "So, Lily isn't getting money like always."

"Nothing wrong with money," Georgie muttered. Just as there was nothing wrong with her.

"It's impersonal." Zach leaned fully into Georgie's side.

Georgie's voice rose. "Money is useful and practical."

"I'm with Zach on this one," Fee said. "It's impersonal."

Georgie glanced around the table. Conner drank his coffee, but his wince remained around his eyes. Lily nodded. Simon picked up a croissant from the plate and shrugged an apology to her. Georgie groaned. "Can we just move on, please? I shopped. It's no big deal."

Fiona raised her hand. "First, when Simon and I get married, we want a real gift, too."

"A really good one." Simon kissed Fee on her cheek. "Although, nothing can top being with Fiona."

That joy sparked off Fee and Simon again. Georgie sighed, refusing to admit it was for her sister's happiness. "Can we concentrate on the hunt? I need the rules so I can figure out how to win."

Lily eyed Georgie. "You don't always have to win."

"What's the point of playing if not to win?" Georgie asked.

Fee lifted her hand, joined with Simon's. "It's really an excuse to spend more time together."

"I don't know." Conner rubbed his chin and tipped his coffee cup toward Georgie. "I'm kinda with Georgie on this one. It's definitely more fun to win."

Conner tallied another checkmark in the hard-to-dislike column. Georgie wasn't sure Conner had any negative qualities.

"Don't worry. We're going to win," Lily declared. "It's our wedding week and all the good luck is with us."

Katie approached their table and set her hand on Georgie's shoulder. The amused delight in her words lifted over the other conversations. "Hey, you guys, we have some excited newcomers over here who believe they can actually win."

Laughter echoed around the room. Chance pounded a drumroll on the table. "Let's get our lists and get this hunt started."

"We're just waiting on Grandma Dot. She had to run back to the house for something." Katie released Georgie's shoulder, pressed one hand to her stomach and stopped in front of Jon and Lydia's Santa's Wish List tree. A scowl settled on her face. "I did not request another goat named Gilly. We have more than enough goats."

"Not according to Billy. He's requested a female goat." Ethan Blackwell unzipped his coat, brushed snow from his dark hair and stepped beside Katie. He plucked the goat wish off the tree and attached it to an even higher branch between two giggling elves.

Katie shoved Ethan. "That's not fair."

Zach stiffened beside Georgie. His narrowed gaze tracked Ethan and Katie. Had he spoken to Ethan already? Had it gone badly? Georgie squeezed his hand hard, drawing his attention to her. She whispered, "You okay?"

He blinked and his shoulders lowered. "Yeah. Too much French toast."

Georgie nodded, but couldn't quite accept his excuse.

He nudged his elbow into her side, disrupting her inquiry. He asked, "Was your family like this?"

"Not as loud." But the good-natured teasing and laughter, the Harrisons had enjoyed that.

Ethan's quick laughter faded beneath his frown. He gripped another Santa wish and hollered, "I definitely did not ask Santa for a range dedicated to bow-and-arrow practice."

"I did on your behalf, Ethan." Hadley raised her hand from across the room. "You can't keep using the side of the old barn."

Ethan set his hands on his hips. "I've been using that very same barn for target practice since I was a little kid."

Georgie and Amanda had faced off in much the same way over the years. Hands on their hips, feet planted. Neither one backing down. The source of their dispute hadn't been a barn, but their shared desk. Amanda had always wanted to examine her animal rescues on the desk. Georgie had always wanted to dissect something under her microscope. Lily had usually ended their standoffs, suggesting that if Georgie helped Amanda she'd be done faster. And, surely, Amanda could give Georgie a hair or a feather to look at under her microscope. Both sisters had won and had fun. Then they'd grown up and the fun waned.

Yet the Blackwells hadn't stopped having fun.

Grace rushed across the dining hall, set her laptop bag on the empty table behind Georgie and Zach. She plopped down onto a chair and looked at Georgie. "Did I miss anything?"

Only a brief dissection of my inability to have fun now. Georgie shook her head. "Dorothy isn't here yet."

Zach added, "They're debating Santa wishes now."

Grace laughed. "This should be entertaining."

Georgie was content with anything that shifted the focus away from her. Could she find her fun again? Could she and her sisters be like the Blackwells?

"Let's ask our resident medical doctor." Ethan waved toward Georgie's table. "Georgie, do you agree that it's healthy to relieve stress on a daily basis?"

Just like that, Georgie had the attention of the entire room.

"I'm sure my sister has done extensive research and a paper on that exact topic," Lily offered.

"Georgie has completed more research than several doctoral candidates combined." Fiona grinned. "We consider her an authority on most things."

Pride and respect framed Fiona's tone. Her words were not intended to sound mean-spirited.

Fiona didn't possess a cruel bone in her body. Georgie winced even as she couldn't stop herself from reciting the facts. "According to the studies, stress can affect clotting factors in the blood and that can lead to a heart attack."

"I shoot arrows at the barn to relieve stress, Hadley." Ethan crumpled Hadley's Santa wish into a ball and shot it into the trash can. "As it's good for my heart, the barn has to stay. Otherwise, if I get heart disease, you'll be to blame, Hadley. Isn't that right, Georgie?"

Not again. Georgie solved theories inside a lab. She never took sides in a family debate. What if she chose the wrong side? "Um…"

"It's not good for the guests' hearts to see an entire barn littered with arrows." Hadley propped her feet on an empty chair, touched her stomach and refused to back down. "You need a new place for target practice and a change in your diet, Ethan. No more fried chicken."

"I'm keeping that barn. It's part of Dr. Harrison's healthy lifestyle orders." Ethan fist-bumped Georgie and ignored the change in his diet recommendation. "Besides, Hadley, you took all the other barns on the ranch from us."

"He's not wrong." Ben came swiftly to his twin's defense.

The sisters had been quick to defend each other over the years, too. Would they defend her decisions now? Sweat broke out on the back of her neck as if she was sitting too close to the massive fireplace.

Ethan gained ground. "You confiscated the large barn for the spa."

"Which you've been seen enjoying more than once since it opened," Hadley challenged. "Spas are also an appropriate stress reliever. Right, Georgie?"

Everyone's focus swung back to Georgie. Her own internal stress increased, initiating her fight-or-flight response. Zach's knee bumped against hers. She scooted closer, until they touched from knee to thigh, and everything inside her settled. She opened her mouth.

But a movement near the Christmas trees had diverted Hadley's attention. "Chance Blackwell, don't you dare." Hadley's sharp tone pulled everyone's focus away from Georgie.

Chance stood in front of Hadley and Ty's DIY tree, his hand wrapped around a plush scarf Hadley had cleverly used as garland. He straightened, not appearing guilty in the least. "My wife is cold."

Katie rubbed her hands together. "Sorry. He's right."

Chance tugged the scarf free and wrapped it around Katie's shoulders. "You can't yell at another pregnant person. It's like a rule."

Hadley poked Ty in the side. "Put some more wood in the fire."

"Now I'm getting yelled at for something my brother did." Ty kissed Hadley on the mouth, rose and added wood to the fire. "Just like old times."

"Some things never change," Ben called out.

Ty snatched a candy cane off Katie and Chance's whimsical Candyland tree.

Katie laughed. "Now I know who's been eating our tree."

Ty tossed the candy cane to Conner and grabbed another one. Ty lifted his eyebrows up and down. "I'm not the only one with a sweet tooth."

Conner tucked the candy cane into his pocket. "The cherry-flavored ones are addicting."

"Conner Hannah," Katie chided. "Wait until next year. I'm going to steal things from your tree."

That launched a lively debate about possible themes for next year's trees. Even Lily and Fee offered their opinions. No one was safe from criticism or censure. Approval was also just as easily doled out. However, the sides kept changing, making it impossible to track who was supporting whom.

Zach looked at Grace behind them. "Is it always like this?"

"Yes. Once you're in with the Blackwell family, you're in," Grace said. "It has nothing to do with blood ties and everything to do with family."

"Have people not been let in?" Zach asked.

"Definitely," Grace said. "Believe it or not, the Blackwells are quite exclusive and extremely protective. Don't let this bantering and carrying on fool you."

"Why weren't the others accepted?" Georgie asked.

"They misunderstood what it means to be a Blackwell," Grace said.

"What does it mean?" Zach asked.

"That's just it." Grace set her hand on Georgie's arm and squeezed. "You have to figure that one out for yourself."

But Georgie hadn't asked to be a Blackwell. Bonding with her extended family had never been a consideration. Even if she recognized the same good humor and entertaining nature that her own family once shared.

Georgie had a schedule to keep.

Ten days at the ranch. Ten days to make certain her sisters were well cared for and in the right place. Ten days to tell her family about her overseas, chance-of-a-lifetime job. Then she had one day to return to North Carolina. Two days to ship her belongings, turn in her apartment keys and fly across the ocean to her new life.

She did not have time in her schedule to figure out what being a Blackwell meant to her.

"Grandma Dot is here," Lily called out. Then she looked at Georgie. "Grandma Dot has the rules and lists."

Rules. Lists. Those were things Georgie preferred. Things Georgie relied on every day. She should be delighted. Thrilled the scavenger hunt was so well organized. Except panic piled up inside her. Now she'd be expected to have fun. To be fun. With Zach. Her sisters would be watching. Expecting them to act like a couple. Georgie pressed her knee against Zach's.

"The theme this year is Twelve Winter Duos." Grandma Dorothy stood in front of the fireplace and opened a three-ring binder.

The entire family settled back into their places at their tables.

"The rules are the same." Dorothy gave the lists to Jon to hand out to the others. "You can only buy two items. You can only photograph two items. The rest need to be handmade with things you find. Everything has to be completed with your partner. First couple to complete their list on or before Christmas Day wins."

Across the table, Lily pointed at something on their list and whispered into Conner's ear. Ethan and Grace moved across the room to strategize. Ben and Rachel retreated behind their tree.

Georgie leaned into Zach and read the list he held. The duos included ugly sweaters, outdoor ornaments, a pair of hot and cold somethings, a pair of animals, cookies and cowboy winter accessories. "I've never seen a scavenger hunt like this."

"Have you ever done one?" Zach asked.

Georgie shook her head. "Have you?"

"At school a couple of times." Zach considered the list. "They'll never see us swooping in and winning it all."

Georgie laughed and released her panic. Perhaps she could have fun. With Zach.

CHAPTER NINE

THE KITCHEN AND dining area cleaned and prepped for lunch, Georgie walked outside, Zach beside her. She asked, "Can you take me into town? I would've asked Fiona or Lily, but they left on an errand run."

"You didn't want to join them?"

She hadn't been invited. "They're heading to the flower shop and grocery store, then stopping at the bakery for chocolate muffins."

"You have something against bakeries?" Zach teased.

"My sisters claim I take the fun out of running errands." Georgie buttoned her jacket under her chin and ignored the common theme. "It's not my fault I like to follow my shopping list. If I do that, I don't get distracted and buy things I don't need."

"But you might miss the one thing you really need." Zach walked beside her to Dorothy and Big E's house and the rental car.

"If I needed it, it would've already been written down." Georgie moved to the passenger side of the SUV. Zach followed and opened her door for her. She dropped into the seat.

"What's on your shopping list?" Zach sat in the driver's seat and set the scavenger hunt paper on the console between them. "We can only purchase two items for the hunt. I vote ugly sweater and the cowboy duo. We could buy matching cowboy hats and shirts."

"We can make the ugly sweaters. The cowboy duo could be a picture of two horses on the ranch." Georgie put her hands on top of her knees. "Before we tackle the scavenger hunt items, I need more pants. As of this morning, my suitcase is now vacationing in Saint Lucia with no return date. I borrowed sweaters from Lily, but that's all that will fit me."

"Let's go to Brewster's Supply Store." Zach buckled his seat belt, turned the defrost to high and waited for the SUV to warm up. "Grace's parents own it. If the Gardners don't have it, they can get it."

"How do you know this?" Georgie tucked the scavenger hunt paper into her jacket pocket.

"I spent the morning with everyone at the stables and then in the dining hall."

She'd spent last night with the same group. She'd learned different details about some of her family, thanks to Rosie's candid nature. "And you asked where to go shopping locally?"

"No." Zach laughed and pulled out of the driveway. "I asked who had local ties to Falcon Creek and who had moved here. Even though the Blackwell brothers grew up here, they all left home. Only Katie and Grace remained true to their roots and stayed in Falcon Creek."

Perhaps, then, her cousins would understand her need to continue on her career path, even if that career path carried her farther and farther away from her family.

"Of course, they all returned home eventually," Zach said. "Because family comes first."

One of Rudy's favorite lines. But Georgie's family was now spread out between California and Montana. The Harrison sisters were no longer rooted in one place. In one home. They hadn't been for years. "Speaking of family, how come you didn't tell me about your brother? I'm really sorry."

"I could ask the same about you."

"I don't have a brother."

He tapped the steering wheel and glanced over at her. "That's not what I meant, but you already know that."

He meant her triplet status and her stranger status with the Blackwells. She should've told him. Just as he should've told her about his brother. Georgie cleared the hurt out of her voice. "Lily and Amanda are my triplets, but they're also identical twins. Peyton is the oldest. Fiona is the youngest. I don't have anything special to claim."

"Having four sisters is pretty special," he said.

"We were close growing up." At least, she'd thought they had been. Until this morning.

"But not now."

"It's different now." Georgie glanced out the window at the snow-filled pastures. The land extended in every direction, vast and beautiful with its pristine layers of snow. "My sisters are in love and want me to be the same." They also wanted her to be fun.

"That's not a bad thing," he said. "They want you to be happy."

"I don't have to be in love to be happy."

"What do you need to be happy?"

"My career," she said.

"And doing research fulfills you?" he asked. Doubt pulled his eyebrows below the frames of his sunglasses.

"Absolutely." What fulfilled her was the knowledge that she was helping others so that families wouldn't suffer the loss of their loved ones.

Georgie, it's your mom... Her dad had never finished his sentence and yet his unspoken words had shattered her world all the same. Four words that had started a coast-to-coast phone call that had ended with the funeral arrangements. Four words that even now haunted her. She rubbed her arms, but the chill of grief remained.

Zach frowned, as if she'd given an incorrect response. "So, you prefer experiments over patient contact."

"My research is done in a lab." She'd been in a lab the day her father had called to give her the news about her mom. She hadn't left. She'd simply sunk to the floor and wept. "It's meant to save lives."

"But lives are lost while you're in your lab experimenting," he said. "Patients are suffering."

She assumed he meant patients like his brother. And she hated that. Hated knowing with every failed experiment, every failed trial, a patient lost hope. Their families stood by helpless, grappling with the potential loss of their loved ones. "In a perfect world, cures and vaccines would be discovered overnight."

"But it's not a perfect world."

The tension in his voice pulled her gaze to him. Pain tightened across his mouth. His jaw firmed as if he fought against it. Georgie ached for him and searched for the right words. "My mom often told me there are only perfect moments and a collection of those makes life worth-while."

His shoulders relaxed. His voice loosened. "Tell me one of your perfect moments."

Georgie flipped through her childhood memories. Their house had been loud and lively. The sisters had argued as siblings tended to do, cried together and laughed. "When I was in middle school, the entire city had a power outage that lasted all day. After sunset, Mom lit a bunch of candles. We crowded around the dining-room table and played board games until past midnight."

Georgie swallowed. That had been the last time she'd joined Harrison game night. Certainly, that hadn't been the last time she'd had fun. Plain, pure fun for the simple sake of fun.

"Did you win every game?" Zach teased.

"I lost more than I won that night." And Georgie hadn't minded. For one night, she had enjoyed herself. Hadn't felt like she'd needed to prove herself. Hadn't felt misplaced. She studied Zach.

He made her feel the very same. Safe and understood. But she didn't really know him. He shouldn't make her feel any sort of way. Yet she kept turning toward Zach to settle herself, not her sisters. Her sisters were overwhelming her with their love and wedding talk. "What about you? Have any perfect moments?"

"Meeting my horse, Rain Dancer, for the first time." Affection smoothed over his face, softening his voice. "He has heart and more will to win than I've ever seen. He's fierce in the arena, then rolling and playing in a mud puddle in his downtime. We earned each other's trust. I've never connected with another horse quite like that before."

"I used to help Amanda with her animal rescues," Georgie said. "But I can't say I've ever connected with an animal like that before."

"We'll visit the petting zoo at the ranch," Zach said. "I'm sure the animals could use the company and you might make a connection."

"That won't be necessary." There was no purpose. Georgie crossed her arms over her chest. Bonding with an animal she'd most likely never see again seemed like all kinds of wrong. "I'm happy despite not having any pets."

"Rain Dancer isn't a pet. Or simply a horse," Zach said. "He's family."

"Right now, I have enough new family around me." Enough people to unsettle and exhaust her.

"For such a big family, the Blackwells are really close," Zach said. "I always wanted that."

Georgie wasn't sure what she wanted, except

their collective blessing on her new job. "Don't you find it all a bit much?"

"Not really." Zach shrugged. "It's comforting, I'd think, to know so many people have your back."

"But it's also a lot of people in your personal business. A lot of people offering their opinions about your life and your choices."

"Big or small, anyone who loves you will have opinions about your life and your choices." Zach pulled into the Brewster's parking lot and turned off the car.

"It's just a lot of people to disappoint." Especially if she loved them and they loved her. Inside her lab, mistakes could be studied and corrected. Mistakes in life, with patients and family, were hard to make right. In two weeks, she'd return to where she belonged. She glanced at Zach.

He'd chosen her today, wanted her on his team. She'd never considered wanting to be with someone long-term. But something about Zach made her reconsider. She opened her car door, got out and inhaled the brisk, biting air.

She was on a scavenger hunt team. Nothing remotely long-term about that.

Frank and Alice Gardner, owners of Brewster's Supply Store and Grace Blackwell's parents, greeted Zach and Georgie inside the main entrance. Alice told them to let her know if they needed anything special. Then the cheerful woman retreated to the checkout counter to assist another customer. Frank unclipped his cell phone from his belt and excused himself to answer a call.

An older gentleman sat in a rocking chair next to a lit fireplace. The carvings in the vintage chair were etched as deep as the man's wrinkles. Both had a timeless air about them. He lifted his arm and waved them over. "You two are new to Falcon Creek."

"Yes, sir." Zach took the older man's hand.

His gleeful cackle disrupted Zach's introduction. "Everyone here, new or old, calls me Pops. Ain't answered to 'sir,' well, ever."

Georgie grinned, liking Pops instantly.

"Legs are too long for riding those bulls." Pops released Zach and considered him. His steely gaze trailed from Zach's cowboy hat to his boots in a slow assessment that matched his thoughtful tone. "Saddle bronc or calf roper?"

"Is that a thing?" Georgie asked. She'd never considered height could ever really be a disadvantage for anything. Especially since she'd spent most of her teen years researching how to grow taller. "Can you really be too tall for a bull?"

"Height isn't always an advantage on a bull,"

Zach said. "Make my living on both saddle bronc and calf roping."

"Got tossed to the ground a few times myself before I came to my senses." Pops chuckled. "Them broncs recognize the unprepared and take advantage."

"Back doored," Georgie whispered.

Pops beamed at her and rolled his hands one over the other. "Tumbling head over tail off the back end of a bucking horse."

"You're riding a bucking horse?" Georgie stared at Zach. *Details matter.* When had she stopped asking questions? Why had she? "That's your event."

Zach nodded. "That's saddle bronc."

"Spectacular show at the rodeo, too," Pops added. "When done right, those eight seconds are a thing of wonder."

"And when it goes wrong in those eight seconds?" Georgie pressed, imagining all the things that could happen to him and his body the same way she predicted the outcome of a scientific test. Only now she was fearful for Zach.

"It's the measure of a man, his resilience, strength and ability to face his fears again and…" Pride lifted Pops's chin. "To get back inside that chute and take another ride."

Or it was the measure of a man with no re-gard for his body or his health. Didn't he care about himself? His future? She cared. And that was why she hadn't asked questions. "Seems like too many unnecessary risks."

"Got yourself a good horse?" Pops rubbed his chin, ignored Georgie's outburst and considered Zach. "Makes all the difference in the roping."

"Rain Dancer and I have been together for more than ten years," Zach said. "He's the best I could've asked for. Trained him myself."

"Time enough to build a solid bond." Pops nodded. Approval flashed in his gaze. "Nothing like the trust between a horse and rider."

There it was again. That special connection between a horse and a person. Georgie had no special connection with another person, let alone an animal. She'd been perfectly fine, too. Until now. Now she wondered if she'd missed out on something, well, special.

"Zach, that was Ethan." Frank Gardner approached. "He was coming down here to help me organize the warehouse. We got supplies sooner than expected. But Ethan got an emergency call in the next town over. Do you think you could help me out? Ethan said you know your way around the stables."

"What can I do?" Zach asked.

"You don't mind?" Frank ran his hand through his gray hair. "We gave the staff time off for the holiday. Wasn't expecting so much heavy lifting this week, but the coming storm changed things up."

"We aren't in a hurry, are we?" Zach looked at Georgie. "I know you like to stick to your list and all."

Georgie narrowed her eyes at Zach.

His grin only expanded.

"No rush," Georgie said. She could change. She could slow down and enjoy herself. If only her sisters were there to see her. "Is there anything I can do?"

"Alice has the store covered." Frank shook his head. "Appreciate the offer, but I'll let you shop."

Frank and Zach headed toward a door marked Warehouse.

Pops motioned to the empty rocking chair across from him. "You don't look like a Blackwell."

"Thanks." Georgie lowered into the rocking chair and noticed the chessboard on the table between them. "I'm a Harrison."

"My granddaughter, Grace, married a Blackwell." Pops harrumphed. "Stubborn lot, the Blackwells."

"I'm not sure stubborn belongs solely to the Blackwells," Georgie said.

Pops's smile creased his perceptive eyes. He

set his index finger on a black bishop on the board. "Do you play?"

"Haven't for a long time." Not since she'd given up board games. Georgie studied the chessboard and realized the game was already in progress. She took in the chess pieces removed from play for both sides, returned her attention to the board and counted her potential moves. She could shop, stick to her list, or she could… "I used to play with my dad."

"Hardly matters how long it's been." Pops slapped his knee. "Frank has played almost every day since marrying my daughter almost fifty-five years ago. Even that hasn't helped his game much."

"Pops, I can hear you," Frank called from behind the checkout counter. He picked up keys from the hook on a back wall, kissed Alice on the cheek and stopped at the warehouse door to holler, "Pops, did you ever consider I've been letting you win all these years?"

"Frank Gardner, you're more of a man than that," Pops yelled. "Don't be denying it now. I wouldn't have let you marry Alice if you hadn't been."

Georgie saw the respect and affection in both men's faces. Heard the same in their gruff voices. She'd never really considered how her father would get along with her husband. She'd been too busy avoiding dating to consider marriage. But she'd want more than her father's approval. She'd want his blessing. She'd want to know he believed theirs was a bond that could last like Alice and Frank Gardner's. If she planned on ever getting married. Which she didn't. Georgie concentrated on the board and decided on her first move.

Pops rocked back in his chair, tugged his worn cowboy hat off his head and scratched his forehead. His gaze remained fixed on the game board.

Looking up, Georgie noted an inflamed lesion on his forehead that extended into his receding hairline above his left eye. She leaned forward, seeking a closer look. Pops settled his hat back on his head, covering the lesion from her prying gaze.

"We might have ourselves a real game." He moved his rook and captured her knight. His cheeks crinkled into a smile. "If you have more than one lucky move in you."

The joy on Pops's face stirred her own. She sank back into her rocking chair and exhaled, letting herself relax. For the first time since her arrival in Falcon Creek, the tension inside Georgie receded. She had more chess moves and she wanted another look at Pops's forehead. "I might have some more luck inside me."

Pops chuckled. "Luck always changes. You can depend on that."

"Great-Aunt Pru always told me to never confuse luck with hard work, diligence and determination."

"Sounds like something Big E would say."

Georgie nodded, surprise hard to find. Pru was really their grandmother and Thomas Blackwell's mother. Just as Big E was the Harrison sisters' grandfather.

"It's certainly more than luck that keeps that man of yours on his horse in the arena," Pops said. "More than luck that makes him good at what he does."

Georgie set her hand on her bishop and eyed Pops. "It's a sport for the adrenaline seeker."

"It's more than a sport," Pops said. "It's a lifestyle."

"It's dangerous and hard on the body." How many injuries had Zach sustained? Broken bones, torn ligaments, concussions. The list of potential injuries was endless. Yet he continued to choose that lifestyle. Continued to push his body, tempting fate and another injury. Who cared for him when he was injured? Georgie frowned. That wasn't her business. She claimed Zach for the next week. What happened after wasn't her concern. Yet the idea of him alone and injured, hurt and in pain, pinched inside her, uncomfortable and unpleasant.

"That's why women and men don't just join the rodeo." Pops lifted his gaze from the game board and leaned back in his chair to look at her. "They're called to the rodeo. It's in their blood."

"Cooks and bakers are in my family tree and I don't prepare anything from scratch. I rarely ever cook." Georgie relied on takeout, fresh fruit and easy travel snacks that wouldn't melt or crumble in her purse. Rolling pins, cookie sheets and aprons weren't her areas of expertise or interest.

Pops removed his hat and massaged the back of his head. Georgie set her lack of culinary skills aside to examine Pops's forehead. Various shades of red and brown discolored the quarter-sized lesion. She was too far away to tell if the surface was raised, yet close enough to know Pops needed to be seen by a specialist as soon as possible.

"Baking is not a calling." Pops scowled as if he'd bit into a burned cookie. He resettled his hat on his head. "That's nothing more than your sweet tooth having a hankering for maple cream pie."

"Fresh-from-the-pot hot chocolate and an apology for Georgie." Alice carried over two mugs and set them on the side table. "Frank and Zach have moved from the forklifts to discussing the best horse feed blends. It's one of Frank's favorite topics. And from what I overheard, Zach knows his feed types, too."

Zach had described Rain Dancer as family. Would he care about his own family with the same dedication? Not the question she needed answered. Georgie dipped the candy cane Alice had hung on the mug's rim into her hot chocolate and swirled it around, then sipped and sighed. Rich, decadent and definitely homemade. Even more to enjoy at Brewster's than chess and good company. "This is delicious. I'll take Zach's since he's too busy talking."

Alice laughed.

"No time to sit and relax. We've a game to finish." Pops captured Georgie's last pawn and waved it over the game board. "Keep those boys occupied in the warehouse a bit longer."

"I'll do my best. Glad you play, Georgie. Dad's been looking for a new opponent." Gratitude lit Alice's smile. "Dad, you can take your hat off inside the store."

"Keeps my head warm and my thoughts clear." Pops shooed her away and adjusted his cowboy hat lower on his head. "Nothing wrong with that, is there?"

Alice squeezed her father's shoulder, affection and love in her tender touch. "Remember

Georgie and Zach are guests in town. We want them to feel welcome, not lectured."

"I'm not lecturing." Pops reached up and patted Alice's hand. "I'm educating. There's a difference."

"Some people come here to shop for ranch supplies and home goods only." Alice leaned into her dad's chair. "They're already educated enough."

"You're educated enough when you get to be my age." Pops's bushy eyebrows receded beneath the brim of his hat. He focused on Georgie. "Until then, you're required to keep learning. You hear me?"

Georgie nodded. She agreed everyone needed to keep learning. The best doctors in their fields were constantly striving to learn more. Discover more. She intended to keep expanding her own knowledge through continuing education programs. To keep pushing and to always honor her mom's memory.

"Pops, you truly are one of a kind," Alice said.

The chimes on the entrance jingled. A woman clad in an ankle-length plaid coat, a cowboy hat and winter boots stepped inside and tugged off her gloves. Alice's greeting included a first-name welcome and warm hug.

The embrace reminded Georgie of the ones

her mom had given her. She missed her mom so very much. With her mom at her side, Georgie had believed anything was possible.

Georgie rubbed her chest. She wanted to return to Brewster's for an Alice Gardner hug. And a moment to remember her mom. Alice linked arms with the woman and the pair headed deeper into the store.

Georgie acknowledged her grief just as the self-help book she'd read had taught her to do. Then she wrapped up the grief and tucked it neatly away. Reminded herself that dwelling in her pain wouldn't bring her mother back. Told her heart to stand down and her mind to focus on her schedule.

"My daughter answered her calling from the start." Pops tapped his stomach. "A calling comes from your very core. And it can't be denied for long."

Georgie picked up the last of Pops's pawns and set it on the side of the board. "Did you ignore your calling?"

"Absolutely." Pops's one-sided grin sparkled in his wide, unapologetic gaze. "It's the privilege of youth. I was young and determined to prove life was more than a run-down ranch, mucking stalls and baling hay."

"What did you do?"

"Simple. Turned my back on my family, my

roots and left town." Pops scratched his cheek. "Lasted until I met my wife."

"She brought you back home," Georgie guessed.

"My wife was my home." Pops set his elbows on his knees, leaned forward over the game board, closer to Georgie, as if to make sure she heard him. "With my wife I finally understood."

"Understood what?" Georgie bent toward him.

"That's a conversation for another time." Pops shifted back into his chair and moved his queen. "Checkmate."

Georgie studied the game board and her king's precarious position. "I did not see that coming."

Pops slapped his knee and chuckled. "It's been a pleasure, Georgiana Marie Harrison."

"You know my full name," Georgie said.

"Of course." He raised his hot-chocolate mug in a toast to her. "We're family."

Simple as that. There was nothing complicated about Pops. Georgie appreciated him even more. She picked up her mug and grinned over the rim. "Then, as family, I can come back and challenge you to another game. A full game, not one already started."

"I'm here every day. Store opens at nine o'clock and closes at five. You know where to find me."

Pops waved to a woman stomping the snow off her boots right outside the open entrance door. "Hey, May. Alice sold one of your saddles. Hope you brought another."

"I did." The slight woman stepped inside and grinned.

Georgie finished her hot chocolate. "Pops, do you know if I can find local honey in Falcon Creek?"

"You sure can." Pops hitched his thumb over his shoulder. "Have Alice introduce you to Ms. Hilda Pittman. Hilda will have what you need."

Georgie stood and acted on impulse. She walked over to Pops and pressed a kiss on his weathered cheek. "Thanks, Pops. I'm glad we met today."

Pops touched the brim of his hat. "See you soon, Dr. Georgie Blackwell Harrison."

"I'm off to find new jeans and Alice." Georgie picked up their empty mugs.

"Women's section is on the other side of the bedding section." Pops unfolded a fleece blanket and draped it over his lap. "As for my daughter, she could be anywhere. But check the gardening section first."

Pops rocked back in his chair, tipped his hat over his face and seemed to instantly fall asleep. Georgie headed to find Alice. She wanted to meet Hilda Pittman and discuss Pops's forehead with Alice. He'd easily dismissed his daughter's suggestion that he take off his hat while not raising Alice's suspicions. Clever gentleman that he was. Yet Pops had convinced Georgie even more that no one in the family had seen the lesion.

Pops had claimed Georgie as family. As his family, she was called to look after him. She couldn't wait to share that argument with Pops over their rematch. Her smile lifted from inside her and spread across her face.

CHAPTER TEN

ZACH STUCK THE paper on which he'd written the horse feed blend Frank and he had come up with for Rain Dancer in his jacket pocket. A blend Frank thought would support Rain Dancer's immunity better. He'd call Wade McKee later and have the ranch manager change Rain Dancer's feed.

Zach had repaired several brackets on the storage shelves in Brewster's warehouse. Driven their forklift to relocate pallets of feed to the newly secure shelves. Unloaded grain and road salt. Then chatted with Frank and enjoyed every minute, glad to be helpful and working. He'd been idle too long.

Georgie and Zach had also helped restock kindling inside the supply store. After Georgie had agreed to wait for Hilda Pittman to return from her property with the honey and herbs Georgie requested.

Next stop was lunch delivery to Grace and Eli, courtesy of Alice. The kind woman had insisted Georgie and Zach eat before they left.

Pops had joined them in the kitchen and informed them that they wouldn't be allowed to leave until they ate every bite. Alice's spicy chili hadn't been hard to finish, even on his second helping.

Georgie opened the door to Grace's accounting office and called out a greeting.

"Come on in," Grace called back.

Zach followed Georgie inside and pulled up short to keep from running into Georgie's stiff back. Grace sat on the floor in front of a large oak desk, her son, Eli, on her lap. Blood stained Grace's cream-colored sweater and Eli's sweatpants. Tissues littered the floor around the pair. Grace had Eli's nose pinched between her fingers.

"It's the second ten-minute compression." Grace frowned at the computer tablet resting in Eli's lap. "I know too much screen time is bad for kids. But I think desperate times should be judgment free, don't you?"

Zach raised the to-go bag Alice had packed for Grace and Eli. "We're only delivering lunch, not judging."

Georgie touched the cloth food bag. "Your mom sent chili and dessert."

Eli's head popped up, dislodging Grace's compression. "Cookies?"

"After we stop the nosebleed." Grace adjusted Eli's head and set her fingers back on his nose.

"My nose likes cookies." Eli wiggled on his mom's lap.

"You have to be still," Grace warned. More blood leaked onto Eli's shirt.

Zach nudged his elbow into Georgie's side and whispered, "Do something. Help them."

"Me?" Georgie mouthed back.

Zach nodded. "You're the doctor."

"In a lab." Heat infused her murmur.

"Consider this your new lab." His whisper matched hers in intensity. "They're your family."

Anger and fear flashed in her gaze. She scowled at Zach, stuffed her phone in her back pocket and turned away from him. She asked, "Grace, do you mind if I try?"

Zach rocked back. None of Georgie's irritation at him dented her calm tone or composed expression.

"Please." The relief in Grace's voice was clear. Worry and desperation were also plain to hear. "Please, could you help?"

Zach stepped forward, preparing to nudge Georgie if required. Yet she inhaled once, as if gathering herself, then knelt on the floor in front of Grace and Eli. The boy had his father's eyes, his mom's twin dimples and a sweetness about him that reminded Zach of his own brother.

Cody had had the same wide-eyed expression, always taking in the world around him as if he'd known, even as a young child, that his time was limited. Zach shifted the to-go bag to his other hand. He'd always been by his brother's side. Cody had always come before a rodeo competition. His brother had always come first. One of the reasons he'd pushed Georgie to help now. Family should never suffer.

Georgie edged closer. "Eli, what are you watching?"

"Zoo Tales." Eli's voice was nasal from his mom squeezing his nose.

"Are there giraffes or monkeys in it? I like to visit them at the zoo." Georgie settled cross-legged on the floor.

Eli lifted his big eyes to her but kept his head tilted forward. "Dragons and unicorns."

"Oh, it's a special zoo. I really like dragons." Georgie looked around, then leaned toward Eli. "Can you keep a secret?"

Eli nodded.

"I had a dragon growing up. She slept under my bed." Georgie pressed a finger over her mouth. Her shoulders edged toward her ears as if she could barely contain her excitement. She added, "My sisters didn't even know about my pet."

Eli giggled and squirmed, scooting off his mom's lap. He dropped the tablet in Georgie's lap and pushed a wad of tissue under his nose. "A big dragon?"

"Really big. She snored like this." Georgie made a loud snoring sound and earned a giggle from Eli for her performance.

Zach watched the pair, surprised. He'd never have guessed Georgie Harrison spoke toddler. And seemingly fluently at that. What other talents did she hide?

Georgie motioned Eli closer. "I can tell you all about my dragon, if you let me look at your nose."

"My nose is in a bad mood." Eli pushed his bottom lip out.

"Can I make your nose happy again?" Georgie asked.

Her voice was patient. She sat at the child's level, her body relaxed and calm as if she intended to play with the toddler. Zach doubted any kid would refuse her. Impressive.

Eli lowered onto Georgie's lap and settled in, the boy's trust in Georgie complete. Had Zach ever trusted anyone, other than his brother, like that? He wasn't certain.

Eli pinched his nose. "Mommy do this."

"That's good." Georgie adjusted Eli and set her fingers below the bridge of his nose, freeing his hands. She glanced at Zach and Grace. "I'm going to need cotton swabs and apple cider vinegar."

Apple cider vinegar. Zach sputtered. And it'd been going so well.

Grace rose and glanced back at Georgie. "Did you say 'apple cider vinegar'?"

Georgie nodded and handed Eli the tablet.

"Fortunately, my husband listened to his grandfather. Big E believes apple cider vinegar is a cure for everything." Grace headed into the back of the house.

Zach crossed his arms over his chest and leaned his hip against the edge of Grace's desk. "Was that your plan to get Grace out of the room so you can realign his nose?" Zach had had his nose adjusted after a full facial collision with the hindquarters of a bronc in the arena.

"His nose is fine," Georgie said. "Straight and completely unbroken."

Zach touched his own nose. "Then what kind of doctor are you?"

Georgie bit her bottom lip. Uncertainty traced through her gaze. "The kind who listens to long-time nurses and doctors sharing their personal home remedies."

"So, you've used apple cider vinegar to stop

a nosebleed before." He tugged a pile of tissues from the box on Grace's desk and handed them to Georgie.

"Never." Georgie chewed more of her bottom lip and accepted the tissues. She replaced the bloody tissues in Eli's hands with the clean ones. "But Loretta, one of the charge nurses on the surgical floor, had seven children and twenty-seven grandchildren. Loretta insisted it worked."

"And if it doesn't work?" Zach asked.

"We come up with another solution," she said.

The panic skimming over her words jarred Zach. He pushed away from the desk, ready to take Georgie's hand and promise her...what? He was a cowboy, better trained to handle horses than people. Still, he'd held his brother's hand during treatments growing up. Never let go until Cody had convinced Zach he was good.

Grace returned with vinegar bottles clutched in her hands and worry creasing her forehead. Grace set the containers and a handful of cotton swabs on her desk. "I have distilled white, white wine as well as apple cider vinegars."

"I just need the apple cider and a damp cotton swab," Georgie said.

Once again, the doubt receded beneath Georgie's neutral expression. Once again, she impressed Zach. He had always set his head on his brother's shoulder or side of the bed. Too afraid to look at the needles. Too afraid to watch another treatment not work. Zach massaged his neck, forced himself to remain present for Georgie. In case she needed him.

"Let's see if your nose is still feeling bad." Georgie pushed on Eli's hands, revealing his nose.

The bleeding had slowed, but not ceased. Zach opened the apple cider bottle and handed it, along with a cotton swab, to Georgie. Grace hovered within reach of her son, her hands clenched in front of her.

Georgie dabbed the piece of cotton into the liquid, then swirled the cotton swab inside Eli's nose and waited. Finally, her words rushed out in a burst of excitement and disbelief. "It worked."

"Happy." Eli pointed at his nose. "Cookies and dragons."

The little boy cuddled into Georgie's lap, his head on her shoulder. Georgie's arms wrapped around his small waist as if she'd always been content holding toddlers and treating bloody noses.

As if she always rescued the scared and sick. He imagined, with the blend of her knowledge and compassion, she could rescue anyone she chose to, even the lonely.

"One dragon story it is." Georgie launched into a fantastic tale about Izzy-Belle, her friendly dragon with rainbow wings who liked chocolate and gummy bears. Eli fell asleep minutes into the story. Georgie transferred Eli to Grace's arms. Her voice was quiet. "I think we wiped him out."

"I'm going to keep a supply of apple cider vinegar everywhere we go." Grace adjusted her son without waking him. "What can I do for you, Georgie? How can I thank you?"

"You just did," Georgie said. "I'm glad it worked."

"Well, I owe you." Grace gave her a one-armed hug. "Big-time."

"It might not work…" Georgie started.

Grace turned away to pick up Eli's blanket and never caught the end of Georgie's warning that the apple cider vinegar might not work the next time.

Zach asked, "Anything else we can do for you, Grace?"

"I'm good," Grace said. "I'll get him settled in his bed and then hopefully get some work done."

"Don't forget to eat." Zach handed Grace the to-go bag.

Outside on the porch, Zach squinted at the

sun reflecting off the snow-covered mountains. "Why aren't you doing patient care again?"

Georgie stepped off the porch. "I treated a bloody nose. It's no big deal. Anyone could've searched the internet for the apple cider remedy."

Not just anyone would've dared to try it. And with such composure. He followed Georgie to the car.

"I got lucky," Georgie added. "Like I told Grace, it might not work again. She should really talk to her pediatrician."

Zach would wager his entire rodeo winnings that Grace would seek out Georgie again for medical advice. Just as the ranch hand, Sean Foster, had tracked down Ethan during breakfast that morning to ask if he should worry or not that his dog, Bruno, hadn't eaten in almost two days.

Ethan had asked several questions, offered his opinion and told Sean to bring Bruno to see him if Bruno hadn't eaten by dinner. Relief had rushed over Sean, the same as it had Grace when Georgie offered her help.

Ethan and Georgie were trained professionals in their fields. Knowledgeable, capable and compassionate. Even more, they were trusted. Trust always mattered.

Georgie picked up a second cloth bag from

the back seat that held the items she'd obtained from Hilda. "Next stop, Rachel and Ben."

Zach parked in front of the law offices of Ben and Rachel Blackwell. He opened the office door for Georgie and followed her inside. Georgie's outstretched hand stopped him from running into her again. He closed the door softly.

Rachel sat behind a modern desk, her face pale. One hand was pressed over her stomach; the other clenched a paper napkin. Her head swayed back and forth. "I can't."

"You have to eat something." Ben traded the deli sandwich on the desk for a soup bowl.

Rachel wrinkled her nose and leaned back.

Ben swept the soup bowl off her desk, caught sight of Georgie and Zach. The soup bowl swayed in his grip. Defeat and concern played across his face.

"I'll get rid of that." Zach jumped forward and grabbed the bowl from Ben. He spied a small kitchen, dumped the soup into the sink and returned to Georgie's side.

"Georgie. Zach. Sorry about this." Rachel rubbed her forehead and grimaced. "I don't know if it's the smell or the look of the food. Or the taste."

"Or all of the above," Zach whispered to Georgie.

Georgie nodded and winced.

"You haven't actually tasted anything." Ben frowned and touched Rachel's shoulder.

"I've never been this sensitive to food before." Rachel released her forehead and waved her hand. "I'm really sorry. You both aren't here to watch our food wars."

"Actually, I'm here to drop off something that might help your stomach settle." Georgie stepped closer to the couple. Her words and movements were hesitant, as if she didn't believe they'd want her help. As if she feared she'd overstepped.

How could Georgie think that offering her help, especially to her family, was an inconvenience? Or an intrusion?

Rachel straightened. "Seriously?"

"You have a cure." Ben grasped his hands together and gaped as if he'd just heard about a miracle.

"A morning-sickness cure hasn't been discovered yet." Georgie shook her head and retreated toward Zach. "But this might help."

"Anything." Rachel motioned Georgie closer. "I'll try anything."

Ben crossed his arms over his chest. Reservation replaced his earlier enthusiasm. He stood guard over his wife and eyed Georgie.

Zach moved to Georgie's side, prepared to defend her.

"What is it?" Ben asked.

"It's honey and other natural ingredients," Georgie said. "Blended into a hot tea."

"Please tell me that you have some with you," Rachel said. Her desperate gaze searched Georgie like a barista looking for the last of the specially grown coffee beans.

"I have the ingredients to make it." Georgie patted the cloth shopping bag Alice had filled with the items from Hilda Pittman. "I just need to use your kitchen."

Rachel rose.

Ben touched Rachel's shoulder and nudged her back into her office chair. "I'll show Georgie where everything is. You sit and relax."

"Take these, too." Rachel pushed a plate of pizza and another of buttered noodles toward Ben. "If you guys haven't eaten, feel free to have some. It's the best pizza you'll ever taste."

Ben gathered the food and motioned for Georgie and Zach to follow him. Ben dropped everything on a small round table in the remodeled kitchen next to take-out bags from the deli and a pastry shop. "Feel free to eat whatever you want. My wife can't eat, so I've been eating everything for the both of us."

Zach pointed at the deep-dish pizza with fresh tomatoes and basil. "Are you sure you don't mind? Because that looks better than anything I've had in Chicago."

"I'll be eternally grateful if you eat everything on this table." Ben patted his stomach. "Pregnancy pounds are clearly not reserved for the mothers only and we're just starting the second trimester."

"Georgie, what can I get you?" Zach grabbed napkins and paper plates from the counter.

"We have chicken salad croissants. Deli sandwiches. Assorted soups. Nachos, plain and loaded." Ben pointed to a bakery box. "Or if you prefer pastries, we have a dozen different kinds to choose from. We even have buttered noodles from the ranch."

"Is there any cuisine you don't have?" Georgie laughed, set the bag on the counter and unloaded the items from Hilda.

Zach found a cutting board and knife, placed them on the counter. Then washed the peppermint leaves she handed him.

"You can't have any Indian food but only because we don't have a good Indian restaurant within twenty miles of here." Ben dipped a chip in a container of guacamole and eyed Georgie. "You think that will work? Even certain smells make her gag these days."

"I have a friend who swears by aromatherapy." Georgie filled a pot with water, set it on the stove to boil and asked Zach to mince the peppermint.

Zach picked up the knife and stepped up to the cutting, pleased he could help Georgie. She was more than capable of handling everything herself. Still, he liked being there for her.

"My friend recommended peppermint. I found a candle at Brewster's." Georgie turned to Ben. "It's in the bag. If it works, I'll have my friend send her special blended essential oils for Rachel to try."

Ben gripped the candle and clutched it between his hands. "Please, let it be as simple as lighting a candle and drinking tea."

"There's nothing simple about pregnancy." Georgie added lemon slices and fresh ginger to the boiling water, then reached into the shopping bag again. "Every pregnant mom is different."

"Speaking of which, I'm going to check on my wife." Ben brushed the chip crumbs off his dress shirt, washed his hands and headed out to the front offices.

"You should eat, too." Zach set a plate with half of a deli sandwich and fresh fruit on the counter beside Georgie. "Where did you learn this? The same nurses?"

"Smoothies got me through medical school," Georgie said. "When I needed to study and couldn't take the time to stop and make a full meal, I blended a smoothie together. I bought the supplies for Rachel to try one if the tea works. Once her stomach settles, she can sip a smoothie and slowly add other bland foods."

Zach sniffed the tea and nodded. "Is this an old family recipe?"

"Great-Aunt Pru loved every kind of tea. She even experimented with her own blends. Some were good. Some not so good." The distance in Georgie's smile hinted that she'd stepped back into a good memory. "But this tea blend I read about in a health magazine while sitting in my genetics professor's office."

"And you remembered it?" Zach asked.

"I have four sisters." Georgie shrugged, her voice casual. "I figured at some point one of them would get pregnant and might need this tea to feel better."

"Or you could drink it when you get pregnant." Zach replaced the lid. He kept his voice as casual and matter-of-fact as hers.

"M-me," Georgie stammered.

"Yes, you." Zach bit into his pizza and considered her. "Don't you want kids one day?"

Georgie picked up the knife, chopped more ginger and avoided looking at Zach. "Maybe."

Her indecision bothered him. He took another bite of pizza and would've blamed his low blood-sugar levels for his reaction. Except he'd already eaten at Brewster's and at the ranch earlier. "You were really good with Eli. Natural and at ease." *Affectionate and loving.*

Georgie dumped the ginger into the pot. Denial scraped into her words. "I didn't do anything anyone else wouldn't do."

Not true. He took another bite of pizza rather than dispute her claim. His mother had offered disregard and indifference as naturally as other mothers offered their children support and reassurance.

You're dirty and bleeding. Go away.

You're always scared of something at night. Go away.

You're always hungry. Go away.

His mother's accusations had always been followed by those same two words, given in the same dull, detached tone: *Go. Away.*

Until he'd finally stopped seeking his mom out and learned to take care of himself. He'd been younger than Rosie. Not yet able to read, but more than able to understand. He had to mind his own business and let his mother mind hers.

He bit off another piece of pizza, refusing to let his past ruin his appetite. Living through his childhood had already soured his stomach enough. "Well, you were good with Eli today and Rosie the other night."

She spun around and stared at him. "And that qualifies me to be a good mother?"

As far as he knew, there were no qualifications to become a mom. Or a parent, for that matter. "Maybe it's the ability to love someone more than yourself that qualifies you."

"Once again, we disagree," she said.

Zach finished his pizza and wiped his hands on a napkin. "You're going to tell me it takes more than love to be a good parent."

"Doesn't it?" she countered.

"Love is the foundation. Without it…" He let his voice trail off.

It wasn't his place to convince her of love's power. He hardly trusted love himself.

It wasn't his place to plead with her to reconsider children and a family. He knew little about a close-knit family—his own had been broken and damaged. He knew only about the kind of family he'd always wanted. The kind he'd always wished for.

It wasn't his place to offer her anything more than the easygoing fake boyfriend she'd requested. Zach peered inside the boiling pot. "At least you have your first tester with Rachel. Now you'll know how well it works before you make it for your sisters."

She frowned at him.

He lowered the lid and studied her. "What did I say now?"

"Nothing." She opened and closed several cabinets until she found a mug.

"You memorized the recipe for your sisters." Zach tracked her around the compact kitchen. "So, you planned to make it for them."

"Of course."

Zach rubbed his chin. He wasn't sure if it was the upbeat declaration in her voice that fell flat between them. Or the way her gaze skipped around the room. But he didn't believe her.

Georgie ladled tea into the mug and stared at the rising steam.

"Looks like everything is ready." Zach moved beside Georgie. She looked anything but ready. "Want me to bring this out to Rachel?"

"What if the tea doesn't help?" Her voice was as thin as the steam.

"Then we'll find something that does help."

"We?" She lifted her gaze to his face.

"Yes, we. You and me." Zach picked up the pot of honey from Hilda Pittman and swirled the wooden stick in the tea. "Honey is good for allergies, sore throats and stomach issues."

"Is that right?" A smile broke through her hesitant tone.

"Yes, it is." Zach drizzled honey on his finger and tasted it. The sweetness coated his tongue and kept the lightness in his words. "You aren't the only one who has read countless health magazines while sitting in offices."

He'd spent more time in medical offices and hospital waiting rooms than he had in his own home, hoping that someone would be able to save his brother. The last *we* he'd been a part of had been with Cody. He hadn't been able to help his brother. Why had he told Georgie he'd help her?

Georgie took Zach's hand as if she sensed his faltering. He stared at their joined hands. He'd been gripping cotton reins and lassos for so long he'd forgotten the power in such a simple connection. Her fingers laced between his, naturally and easily. And quickly the past, the pain, the powerless feelings that had kicked up inside him, settled. Her soft, sure hold tethered him firmly to the present.

"Let's bring Rachel the tea before it gets cold." She tugged on his hand, guiding him into the front offices.

And with her hand in his, for the first time in years, he considered something more than a temporary connection.

CHAPTER ELEVEN

GEORGIE CURLED HER toes in her fleece socks, covered her yawn and peered into the enclosed sunporch. The sun had yet to rise and only two side-table lamps lit up the comfortable, homey space.

Zach sat in the rocking chair Dorothy had warned them not to use. It'd been broken for more years than Dorothy could remember. Tools were scattered around the rug. Zach's fingers wrapped around the armrests, his grip stiff and unyielding. His boots sank into the thick rug as if planted. A quiet strength enfolded him, holding him straight in the chair. His chin sank toward his chest. Loneliness splintered his stillness and pulled her fully into the sunporch.

She stopped, holding herself just outside touching distance. "You're up early."

"I could say the same about you." His head lifted, but his gaze remained hooded.

I felt you leave the room. Wanted you... "Occupational hazard. Research requires long hours with early mornings and late nights." She pointed to the rocking chair. "You fixed it."

He shrugged. "It was nothing."

"Anyone could've done it." She repeated her words from yesterday at Grace's office after she had stopped Eli's bloody nose. Her heart warmed at his generosity. "With an internet search, how-to video and the right tools."

"Something like that." He wiped his hands over his face as if rubbing away a bad dream.

"Why are you out here?" *Did you mean it when you referred to us as a* we *yesterday?*

"It's the most peaceful, beautiful time of the day."

He looked isolated and alone and far from peaceful. She sat in the cedar porch swing, curled her feet underneath her and watched him. And waited. *I want you to mean it. I want to reach for you. For us.*

He leaned back against the hand-carved headrest. His gaze remained fixed on the windows, still darkened in the predawn hour. "It wasn't a two-story house on a cul-de-sac. There was no basketball hoop out front. No sandbox in the backyard."

Georgie folded her arms over her chest, blocking the chill skimming across her. "This was your childhood home in Cincinnati."

"It was a two-bedroom ranch on the edge of

the city limits." He set the chair in motion. The slow rocking matched the wryness in his words. "A step above the trailer park. Mom always took pride in that."

The bleakness on his face plunged that chill deep inside her. Childhood memories should be unable to hurt an adult.

"My brother, Cody, and I always woke up at sunrise." His chair slowed. His words continued, "Mom was always passed out then. We could eat without the constant accusations. *You boys ruined my life. Stole my dreams. Selfish and greedy. Ungrateful.*"

Georgie pressed her knuckles against her mouth, knocking back her gasp. "How old were you?"

"Seven. Cody was five." His fingers uncurled from the armrests. "We were always the first ones on the school bus and the last ones off."

"Where was your father?"

"Dad was a cross-country truck driver." Zach rose and flipped the rocking chair over in one swift motion. "He was always hauling loads from one state to another."

And left his sons to fend for themselves. Georgie grimaced.

Zach picked up a hand sander and drew it across the runner. Back and forth. Steady and smooth, the motion almost dulling the sharpest parts of his memories. "Dad did his best for us. He always told me, *Son, don't forget your hands. If all else fails, you can use your hands to provide for your family.*"

"And did he follow his own advice?" she asked. "Did he provide for you and your brother?"

"He provided the money for Mom's vodka." His hands stilled as if the sandpaper had caught on a nail. "If I got to the mailbox first, then we had food, too."

Georgie pushed off the swing, wrapped her arms around her stomach and wandered across the porch. She willed the sun to rise faster. Looked for anything to drive the cold away. "How did you and your brother...?"

"Survive," he cut in. He ran his palm over the runner. "I learned to use my hands. The neighbors never asked questions if the yard was mowed. The front door painted. The blinds straight and the screen repaired."

"But you had to eat. You were children." Not once had she ever worried about food or gone to bed hungry. Not once had she been scared to go home. Afraid in her own house.

"My dad taught me about woodworking and tools," he said. "When I got older, Dad brought home old dressers, tables, chairs, whatever fit in his truck. I fixed them in the shed in the back-yard. Then we sold them."

"We," she said.

"Dad took pieces to the different towns and sold them." Zach flipped over the chair again, set it right. "I mowed the neighbors' lawns and repaired things for them. Cody raked leaves. Whatever they needed."

"But you shouldn't have had to work." Anger trembled through her words. "You were children like Rosie."

"It made me who I am." Zach picked up the scattered tools.

"And who is that?" she challenged.

He was so much more than the laid-back cowboy she'd met on the plane. And his sixty-second short was just that—entirely too short. He'd kept up his childhood house for appearances. Refurbished furniture for food. Worked as a child to support his family.

"I'm a man who doesn't dwell in the past." He set the tools inside the toolbox he'd left in the corner of the sunporch.

But the past dwelled inside him and he suffered all the same. Still. Loneliness and pain bracketed him like steel grips. She asked, "Remind me again—why the rodeo?"

He shook his head. "It started with a girl and then I made a promise to my brother."

The sun finally slipped above the horizon. The rays pulsed against the windows, shining into dark corners of the porch. The more the day awoke, the more Zach closed down. No more secrets would be revealed this day. She said, "My dad made a promise to my mother to see their daughters happy and married."

"That's why I'm here." A slight tease had returned to his voice.

"I don't intend to get married," she said.

He set his hands on his hips. "Then your dad will break his promise to your mom."

"He's not my biological father. Thomas Blackwell, Big E's son, is." She brushed her hair off her shoulders. Clearly, her secrets weren't safe during the daytime. "None of us knew the truth until a few months ago."

"That explains the part about you not having met any of your Blackwell relatives." His eyebrows drew together. "But not the part about marriage."

"My parents lied to us. Mom even asked my oldest sister, Peyton, to lie." Georgie twisted her hair into a bun. "Dad could've lied to Mom about seeing us settled into happy married life, too."

"What did your dad do?"

"Career military," she said. "Rudy Harrison was an admiral in the navy."

"That's impressive," Zach said. "He didn't lie to your mom. Men like him live by a code. He intends to follow through on his promise."

"Dad will have to break his promise," she argued.

"Or you'll have to fall in love."

She opened her mouth. *Love.* Her mouth closed. *About that we.* She shook her head. "Why are we talking about this?"

Zach spread his arms wide. "It's a new day. Time to face what the day brings."

But she didn't have to face certain truths. "I need coffee to face this day."

"Coffee is already brewing." Dorothy walked into the sunporch, dressed for the day in a thick cable-knit sweater, pants and fur-lined boots.

"I hope we didn't wake you." Georgie accepted a quick morning hug from her grandmother.

Dorothy laughed. "And I always considered myself an early riser." Her gaze shifted to the rocking chair. She gasped.

"Zach fixed it," Georgie announced. "Hope you don't mind."

"I don't mind in the least. May I?" Dorothy motioned to the chair.

"Please," Zach said.

Dorothy lowered into the chair and sighed.

Pleasure filled her face, and she whispered, "My mother rocked all her babies to sleep in this very chair."

The tradition touched Georgie. And Zach had given Dorothy a piece of her family history back. She reached for his hand, grateful for the gift he'd given her grandmother.

Dorothy ran her hands over the armrests. "I thought Mama's chair would have to go to the Once Was Barn. But I wasn't ready to lose the connection to her, so I hid the rocker out here." Dorothy wiped at her eyes. "Such silliness over a simple chair."

Not silly. Not in the least. Georgie wore a simple bracelet that had belonged to her mother every day. Georgie asked, "What's the Once Was Barn?"

"It's where all the best memories go." Dorothy chuckled. "It's really where all the meaningful but no longer useful furniture and trinkets go after they've been retired from use. Things have been piling up for years in that barn, especially as we seem to favor the new over the old more and more these days."

Georgie squeezed Zach's hand. "Can we see it?"

"After coffee and the last of my homemade bourbon cinnamon French toast." Dorothy rose and walked into the kitchen. "I'd like to take a walk through the Once Was Barn, too. Been too long."

CHAPTER TWELVE

WHY HADN'T GEORGIE walked away? Gone back to bed? Zach had told her the truth about his childhood and his parents. He'd revealed the sorrier side of his past in the dark. She hadn't turned away. She'd sat on the porch swing and listened. No judgment. No pity.

He'd rambled even more, as if safe in the predawn hour inside the enclosed sunporch with Georgie Harrison. As if they'd crossed an invisible barrier. As if they were more than pretend and building toward something more than short-term.

But he was safest when alone. Keeping his own counsel and his own secrets.

Georgie was lightness and good. He was ruthless and harbored too many shadows.

He'd tallied favors owed. Selfishly and intentionally. He'd repaired a Blackwell family heirloom. Helped at Grace's family store. Joined Georgie to assist Eli and Rachel.

Never mind that he'd really liked working with Frank Gardner and would help the Gardners again. Anytime. No favors required in return. He thought Eli was adorable. And he liked Ben and Rachel—two strong individuals who together made an even stronger couple.

He wanted the Blackwells to feel slightly indebted to him. It was entirely wrong. He was entirely wrong for Georgie. Certainly, she'd recognized that on the sunporch that morning, too.

Zach pushed the ATV faster. Dorothy had insisted he take the vehicle and he followed the directions she'd given him to the Once Was Barn. The barn stood by itself in its own private corner of the Blackwell property, far away from the guest lodge and activity on the working ranch. As if the old barn and its occupants deserved a peaceful last resting place. There was resilience to the old barn despite the icicles dangling from its weathered roof and the snowdrift leaning against its faded exterior wall.

Zach parked and grabbed the flashlight strapped behind the passenger seat. A path had been shoveled to the double doors recently, so his boots only sank into the snow several inches rather than up to his knees.

He eased inside and spotted the light switch immediately. With the lights turned on, the barn was lit from the rafters, highlighting the space. Furniture and oversized pieces filled the ground level. Plastic bins, their tops color coded, sat stacked in rows up in the loft.

The barn wasn't as forgotten as Dorothy had led him to believe. Zach rubbed his hands together. His gaze skipped from a claw-foot tub to tractor parts, to a half dozen brooms leaning against the wall. Doors and window frames had been propped against another wall. Furniture from past decades, some pieces broken, some pieces simply outdated, huddled together as far back as Zach could see.

Had he been given access to such a barn as a kid, he'd have had a continuous stream of projects and items for his father to sell on the road. The barn was a treasure trove of links to the Blackwell past and he was merely trespassing.

Still, he couldn't quite keep from working his way around the furniture, running his hand over the large scroll swerving through an aged wrought-iron headboard and imagining.

"Zach, did you get lost in here?" Dorothy called out.

Zach worked his way back to her and stopped beside a sturdy oak headboard and footboard. His fingers curved around one of the twisted posts of the headboard. Dorothy hadn't arrived alone. Grace, Hadley and Georgie stood around a pair of dining chairs and examined the cracked leather seats. "This is quite the barn, Dorothy."

"There are pieces here from before Big E and I were born." Dorothy unwound her scarf. "Buried, I'm sure, underneath the items we considered all the fashion at one time."

"Everything becomes popular again at some point." Hadley pressed on a chair's leather seat as if testing its durability.

"What's old is new." Grace tapped a broken wood bucket with the toe of her boot. "Unless you're like me and can't quite see how to make the old new again."

Georgie stepped beside Grace. "You're not the only one who can't see it."

"That's a relief." Grace grinned. "Why are we here, anyway?"

"I wanted to revisit the barn." Dorothy clasped her hands together and walked closer to Zach. "And I wanted Zach's advice on several pieces."

"If it's the value you want to know about, I can't help you." Zach studied the vine carving following the curve of the headboard's frame. "You'll need an appraiser and more qualified eye for that."

"The value of these pieces is in the memories." Dorothy set her hand on the intricate headboard. "And the idea that they could be useful once again."

Zach eyed her. "What do you have in mind?"

"This headboard once belonged to my grandmother. Hand-carved by my grandfather." Dorothy traced her finger over the vine design.

"Grandma Dot, you shouldn't have let me put this out here." Dismay spread through Hadley's voice.

"Nonsense," Dorothy said. "It had no place at the lodge. It's quite bulky as a king bed."

Zach studied the solid wood construction and the handcrafted workmanship of the headboard. One-of-a-kind pieces shouldn't languish in an old barn, unseen and unappreciated. Cody had claimed that they'd crafted unique pieces all those years ago. Zach had only been interested in earning a few dollars and sneaking to the store for a frozen pizza. He hadn't let his mind simply envision possibilities since his dad had given him a crate and told him to make it into whatever he wanted. He'd made it into the seat of a tree swing for his brother. "You could take the headboard and footboard to make a bench."

The four women crowded around Zach.

"Is that possible?" Georgie wedged in beside him.

"It would make a stunning entryway piece," Dorothy said.

"You can do that?" That from Hadley.

Zach shrugged. "I could with the right tools."

"We have tools." Grace chuckled. "A lot of

tools all around the ranch, and there's power in here, if you wanted to work inside the barn."

Hadley shifted toward him, her movement more of a shuffle as she tried not to bump her stomach. "Could you repurpose other things in here?"

"We have several cabins to update." Grace's eyes widened behind her glasses. "If we used what we already own, we'd save money."

"Money that we can use to build the next phase of cabins," Hadley added.

"That's brilliant," Grace said. "The accountant in me is singing right now."

Zach wasn't singing. He would be leaving in less than a week. Repurposing or refurbishing the furniture inside the Once Was Barn would be an ongoing project with an unending to-do list. The idea appealed.

He stuffed his hands into his pockets and walked away from the women. This wasn't his barn. His family. And these weren't his heirlooms to repurpose or fix up. He'd have to move on.

"Well, we're starting with my bench," Dorothy said. "You can make the bench, can't you, Zach?"

He turned and his gaze skipped from the veiled delight on Dorothy's face to Georgie. She touched her grandmother's arm as if she'd heard the fragile hope in Dorothy's voice, too. Then she looked at Zach and his breath stuck in his throat. Disappointing Georgie became the last thing he wanted to do.

"Of course he can." Georgie's chin dipped ever so slightly, as if she wanted his consent. Wanted to know she hadn't overstepped.

He'd overstepped. In more ways than he could count. And staring at Georgie, he wanted nothing more than to cross more barriers. But holding her in his arms, kissing her, would be like climbing onto a bronc without the cotton rein to hold. He'd never recover from a fall like that. "I'd be more than happy to make the bench."

Pleasure stretched Georgie's smile into brilliance, bursting into her gaze and overflowing into Zach. He captured her look, recorded it to memory. Months from now, stretched out in the bed of his truck with only the stars as company, he wanted to be able to close his eyes and see her face. Remember how she'd looked at him—a drifter cowboy—with such admiration and affection.

Dorothy hugged him and turned to Grace and Hadley. "If you two like Zach's work, you can talk to him about other projects."

"Deal." Hadley set her hands on her stomach. "While I'm seeing this barn in a whole new light, I need to get back to the house and put my feet up."

"Are you feeling okay?" Georgie asked.

Zach smiled. Georgie might claim to want to be inside a lab, but the nurturer inside her kept surfacing. She cared about the people around her. Zach cared about her. His smile faded. No harm in caring about someone. He just had to make sure he stopped there.

"I'm ready for this little one to arrive," Hadley said.

Grace curved her arm around Hadley's waist. "Let's head back and run some numbers. Numbers will get your mind off your swollen feet."

"Or put me to sleep." Hadley laughed.

"I'll join you." Dorothy linked her arm around Hadley's. "I promised Ty I would help him with the last of the nursery setup."

"Georgie, you want to come with us?" Grace asked.

Georgie shook her head. "I think I'll stay and explore, if you don't mind."

Zach minded. Very much. He'd be alone with Georgie. Again. And every time he was alone with her, he spilled more truths. Revealed parts of his life he'd never wanted to share. Every time he was alone with Georgie, the lines blurred, and he forgot he was only supposed to be pretending to like her.

"Stay and enjoy, you two." Dorothy tucked her scarf inside her jacket.

"I'll let you know if I find any treasures," Georgie said.

"If you do, it's yours for the effort," Dorothy said.

The women stepped outside, and the barn doors closed.

Georgie spun in a slow circle. "Where should we start?"

With me taking your hand. Pulling you into my arms... Zach coughed. "I'm going to check the ATV for tools, a tape measure." And something to disconnect his unwise attraction to Georgie.

Twenty minutes later, Zach had taken the measurements of the headboard and footboard. He had a basic idea of his plan and a list of supplies he'd need. And one ear listening to Georgie's every move through the barn, taking note if a cabinet door opened or a hinge squeaked. Two muffled grunts had him dropping his tape measure and heading into the furniture to retrieve her. Only her calls of "I'm fine, really, I'm fine" kept him from intervening.

"I found it." Georgie emerged from the back of the barn, dust on her pants and cheeks, her ponytail crooked and her full smile all too appealing.

Zach set the tape measure on a round table and brushed off his hands, but not the pull he had to be closer to her. "What?"

"Our lock-and-key item. For the scavenger hunt." She held up a tall antique jewelry box. Wonder flickered in her hazel eyes. "Look, the little key is still in the door."

The door that was no longer attached to the jewelry box. She held the door in her hand and gave it to him. He pulled his gaze away from her and studied the frosted glass door. "I can't believe the glass isn't broken."

"I know." She stepped closer, clutching the jewelry box like a valuable possession and not a scavenger hunt find. "Can you fix it?"

"Sure." He swapped the broken door for the jewelry box. "We can take it back to Dorothy's. The light is better there. Are you planning to take it home with you?"

"What?" She shook her head. "I couldn't."

"Dorothy told you anything you found in here was yours to keep." The jewelry box, even broken and dirty, had charm and history.

"I have no place to put it."

"Doesn't match your decor?" He figured her for modern lines and a clean, sleek style. No unnecessary stuff and only the essentials. He brushed the dust off the top of the box. Dirt and clutter would only clash. The same way he and she did.

"I don't have decor." She took the jewelry box back as if worried he'd drop it. "I have an apartment that barely qualifies for a one bedroom. Everything I own has been packed into five boxes."

"For London." Where she was moving to start a new life. One that would not include him. The reminder should have weakened his interest.

"I don't know how I'd get the jewelry box to London without damaging it," she said.

He could deliver it. If he lived in another world and this was another life. "It still works perfect for the lock-and-key item." Zach tapped the round table as he tapped his impossible thoughts back into the impractical category. "Set it down. Let's take a closer look. Who do you think owned it?"

"I'm not sure." She stared at the broken door. "I don't know much about the Blackwell family tree."

"Then make something up," he teased. He wanted the wonder and affection back in her smile. Back in her tone. He wanted her to forget London, if only for right now.

"Okay." She set the broken door on the table and touched the key. "It probably belonged to Dorothy's mother."

Zach shook his head. "It's on Big E's side."

"How do you know?"

"Dorothy and Big E recently remarried," he said. "Dorothy's things are in the front of the barn. You got that from the very back."

"Were you following me?" One corner of her mouth tipped up. Almost the smile he wanted. She added, "Making sure I didn't break anything?"

"I didn't need to. You were loud enough I could've tracked you from outside." He brushed the dust off her cheek, captured her full attention and her exasperation.

"I wasn't that loud." Her voice lowered. Her warm gaze locked on his.

He trailed his fingers down her neck. "Want to try again?"

"Try what?" Her voice faded.

Try to test the boundaries of fake. Try to discover what's real between us. He pulled his hand away. Real was Georgie moving to London. Real was Zach heading out for the rodeo tour. He dragged his palm over his rough beard. He needed a shave and to realign his priorities. "Who else might have owned the jewelry box?"

She was slow to pull her gaze away from him, as if she'd been focused on something else, too. Her hand fluttered over the jewelry box. "It probably belonged to one of Big E's sisters."

"That's all you've got?" He shook his head disapprovingly.

She straightened. "What's wrong with that?"

"Everything." Everything was wrong with the way he liked watching that spark of defiance flicker across her face. Everything was wrong with the way he liked everything about her. "Where's your creativity? Where's your story?"

"You think you can do better?" Her hands gripped her waist. One eyebrow arched. Challenge issued.

"I can definitely do better." And he could definitely get used to accepting her challenges. Not important. He opened and closed several of the drawers inside the jewelry box. "This belonged to Big E's mother."

Her fingers drummed against her hips. She opened her mouth.

He lifted his hand, stopping her response. "There's more. It was a favorite piece. The metal on the handles is worn away from someone using the drawers a lot." He pinched one of the small round handles to show her. "There are still impressions in the velvet padding from rings being set into the slots in the drawer."

"You saw all that?" She moved next to him and peered more closely at the jewelry box. Her shoulder bumped into his.

"When I was a kid, I studied every piece my

dad brought home. If I couldn't find the story on the furniture itself, I made it up."

She turned to face him and set her hip against the table edge, curiosity and interest in her steady gaze and face.

"I'd tell the stories to my brother." Why was he telling her such a silly thing now? What did it prove, other than that he and his brother had always imagined a different home than the one they were stuck in? He paced away. "Then Cody would add his own details. Before we knew it, we had a piece of furniture with a history and a vision for its future."

"You were two historians in the making." She tipped her head toward the furniture. "Now you'll keep the tradition for the headboard and footboard, and reimagine its future."

"No. That's Dorothy's vision." And not his tradition. The stories had been an escape for two young boys. Nothing more. "Dorothy and I talked about her wanting a bench for her entry-way this morning while you were changing." He wanted to move closer to Georgie. Bad idea. He stepped around her and walked deeper into the Once Was collection. "I did find something earlier you might like."

She trailed behind him, close enough that, if he turned, she'd run right into him. He kept moving forward and stopped in front of an armoire wide enough to fit a sizable flat-screen TV. He opened the doors and took out a plastic crate. "Found these when I was looking around."

Georgie reached into the crate and took out a rose-colored bottle. "It's a perfume bottle."

"I think they all are." Zach adjusted his grip on the box. "There are a lot in here."

She replaced the rose bottle and removed two squat frosted bottles. "These are a pair and the glass stoppers are still in both."

"You said your Christmas presents were in your vacationing suitcase." Zach paused. What had he been thinking? Vintage perfume bottles. He held the crate, Georgie next to him, and his idea sounded foolish, like the stories he'd told his little brother to scare away the monsters under the bed.

Her gaze lifted to his, locked on and searched.

"I thought you could use these as gifts for your sisters." Zach cleared his throat. "Or not. They're old glass jars. Probably chipped and cracked. Need to be cleaned."

She reached up, placed her hand on his cheek.

Her warm, soft touch stalled his rambling and his heart.

"They're perfect." She set her other palm against his cheek, framing his face. "Thank you for thinking about me."

He shifted the crate. She moved closer. His

heart kick-started into a race. He leaned forward. She leaned in. One more inch. One
more...

"Georgie! Zach!" Her sister's voice echoed up
into the rafters. "Where are you guys?"

Zach jerked away. The glass perfume bottles
clinked against each other.

Georgie jumped back. "Lily. We're over here."

"Where?" Lily hollered.

"Wait there," Georgie shouted. She grabbed
several dish towels from the armoire and covered the perfume bottles. "We'll come to you."

And Zach would come to his senses. He'd
almost kissed Georgie again, his pretend girlfriend. And all he knew was there would have
been nothing pretend about their kiss.

CHAPTER THIRTEEN

"WHAT WERE YOU and Zach doing, exactly, in the back of the barn?" Lily started the truck and glanced at Georgie in the passenger seat.

They weren't *exactly* doing anything. She'd been about to kiss her cowboy. Then Lily and Fee had arrived. Yet now Georgie wasn't certain if she welcomed or regretted her sisters' interruption. "Zach found something he thought I would like."

"Well, tell us what he found." Fee leaned between the front seats.

"I can't." Georgie adjusted her scarf around her chin, wanting to hide the blush she knew still lingered. The same as her urge to kiss Zach stuck to her, too. "They might be gifts for you guys."

"You found gifts for us in an old, dusty barn," Lily said.

"Zach found them." For her. Georgie caught her sigh. Her sisters sighed, not her. "He knows my Christmas gifts are in my missing suitcase."

"You mean our gift cards are in your missing suitcase," Fee clarified.

"There's nothing wrong with those." Meanwhile, there was everything wrong with kissing Zach. She was moving to London. Wanted to move overseas for her career and continue to honor her mom in the only way she knew how. Zach would become a memory. She didn't need to add color and depth to those memories with hand holding and stolen kisses.

"We appreciate those gift cards every year. We really do." Lily set her hand on Georgie's arm. Sincerity bolstered her words. "You could've easily replaced the gift cards."

"It's just surprising you'd opt for gifts found in the Once Was Barn. Things in there are essentially family heirlooms." Fee touched Georgie's shoulder. "You're not the most sentimental Harrison sister."

But she could be thoughtful, give a gift with intention, couldn't she? Give a gift for the meaning rather than its practical purpose. Georgie tugged on her seat belt and squirmed in the captain's chair. Zach had found the perfume bottles, not her. She should return to her typical gift cards. Keep the expectations the same as they'd always been. "You're right. It was a silly idea."

"But," Fee said.

"Let's talk about this afternoon." Georgie interrupted her sister. "Where are we going? You only told me it was a wedding outing."

"Jem Salon." Fee squeezed Georgie's shoulder. Her excitement shimmied around the truck cab. "For our practice session."

Lily joined in, sprinkling her own delight. "We're getting our hair styled, nails and toes done. And full makeup."

Georgie visited a salon once every twelve weeks to get the split ends on her long hair trimmed. Her appointment lasted thirty minutes and she always brought work with her to make the most of her time in the chair. "How long are we going to be there?"

"Anxious to get back to Zach and the barn." Fee laughed.

"This is our sister bonding time." Lily parked the truck on the street beside a barber pole. "It doesn't matter how long we're here."

Except Georgie had never joined her sisters for their impromptu nail sessions in their bedroom as kids. She'd never sat still long enough for Fee to braid her hair. She'd never borrowed Amanda's clay mask and joined her to read teen gossip magazines. Instead, she'd retreated to the library or opened a medical journal. Georgie followed her sisters inside the Jem Salon.

A deep brown couch and coordinating chairs surrounded a table filled with an assortment of hair magazines. Georgie took a step toward the empty waiting area.

Fee grabbed her arm, stalling her retreat. "We have appointments."

"Lily, welcome." A woman, her long, straight black hair swept back in a neat low ponytail, stepped around the antique display case turned reception desk. "Are you ready for an afternoon of pampering?"

"Emma." Lily acknowledged the stylist. "More than ready."

"Who's going where first?" Emma glanced at them.

Georgie's eyes skimmed over the black-and-silver styling chairs facing large mirrors attached to an exposed brick wall. A woman, wearing a suede vest with an eye-catching wide fur collar, reclined in a pedicure chair. Her black slacks had been rolled to her knees, her bare feet were immersed in the water bath and cucumber slices rested on her closed eyes. Across from her, a petite older woman sat in the dryer chair. The dryer had been angled high above her head.

"Nails." Georgie pointed to the empty manicure station. "I'll start with nails." That would surely ease her into the all-day pampering.

"That leaves two chairs open for hair styling." Emma swept her hand toward the available seats. "Ladies, take your pick. We're enjoying a quieter Sunday before the rush this week to be picture-ready for Christmas."

There were at least a dozen customers in the salon. Stylists wove around chairs. Georgie wondered what a busy afternoon looked like.

Lily stepped up to the nail polish display and picked up two colors. "These are the ones Fee and I decided work best with the dresses. You choose."

One bottle sparkled silver. The other shimmered a deep crimson. And both looked as if they belonged on her sisters, not Georgie.

The petite woman under the dryer set a magazine on her lap. Ocean-blue eye shadow and perfectly sculpted eyebrows added depth to her pale eyes. "You're the new doctor in town."

"I'm Lily, the bride-to-be." Lily tugged Georgie into her side. "My sister Georgie is the doctor."

The woman in the pedicure chair lifted both cucumber slices away from her dark eyes to peer at them. "Elias's granddaughters?"

"Yes, we are." Fiona dropped into the nearest salon chair and smiled.

"Ladies, please meet Iris Lane and Estelle York, two of our favorite and most loyal customers." Emma retied the black apron around her waist. "Estelle has been perfecting her pedicure experience. Today we added a scented oil to the water."

"Elias wasn't exaggerating." Iris dabbed a clear shimmery lip gloss onto her bottom lip. "You're all quite lovely."

"Thank you." Georgie took a seat at the manicure table.

Iris looked closer to seventy than sixty, wore stylish leggings and wedge fur boots with pompom tassels. Her gray pixie-cut hair looked to have layers dyed purple. The woman's entire look was chic and fashionable. Georgie borrowed a pinch of the older woman's boldness and took the silver nail polish from Lily.

"You're the doctor who sent Hilda an aloe plant." Estelle pressed a button and lifted the pedicure chair out of the deep reclining position.

Surprise caught Georgie. She'd ordered the plant yesterday and it had already arrived in Falcon Creek. Surely Georgie's suitcase could've arrived by now, too. "Hilda has quite the green thumb. I thought she might like her own natural treatment for burns, bug bites and blisters." And more specifically for the nicks and scratches that marred Hilda's hands and wrists. One conversation with the kind woman and Georgie had realized Hilda would appreciate a natural ointment to anything store-bought.

"And Georgie cured Rachel, the poor dear."

Iris's head swayed from side to side in slower motion than the dryer above her head.

Emma turned from Fee's chair and grinned at Georgie. "Rachel was in here earlier, praising you and your magic tonic."

Estelle set her cucumber slices on the glass dish on the table beside her. She wore several silver necklaces of different lengths that elevated her look into evening wear. "Would you happen to have a tonic to improve digestion?"

"Great-Aunt Pru always claimed dandelion root tea was the secret." Georgie placed her fingers in the soaking bowl the nail technician set on the table. "One and a half cups every afternoon."

"Granddaddy used to make dandelion wine." Iris's thin shoulders lifted toward her ears as if she suppressed a full-bodied laugh. "He'd let me sip from the bottle as a child. One of my favorite memories."

"Must have been before everyone had to be twenty-one years old to imbibe." Estelle chuckled.

Iris brushed her hand through the air. "There's a birth date printed on my driver's license, but I don't pay it any mind."

"Don't forget, dears." Estelle's snowy-gray precision-cut bob angled past her jawline, adding polish to the already graceful woman and challenging anyone to guess her age. "We were born before computers and cell phones. There's no telling how many birth dates were recorded incorrectly in pencil back then."

"Very true," Iris added. "I can't tell you how many times I've written down the wrong date on things. Mistakes happen."

Like kissing Zach. Or not kissing him. Georgie wasn't sure which one she'd regret more. Perhaps the mistake was that she still thought about kissing Zach. The mistake was letting Zach intrude on her sisterly bonding time. She lowered her shoulders and relaxed her fingers in the warm solution.

"Iris and I were born at home, too," Estelle added. "I'm the youngest of twelve. My mama forgot her kids' names daily. Surely she mixed up a date here and there."

Twelve home deliveries. Georgie praised the mother's strength and the people who'd assisted in those home births. Estelle's siblings would have probably been involved.

"All that to tell you not to pay your birth date any mind." Iris tipped her chin at Georgie. "You've got to live life according to your heart."

Estelle hummed her agreement. "Your heart doesn't collect years. It collects people and experiences."

Georgie lived life according to her goals.

Once she achieved one, she set another and challenged herself again. Her heart experienced the joy of accomplishment. Her gaze jumped from Estelle to Iris. Both women wore intricate wedding rings. The two lovely women would most likely disapprove of her point of view.

"Is that the secret to staying young?" Emma twisted away from Lily, a curling wand clutched in her hand. "Surround yourself with younger people?"

"Surround yourself with good people," Iris corrected. "That's what I tell my grandchildren. The good ones make every minute worthwhile."

Zach was a good one. He'd made the last few days on the ranch bearable. More than bearable. And the Blackwells, they were good, too, welcoming herself and Zach, their arms and hearts open.

Georgie wasn't a good one. She was deceiving everyone. She yanked her fingers out of the solution, the warmth no longer soothing, and wiped her hand on the towel.

"What about your sister?" Estelle leaned closer to Georgie. "Is she marrying a good one?"

"Conner Hannah." Georgie shifted her gaze to her sister. She hadn't seen Lily quite so happy in years. Yet even more, there was a confidence in Lily now. As if her sister had found a strong foundation and knew she could bloom without second-guessing herself. With Conner, Lily wasn't alone. "Conner seems like he's good."

"That makes my own heart full." Iris smiled warmly.

Was Georgie's heart full? A full heart wouldn't further her career, would it? Or honor her mother's memory. Only helping people not suffer the same unexpected loss of a family member would do that. She hadn't needed a full heart in the past. Still, she glanced from Fee to Lily to Iris. All three women had full hearts. All Georgie had was a tweak of regret.

"What's your full name, Georgie?" Iris took out a pen and piece of paper from the tote-style purse on the seat beside her.

Distracted by her partially full heart, Georgie recited her full name.

"It'll fit nicely." Iris wrote something across the paper, then presented it to Estelle, who nodded.

"What will fit?" Georgie asked.

"Your name on Dr. Cummings's office sign." Iris shifted and displayed the paper to Georgie and the others. "His full name is Theodore Laurence Cummings. There are two more letters in his name than yours. This will work out just fine."

"Dr. Cummings's offices are half a block from the Silver Stake Saloon." Estelle pointed

at the front window. Her pretty dangle brace-
lets slipped down her arm. "Make a right at the
stop sign. Then a left when you come to Pos-
sum Trail Park."

Georgie forgot her heart and considered the
women. "Isn't Dr. Cummings using his offices?"

"Only at his convenience." Emma caught
Georgie's gaze in the large mirror and frowned.
"And that's not frequently."

"He spends more time in Livingston at his
other offices these days." Estelle shook her
head. "As if Livingston has more going for it
than Falcon Creek."

"We've got Pops watching for his car," Iris
said. "It's a sunburst yellow color and very hard
to miss."

"If Pops spots the doctor's car, a signal goes
out," Emma explained. "I'm convinced it's
speed dialing or some such thing by how fast
the word spreads throughout town, but Pops
won't reveal his messaging ways."

Georgie grinned. Finally, something that
made sense. Pops being evasive about his methods and ways. Georgie wouldn't put it past him
to have a superpower.

"Front and Back Streets fill with cars," Estelle said. "Looks like the Fourth of July parade

with all the cars trying to get into the doctor's parking lot."

"You could take over Dr. Cummings's offices and open your own practice," Iris said.

"That's…" Lily gasped, then slapped her palm over her mouth. Her gaze widened in the mirror as if she considered the suggestion and liked the merits more and more with each passing minute.

Georgie blinked and forced herself not to flinch. Not to disrupt the precision nail painting being applied to her fingernails. Open her own practice? In Falcon Creek? She'd gone from sisterly bonding to the improbable. Impractical. Impossible.

"If you had normal patient hours, you could see everyone and still walk across the street for happy hour at the Silver Stake," Estelle continued, as if Georgie had agreed to the idea. As if Georgie had jumped on their implausible doctor train. "The bar has even extended its happy hour."

"My grandson Roman works there." Iris lifted her eyebrows at Georgie. "Be sure to meet him. He claims to be happily single."

Estelle shook her head. "No one is truly happily single."

Georgie wanted to raise her hand. She was happy. Truly happy.

"Georgie has a boyfriend," Fee offered and moved two chairs closer to the conversation.

"He's a cowboy in the rodeo," Lily added.

"He'll do just fine." Iris nodded. Estelle agreed, another low hum.

"For what?" Georgie asked.

"Sticking around, dear." Iris tapped her fingers on the leather seat.

"Hasn't been a cowboy who came to Falcon Creek and left," Estelle said. "They all plant their boots and grow roots here."

But Georgie wasn't sticking around. Or putting down roots. Her boots were boarding a plane to England. In a little more than a week.

CHAPTER FOURTEEN

Could you pick me up at Jem Salon?

Sure. Be there in five. Everything okay?

GEORGIE STARED AT Zach's reply to her text message. Cursor flashing as if mocking her. How could she explain she was both okay and not okay all at once?

Her hair, intricately twisted around her head with wispy strands curled to frame her face, and her makeup, expertly applied to appear natural and enhance her eyes, made her appear bridal party perfect. Picture-ready. Her glossy nails shimmered like frozen snow.

Inside, her heart ached. Between the talk about opening her own practice in town and last-minute wedding particulars, Georgie had sipped champagne, snacked on cheese and bonded with her sisters. Selfies of champagne toasts and the sisters wrapped in a group hug had been sent to Amanda and Peyton, *wish you were here* tags attached. They'd pulled up funny family photos on their phones of bad hair days and awkward teenage years, laughed and cried at pictures with their parents. Shared old dating stories and things they hadn't known about each other. Mostly, they'd reconnected.

But Georgie was moving out of the country soon. That ache settled deeper. She knew she'd miss her sisters and her family. She'd accepted that. It shouldn't be possible to miss them even more, when she hadn't even left yet.

Georgie clutched her phone. She would honor her mother in the best way she knew how. And if she hurt, so be it. She typed: I'm fine. Finished here.

On my way. Zach's reply came quickly.

And with no more questions asked. Georgie rubbed her chest. She'd miss Zach, too.

Georgie tucked her phone into her purse and hugged her sisters. If she held on tighter than usual, no one stopped her. "Zach is coming to get me."

Lily lifted her eyebrows up and down. "Hot date night."

Fee clinked her champagne glass against Lily's. "We want details."

"Don't blush, Georgie." Lily laughed. "I'm going to find Conner and get him to take me out, too. I don't want to waste all of this."

The salon door opened, and Zach stepped inside. Lily and Fee greeted him from their salon chairs.

Georgie thanked Emma and the stylists, hugged her sisters one more time and walked toward Zach, suddenly unsure if calling him in for an escape had been her best idea.

"I feel like I should be taking you out for a night on the town." Zach tipped his hat up and settled his intense gaze on her. "You look incredible."

"Thanks. It's just hair and makeup." Only Zach looked at her as if he didn't want to stop looking at her. Her stomach fluttered the tiniest bit.

Behind her, Lily and Fee offered their encouragement for a fun evening alone.

"I'm feeling a little underdressed." He ran his hands over his jacket. "And unprepared."

"I hope I didn't pull you away from something." She'd been the one wanting to be pulled away. Needing to be pulled away. Now she was being pulled again. Only this time toward Zach.

"Just the Once Was Barn. Nothing that couldn't wait." He opened the door to the salon, waved goodbye to her sisters and stepped outside. "Where can I take you?"

"Can we not go to the dining hall tonight?" Georgie asked.

"Sure." He shrugged. "It's so crowded, they'll probably not even notice we're missing."

"I love them. I really do," she said. "It's just a lot sometimes."

"I imagine the Silver Stake will be a bit much, too." Zach pointed down the street toward the bar and restaurant. Cars lined the street, the bar's parking lot already full.

"My dad, grandfather and sisters will be arriving in two days." She stuffed her gloved hands into her jacket pockets. "Is it wrong to want a minute? I know it makes no sense. There's no purpose to it."

"No, it's not wrong." He adjusted her scarf under her chin and grinned. "If you don't mind takeout, I have an idea."

"What do you have in mind?" *And will you continue to look at me like I'm the one you've been waiting for all your life? Make me believe for one moment we could be more than pretend?*

"Spaghetti or hamburgers for dinner," he suggested.

"Definitely Italian." The dinner decision was easy. Deciding what to do with the expanding flutters in her stomach and the race in her pulse was another thing entirely.

TAKE-OUT CONTAINERS FROM the Tuscan Tomato Ristorante waited in the back seat of the SUV, as Zach and Georgie drove through the Blackwell guest lodge gates. Zach parked in Dorothy and Elias's circular driveway and took her hand. "It's not the dining hall, Georgie. You don't have to talk at all if you don't want to."

"Thanks." Georgie relaxed and curved her fingers around Zach's. "I owe you."

"It's takeout. Nothing fancy about it." His fingers tensed around hers quickly before he let go. "Now, wait here."

"Where are you going?" she asked.

"Give me five minutes to get things set up." He reached into the back seat and picked up their to-go order.

"So, we're not eating in the kitchen?" she asked.

"I have something different in mind." He turned up the heater and aimed the vent at her. "Five minutes. Stay warm in here."

Zach returned in four minutes, opened her car door and held out his hand. "Our dinner for two is ready."

Georgie set her hand in his and let him pull her into his side. He led her around the outside of the house. The light from the full moon highlighted the shoveled gravel path, curving toward the creek. The evening was cold, the winds calm.

Georgie's nerves fired a sudden warmth through her. "How did you know this was here?"

A screened cedar-log gazebo stood near the creek. A fire blazed in the firepit inside. A welcoming sanctuary for those seeking privacy or solitude. Tonight, she thought, she'd reach for one of those perfect moments her mother had so often spoke of. Tomorrow was soon enough for logic and all the reasons her heart shouldn't skip and those butterflies inside her stomach shouldn't flap.

"I spotted the roof of the gazebo from the sunporch." Zach opened the log-framed door and motioned her inside. "I asked Dorothy about it."

Blankets and pillows had been piled on one of the benches. Their takeout waited on a small folding table. "And all of this was just in here, waiting to be used?"

"No." Zach laughed. "I had to borrow things from the house."

Georgie adjusted several of the pillows and sat on the wide bench. "This is beyond anything I imagined." Or expected. Her cowboy set a high bar for a dinner for two.

Zach covered her legs with a blanket, then moved the folding table closer. "I'm ready to eat. Where should we start?"

"The cheesecake." Georgie opened containers

until she located the slice of tiramisu cheese-cake. She handed Zach a plastic fork. "I'm breaking rules tonight. Want to join me?"

Zach took the fork. His grin reached his green eyes. "I always thought dessert should be the first course."

They ate in silence, but Georgie felt the warmth and intimacy of the moment down to her toes. Cheesecake finished, every last bite of bread dipped in olive oil devoured and the baked ziti container scraped clean, Georgie leaned into the pillows, and Zach, then tugged the blanket higher. "This could easily become a favorite reading spot."

"Do you have a lot of those?" Zach stacked his feet on the edge of the firepit. His arm dropped around her shoulders.

"I have a park bench under a big tree close to my apartment." She smoothed her hand over the fleece blanket and watched the flames in the firepit.

"Do you go to your bench often?" His voice was low and relaxed.

"I haven't been in months." Georgie frowned. She couldn't remember when she'd last been to her park bench. Or the last book she'd read that wasn't devoted to medicine. She'd been completely wrapped up in her lab and her work for so long now.

"Then it's probably not your bench anymore." He squeezed her.

She had to let go eventually. She set aside her lost park bench and the twinge that letting go jabbed inside her. "I can't remember the last time I did this."

"Ate pasta from a tin take-out container." Humor skimmed over his words.

"Takeout I recall. It was the night before my flight to Bozeman." She took his hand, linked their fingers together. "I mean this."

"Outdoor dinner." His thumb drew a slow circle across her palm. "A fire and a full moon."

"And good company." She tipped her head up to look at him.

"Did you just call me good company?" He tucked a piece of her hair back inside her knit hat.

"Yeah, I believe I did." Friends made for good company. And Zach was a friend. "Don't let it go to your head." And she wouldn't let Zach, her friend, get to her heart. Even in this one stolen moment.

"You're okay, too." His gaze dipped to her mouth.

Her throat dried. Her pulse kicked up. "Just okay?"

He reached out, smoothed another strand of

her hair off her cheek. His touch soft. Gentle. Nerve-firing.

Georgie held her breath.

His gaze searched her face, then settled, locking on hers. Intense and consuming. "You're so much more than just okay."

Tomorrow she'd blame the heat from the fire. The starlit sky. The wine they'd shared over dinner. Tonight, reasons drifted by, uncatchable, like the falling snowflakes.

It was only Zach. Only her. Alone in the gazebo.

And Georgie wanted to break one more rule.

She leaned in. Zach met her halfway. And, finally, their lips met.

CHAPTER FIFTEEN

ZACH OPENED HIS eyes before sunrise. Restless and unable to stop replaying his evening with Georgie. Specifically, the kiss they'd shared. The one now imprinted on him like a mark from a hot branding iron. He rose and stretched the kinks from his back, added a blanket over Georgie, who was curled on her side in the bed, then gathered his clothes and left.

The power tools he'd borrowed from the shed loaded into the ATV, Zach retreated to the Once Was Barn to work on Dorothy's new bench. A fitting place for him to spend his morning, as he had to start considering his future.

One time-stopping, breath-stealing kiss aside, his relationship with Georgie had a time limit. And the end was fast approaching.

He had to remember why he'd come to Falcon Creek. It wasn't to find a home or a woman to give his heart to. He'd made a promise to his brother.

Promise me, Zach. No regrets. Make your life

count. It's not too late to have the life we always dreamed about.

How many hours had Cody and he spent in the hospital room or in their small cabin, watching the rodeo on TV, imagining Zach on that same national stage? Cody had researched training methods for Rain Dancer as a yearling, a colt, then a gelding, and collaborated with Marshall to train the horse for a successful calf-roping career. Zach had honed his own riding skills and deepened his bond with Rain Dancer. And all the while, the brothers had envisioned their own home. Their own land. Their own stables. Zach had only to enter the arena and win.

After Cody's death, Zach had finally dedicated himself to the rodeo and the brothers' dream. He was close to achieving everything they'd wanted. But not without his horse.

Zach parked the ATV outside the Once Was Barn and texted Wade for an update on Rain Dancer. Next, he had to approach Ethan Blackwell. He had a promise to keep.

Several hours later, the sun fully awake and his system requiring sustenance, Zach loaded the pieces of the bench into the ATV and stopped by Ethan's large-animal clinic. The Blackwell vet wasn't in the clinic or on the property. Zach needed a shower and change of clothes, and hoped that Georgie, like Ethan, was elsewhere—

there could be no more kissing Georgie. He returned to Dorothy's house.

Georgie swung open the door and greeted him. "Good! You're back. We have work to do."

"What kind of work?" He eyed her. She'd scrubbed off yesterday's makeup and replaced it with very little, returned her hair to its usual ponytail and wore another of her sister's oversized sweaters. The cuffs were rolled above her wrists and the high collar was bundled around her chin. She looked just as striking and even more appealing in the morning light.

Just like that, he misplaced his own warning to himself. He reached for her, wrapped his arm around her waist and kissed her, fully and soundly.

She leaned back and touched his cheek. A smile, soft like a secret, curved her lips upward. "Good morning to you, too."

"*Now* I'm ready to work." He released her. "But first, I need to unload the ATV, then find some food."

She followed him outside.

"What are you doing?" He turned around and frowned at her. "You don't have a coat on."

"Helping you." She hopped from one booted foot to the other and smashed her bare hands together.

He was used to working alone and hardly

ever asked for help. Hadn't asked her now. He shouldn't have kissed her again. Shouldn't have refreshed his memory. None of their relationship was real. But when she was in his arms, it felt real. "You're freezing. Go back inside."

And he would go back to his old ways. The ones that didn't include morning kisses and turning takeout into a romantic dinner.

"It goes faster with two people." She stepped beside him and pressed a kiss on his cheek as if she understood his hesitation and wanted to shatter it. "Now, show me what we're doing. It's freezing out here."

Once the pieces of Dorothy's new bench were inside the entryway, Zach poured a cup of hot coffee and grimaced at what Georgie was holding. "Please tell me that is your ugly sweater for the scavenger hunt and not something you plan to wear."

Georgie's laughter bounced around the kitchen. She hung a red sweater, its sequined candy canes twinkling, over the back of a kitchen bar stool. She placed a green sweater on the next stool and adjusted its thick collar. On the sweater, twin bucks faced off at the waist and an odd snowflake pattern circled the chest. "Dorothy felt the same about Big E's green sweater and seemed thrilled to be donating it to our ugly sweater cause."

"Then that's another item off our scavenger hunt list." He picked up one of the cranberry-orange muffins Dorothy had brought over from the dining hall earlier.

Georgie plugged in a hot glue gun and set it on the counter. Then she unloaded a box of Christmas trim onto the kitchen island, each bit tackier than the next. He leaned toward her. Was she humming, too?

He listened closer, certain he caught the notes from "Jingle Bells." He poured another cup of coffee, suddenly convinced more caffeine was required. Georgie was humming a Christmas carol and he had the urge to join her. "What are you doing now?"

"Getting our supplies out." She unloaded another bag of Christmas decorations onto the wide counter. "We can't leave the sweaters like they are."

"Why not?" Why couldn't he press Pause and stop things right where they were? No more talk of moving to London. No more worsening of Rain Dancer's condition. No difficult good-byes or ending of what was becoming quite an incredible, extended moment.

He'd learned the truth during Cody's final battle. Time refused to slow. There was no freeze button. And minutes were wasted wishing for impossible things. Life had to be enjoyed in the now.

"We can't leave the sweaters as they are because those aren't the scavenger hunt rules," she said.

And the only rule that applied to life was that things always came to an end. "What's the plan?"

"You decorate my sweater." She handed him a roll of blue-and-silver tinsel. "I'll decorate yours."

And he'd enjoy their moment because it hadn't come to an end yet. "I can do anything I want to this sweater?"

"We still need to be able to wear them to the party on Wednesday night also," she warned.

The sisters had decided to throw a family-style joint bachelor and bachelorette party on Wednesday night. The theme was Ugly Christmas Sweaters, since they had to have them for the scavenger hunt anyway. Everyone had been told to get their ugly on their sweaters to celebrate Lily and Conner's upcoming nuptials. Zach unwound the tinsel and plotted his attack on Georgie's sweater.

Thirty minutes and several hot-glue sticks later, Zach stepped back to admire his effort. "I think mine might be uglier than yours."

"Lily is not going to want her sweater back.

I'll have to get her a new one." Georgie used the edge of her scissors to curl more ribbon, reminding him of a crazed, gleeful designer. "You can't take the title yet. I'm not finished."

"I hope you like the scent of artificial pine." Zach reached into his back pocket and crinkled the wrapping of a value pack of air fresheners.

"Where did you get those?" Georgie wrinkled her nose.

"Dorothy." He smiled and attached the air fresheners to the garland he'd looped all around the sweater. "She hid them from Big E and thought we might need them for scavenger hunt supplies."

"Dorothy provided me with these." Georgie revealed a dozen bells and set them jingling in her hands. Her laughter edged into a cackle.

"You don't have to use all those." He scowled at the bells.

"Did you use all those scented trees?" One eyebrow arched. The bells jingled louder.

"Definitely." He laughed. "You can't ever smell too fresh."

"Or jingle too much." She went to work, attaching the bells to the giant reindeer antlers she'd hot glued to the shoulders of the sweater.

Mini blinking lights woven through both sweaters, every scrap of sparkly tinsel and glit-

ter hot glued onto the sweaters, Georgie and
Zach high-fived and admired each other's work.

Dorothy came through the back door, dropped
a collection of paint cans and paintbrushes on
the kitchen counter and caught her laughter behind her hands. "Those are quite awful, aren't
they? I think you two have outdone yourselves."

"That was the plan." Georgie walked toward
her grandmother. "Can we help you?"

"I'm going to decide on a paint color for my
bench and get started." Dorothy sorted the half-
dozen sample cans on the counter. "Then Zach
can put it together for me. It's like an early
Christmas present."

"We put down the tarps like you wanted and
set everything up in the sunporch for you," Zach
said.

"Then that's where I'll head." Dorothy grinned
at them. "What's next on the scavenger hunt
list?"

Georgie pulled out their list and glanced outside at the heavily falling snow. "Can we push
building snowmen off until tomorrow?"

"Alice Gardner gave me an extra-large bag
of birdseed in exchange for helping Frank fix
the forklift yesterday. We can use it to make our
outdoor ornaments." Zach knew he should be
hunting down Ethan, not offering to check off
another item on their scavenger hunt list.

But he feared Ethan would escort him off the ranch once Zach spoke to the Blackwell vet. Once he confessed to Ethan his real reason for being at the ranch. And if he was honest, he wasn't quite ready to leave yet. Selfish as he was.

"Birdseed ornaments it is." Georgie stuck the scavenger hunt list back inside her pocket. "How does this work?"

Dorothy made the motion of sealing her lips. "I can't help you. But I can tell you that there are cookie cutters stored on the top shelf in the pantry."

Georgie picked up her phone and opened her internet browser. "There's a how-to video on everything online. Surely we can find one."

"I'll get the cookie cutters." Zach headed to the pantry, located the cookie cutters, then retrieved the birdseed from the rental car. He returned to find Georgie already well into the ornament-making process.

"I'm going to mix this with flour." Georgie stirred a liquid solution around inside a large pot on the stove. "Then you add the birdseed and we make ornaments."

Zach followed Georgie's instructions, added birdseed to the bowl and mixed everything together.

"Now, according to the video, we fill," Georgie said.

They worked in tandem, pressing the mixture into the waiting cookie cutters that they'd set out on a large cookie sheet. Their rhythm was quick and efficient. He liked that about Georgie. She set her mind to something and accomplished it, big or small. He liked working beside her. He liked making ugly sweaters and birdseed ornaments. He simply liked being with her.

The truth was Zach liked Georgie too much.

He moved around to the other side of the kitchen island, as if that would lessen her appeal and his feelings. If anything, the new position gave him a better view of her face and more reasons for his gaze to keep tracking to her.

He concentrated on his cookie cutters and scrambled for something to distract him.

Fortunately, Dorothy emerged from the sunporch, white paint coating her hands and paintbrush. "I'm down to two colors. Going to let the sample sections dry, then see if I can decide."

"What are your choices?" Georgie's Christmas carol humming lowered.

"White and off-white." Dorothy laughed. "There's too many shades."

"With sandpaper and stain, the bench can be antiqued." Zach swiped sticky birdseed mash off his fingers.

"I never considered that." Dorothy piled the paintbrushes in the kitchen sink.

"That would look terrific." Georgie finished filling another cookie cutter, seemingly not bothered by the gooey mash sealing her fingers together. "We could help, if you'd like."

We. There she was, offering Zach and herself up as if they were a team. As if they came together. Were meant to be together. Zach scooped more birdseed from the bowl. And there he was, again liking the sound of *we.* If it involved her and him. He had to stop. He'd finish the birdseed ornaments and retreat to the Once Was Barn, lose himself and his hazardous feelings among the broken and forgotten furniture.

"I saw Iris Lane outside White Buffalo Grocers this morning." Dorothy washed paint off her hands. "She showed me the paper sign, proving your name fits."

"She did?" Georgie knocked a wooden spoon and bell-shaped cookie cutter onto the floor.

"Who is Iris?" Zach packed birdseed into a gingerbread man cookie cutter. "What is she proving?"

"It's nothing." Georgie waved the wooden spoon around as if swatting away an aggravating horsefly.

Judging from the alarm in her gaze and her

hasty words, Zach assumed it was more than nothing.

"It's not nothing to Iris and Estelle." Dorothy dried her hands. Her kind gaze followed Georgie around the island. "The two women suggested Georgie could open a medical practice here in Falcon Creek, using Dr. Cummings's offices."

Zach's fingers stilled inside the birdseed bowl. Georgie living in Falcon Creek, Montana, not London, England. Georgie practicing patient care, not working in a research lab. That was everything Zach could see for her. Yet nothing Georgie wanted for her future. "When was this suggested?"

"Yesterday at the salon." Georgie swung her wooden spoon in a cutting motion, striking through the idea.

Zach held on. If Georgie remained in Montana…maybe they could… He smashed his fingers in the birdseed and squashed the thought.

"Iris wrote Georgie's full name on a piece of paper to show Georgie that her name would fit nicely on Dr. Cummings's office sign outside his building." Dorothy picked up a wooden skewer and poked holes in the tops of the filled cookie cutters for the string hangers to be looped through. "It seems the two women have been sharing their idea around town."

The wooden spoon clattered on the counter. Georgie paled. "I never agreed to open a medical practice here in Falcon Creek."

She'd only agreed to move farther away from her family. Zach stuffed birdseed into a stocking-shaped cookie cutter. His own Christmas spirit—the one he'd recently been discovering—fizzled. Georgie wanted her research lab in England. Not her family in Falcon Creek. Or her sisters in California. Or him.

"Folks in town tend to get an idea and run with it." Dorothy reached across the island and clasped Georgie's hand. Her voice was kind and reassuring. "They mean no harm."

Zach and Georgie would cause their own kind of harm when the truth came out. He reached into the bowl and wadded the birdseed into palm-sized balls.

"I just don't want to disappoint them when I leave." Georgie held her grandmother's hand. "And I am leaving."

"Of course you are, dear." Dorothy released Georgie and picked up the skewer again. Her voice returned to cheerful and positive. "You have a life outside Falcon Creek to live. We're just lucky to have had you here for this long."

Georgie stepped around the counter and hugged her grandmother. "Thank you for understanding."

Zach understood, too. Reminded himself again that their *we* was only temporary. He frowned and formed another birdseed ball.

Georgie spun around and gaped at him. "What are you doing? Those look large enough to play softball with."

Zach glanced at the birdseed snowball in his hands. Laughter curved inside him, a welcome relief that settled him back into the moment. One of the few he had left with Georgie. "Or it's large enough for our snowman to hold tomorrow."

"Hmm, not bad." Georgie smiled.

Zach shrugged. "We can't waste the bird feed and we're out of cookie cutters."

"You seem to be enjoying this quite a bit." Georgie tapped her fingers on the counter. "You know Estelle told me yesterday that cowboys who come to Falcon Creek never leave."

"Is that so?" He tossed the birdseed ball from one hand to the other. The snow would be thawing before the birdseed snowballs were finished.

"That's what she claimed." Georgie tipped her head at him. "You could stay here in Falcon Creek."

Not without you. "What would I do in Falcon Creek?"

"Restore and build furniture," Dorothy suggested. "I've got a list. And I wouldn't put it past Hadley and Grace to have made lists of their own."

"Work on the ranch," Georgie offered. "Katie told me yesterday how good you are with the horses. How she needs someone like you on her full-time staff."

He wasn't interested in Katie. He was interested in Georgie. And if she could ever want someone like him. "There's not a rodeo in Falcon Creek."

"Then bring one here," she said.

She was serious. He heard it in her tone, saw it in the set of her chin. He dropped the birdseed ball on the cookie tray. "Like you, I have a life to live outside Falcon Creek."

Disappointment collapsed across her face. She spun away from him. "Dorothy, should we check the paint samples? See if they've dried and whether you like one color more than the other."

"Yes. I'm quite excited to see the finished product." Dorothy and Georgie walked into the sunporch.

Zach cleaned up and put the kitchen back as it had been. If only putting his thoughts together were as easy as stacking the stainless-steel bowls inside the cabinet.

Should he have told Georgie he wanted to stay in Falcon Creek? Then invited her to join him? Invited her to give up her dream job and career to be with him—a wandering rodeo cowboy? As if he believed she'd ever choose him first.

Georgie had already made her choice.

CHAPTER SIXTEEN

Ugly sweaters hanging in the bedroom closet and warm in her borrowed flannel plaid pj's, Georgie picked up her phone to plug it into the charger for the night. A new text message alert flashed on her screen.

Her dad's text read like a military brief, short and to the point: Arriving tomorrow. Before 1700 hours. Pending weather delays.

Georgie replied: Please be careful. See you soon.

Her father responded: Will deliver updates tomorrow.

And Georgie would deliver her job update in the dining hall to her father and the rest of her family, Harrisons and Blackwells together. Peyton and Amanda were scheduled to arrive tomorrow, but they'd already been alerted by the airlines to a possible weather delay due to an approaching winter storm. Still, Georgie couldn't wait.

She had to put down boundaries and tell everyone, including herself, what was happening. She was moving to London. Her plans had not changed. Perhaps if she spoke to the entire dining hall, her heart would hear her and stand down, too.

Her feelings for Zach were too strong. Too fast. Everything she felt for him went against every rule and guideline she'd ever imposed for relationships. Love was a conscious decision two people made after years together. First as friends, learning about each other. Then as a couple, dating and exploring their compatibilities and acknowledging their differences. Then as a seriously committed couple who knew how to communicate and designed a future together, one that included marriage and kids.

Love was like a long-distance coast-to-coast drive. Love was the destination the car arrived at. Love wasn't a passenger, picked up at the first stop.

Love wasn't what she was feeling.

The bathroom door opened, and Zach stood on the other side of the bed. "You okay? It was those jalapeño poppers at dinner tonight, wasn't it? Those had a kick stronger than swallowing a tablespoon of raw chili powder."

The most ridiculous urge to smile overtook her. But the dry mouth, weak knees and stomach butterflies were not love either. That was simple attraction and attraction faded. "I never had any poppers tonight."

"Good choice." He touched his stomach and peered at her. A plea in his voice. "Maybe next time you could tell me to skip those, too."

Next time she would skip inviting a charming cowboy to her family's home. Next time she would skip the holiday family reunion. Next time she would skip the falling in love.

In love. Heat crawled from her chest, circled her neck and lit even her earlobes as if she'd eaten a dozen jalapeño poppers.

Her phone slipped from her hand, smacked against the bedside table and clunked on the floor. Georgie dropped to her knees and hitched forward on all fours, escaping from Zach's view.

She was not in love.

Sure, she liked Zach. Found him attractive. Wanted to spend more and more time with him.

That hardly qualified as love.

Love was gradual. A natural building of feelings. One atop the other—friendship, respect, loyalty.

Love would render her exhilarated and ecstatic, like her sisters. She was short of breath, miserable and definitely not in love.

"Need help over there?" Zach asked.

He'd done more than enough. He'd made her

love him. "No. My phone just slid farther under the bed than I expected."

And she'd fallen harder than she'd ever thought possible. She clutched her phone. It wasn't possible. She had not made the choice to be in love. She was not making it now. So, it was rather simple: she was not in love.

She set her free hand on the mattress, rose and forced herself to inhale through her clogged throat. "My dad and grandfather will be here tomorrow."

Zach nodded. "Are you worried about meeting your grandfather?"

"I'm worried about telling them that I'm moving to London." *I'm worried my heart might not forget you.*

"I didn't know that was the plan for tomorrow." He spread out the blankets he'd been using on the floor.

"I have to tell them." Georgie thrust her hand through her hair and loosened her ponytail. Nothing felt right, all of a sudden, from her too-tight hair band to her borrowed pajamas. "You heard Dorothy this afternoon. Iris and Estelle are talking about my name on Dr. Cummings's sign."

"How many people could two women have told?" He unfolded another blanket.

"Lydia told me at dinner that the pharmacist at South Corner Drug asked her about me today." Georgie crossed her arms over her chest. "Rachel heard about it at the Clearwater Café. And Ty mentioned overhearing customers talk about me at the bank."

"I guess it is true." Zach dropped a pillow on his makeshift bed. "Gossip really does travel faster than the speed of light in a small town."

"I have to tell my family and let them correct the locals." And stop herself from considering Iris's absurd suggestion. She belonged in a research lab, not patient care. How could she honor her mother's memory if she let her own patients down? If she failed her own patients like she'd failed her own mom?

"What can I do?" he asked.

Stand beside me. Hold my hand. Come to London with me. She blinked at him. "Help me convince my family this is the best career move for me, like we agreed."

They'd also agreed their entire relationship was fake. And she hadn't held up her side of that deal. It wasn't too late for a course correction. She would help Zach and his horse. Make it her parting gift. "Have you spoken to Ethan about Rain Dancer?"

"Not yet." Zach folded his jeans and avoided looking at her.

"But you've been helping in the stables every

day. Surely you've run into Ethan." Georgie pulled the comforter back and sat on the bed. "You told me Rain Dancer needs help soon."

"He does." Zach ran his hands over his head. "Ethan's busy with his own patients and family."

"But Rain Dancer should be his patient, too," Georgie argued.

"Let's get through your family announcement first. Then I'll talk to Ethan," he said.

"Fine," Georgie agreed. Then she silently decided she'd talk to Ethan herself.

"I have something that might help tomorrow." He walked out of the bedroom and into the living room.

He returned holding the jewelry box she'd discovered in the Once Was Barn. The door had been reattached, the glass cleaned and the entire box stained a rich cherry color. She walked over to him and accepted the jewelry box as if he was presenting her with a career achievement award. "You fixed it."

"I know it's not your mother's bracelet, but it's old and a piece of your family history." He touched the top. His voice touched her heart.

She hugged the jewelry box, rather than embracing Zach. If she wrapped her arms around him, she'd forget. Forget she didn't love this kind, generous man. "It could be Lily's something old."

"Maybe it'll take the sting out of not having the charm bracelet to give her." Tenderness and affection tempered the green in his gaze.

The thought of not having Zach in her life stung, piercing right into her chest. She wasn't certain anything would remove the pain.

She lifted onto her toes and pressed a kiss on his cheek. The last kiss she would ever give him. "Thank you."

CHAPTER SEVENTEEN

"PUT YOUR PHONE over there on the workbench." Zach pointed at the wide workbench against the wall of Dorothy and Big E's garage.

"My dad is going to send another update soon." Georgie's knuckles were white from her rigid grip on her phone. Tension hunched her shoulders to her ears and stiffened her voice.

The woman was more agitated than a rattler's tail before the snake attacked. Her father had been texting hourly progress reports and location updates all morning. She'd been staring at her phone's screen since sunrise. Reading aloud her father's text messages, then simply rambling. First about the weather. Then her sisters' arrival the following day. Then reading the advisories included in a snowstorm warning. In the kitchen, she'd added pacing to her ongoing rambling. Every mile marker closer to Falcon Creek that her dad and Big E drove, the more anxious Georgie became.

Now it was the lunch hour and Zach determined he had to channel her nerves, or she'd combust well before dinner.

He walked over to her and pried her phone out of her grasp. "We're antiquing Dorothy's bench. You need both hands free."

"Right." She opened and closed her hand as if working out the stress. "What do I need to do again?"

He stuffed her phone in his back pocket and placed his hands on her shoulders. "First, you need to breathe and relax."

"I know." Her forehead dropped onto his chest. Her words came out muffled. "But I don't know how. My mind won't stop."

"Good thing I'm here." He ran his hands up and down her arms. He wasn't pulling her against him to hold her. Or pulling her in to distract her with a kiss. He was offering her support. Nothing that involved emotions or deepening connections. "We're going to focus on staining and making Dorothy's bench perfect for her."

"Yes. Right." She nodded against his chest. "That's your plan."

"Our plan," he corrected.

She lifted her head. "How, again, is antiquing a bench going to prepare me to tell my family about my upcoming move to London?"

"Antiquing the bench is going to help me finish faster." He released her and set her phone facedown on the workbench.

"So, this isn't about helping me at all." She frowned, but a hint of humor tinged her tone.

"Working with me is going to give you something else to focus on." Not that he wanted her to focus on him. He cleared his throat. "I meant working on the bench."

"I need to practice what I'm going to say." She followed him over to the tarp where he'd arranged the pieces that would become the new bench.

"Why not speak from the heart?" He handed her a paintbrush and a can of stain. "If they understand what it really means to you, they'll have to support you."

"I speak logic and data," she said. "Not heart."

Except with him. He'd told her about his mother and his past. Georgie hadn't given him the scientific evidence proving addiction was a disease. She hadn't listed the scientific reasons to explain away his mother's behavior. She'd listened and had gotten angry on his behalf. That had been her heart speaking. "If your mom was here, what would you tell her?"

"My mom." She lowered onto her knees and dropped the paintbrush in the stain can.

Zach clenched the stain cloth in his fist. He'd overstepped. Should've left well enough alone.

His throat dry, a scratch cracked through his words. His mouth clearly refused to leave it alone. "My brother, Cody, was my person. He knew everything about me, knew me the best."

"Like my mom," she whispered. "She knew me the best."

He nodded and loosened his grip on the cloth. "Even today, years after his death, I still ask myself...what would Cody tell me? What would Cody want me to do?"

"My mom always told me to spread my wings and fly." Georgie stirred the paintbrush around the can, as if inside the liquid she saw her mother's face. Heard her mom's encouraging voice.

"Cody always accused me of trying to fix everything and help everyone."

She touched his arm. "That's not a bad quality."

But he hadn't been able to help the one who had mattered the most: his own brother. He hadn't been able to fix everything after all. Zach wiped off the excess stain from a corner of the headboard. His frustration and grief proved harder to remove. "Wanting to spread your wings and fly isn't a bad thing either."

"My mom would've supported my dream." She picked up the paintbrush and spread stain across the bottom of the headboard.

"And London is your dream," he said.

"The job in London is my goal."

He caught the drips of stain in the cloth and the confusion in her voice. "Aren't those the same?"

She paused and passed the paintbrush from one hand to the other. Her gaze, bewildered and clouded, collided with his. "I don't know."

The door leading from the garage into the house opened. Dorothy appeared, bundled in snow pants, a puffy jacket and heavy boots. Concern pulled her mouth into a firm frown. "The storm is arriving sooner than expected. The forecasters have now upgraded us to a blizzard warning."

Zach pressed the lid onto the top of the stain can and rose. "What can we do?"

Dorothy pulled several heavy-duty flashlights from a shelf beneath the workbench. "It's all hands on deck to get prepared."

Georgie set her paintbrush in the work sink and wiped her hands on her leggings. "We just need our jackets and we'll go with you."

Jackets, scarves and gloves on, Georgie and Zach joined Dorothy in the driveway.

"Thank you. We can use the extra help. Jon, Conner and Ben are at their homes prepping." Dorothy opened both passenger doors on the ATV and climbed into the rear passenger seat.

"We're meeting in the dining hall to divide up the work."

Zach tugged a knit hat over his head and glanced at Georgie.

"Zach has been driving these roads all week just fine." Dorothy waved them inside. "I'm more than happy to be a passenger."

"Dorothy wins." Georgie climbed into the front seat.

Zach shut Georgie's door, rounded the ATV to the driver's side and drove toward the dining hall. Flurries already fell, thick and wet, curtaining the ATV in a dense snow shower.

"How much snow is expected?" Georgie rubbed her gloved hands together.

"Eight to twelve inches," Dorothy said.

"It's the heavy snow and ice accumulations that'll cause the most concern." Zach slowed the ATV going around a curve.

Dorothy leaned forward and patted Georgie's shoulder. "We'll ride out the whiteout conditions safely here, as Blackwells have done every winter for generations."

"What about my dad and Big E?" Georgie's worry extended into the misty puff of her breath.

"They checked in not thirty minutes ago," Dorothy said. "The roads are still open on their route, although they've had to slow down."

Zach parked outside the dining hall and

grasped Georgie's hand. "Your dad and grandfather aren't reckless. They'll take precautions."

"Reckless is your grandfather's middle name," Dorothy said. "Fortunately, even he knows his limits, and battling a blizzard isn't a challenge he'll willingly take on."

Dorothy rushed inside the dining hall, leaving Zach and Georgie behind.

Georgie kept her hand on her door handle. "Was Dorothy trying to make me feel better?"

"I'm not sure." Zach shook his head. "But I meant what I said. I don't think they'll keep on driving in whiteout conditions." The corner of her bottom lip disappeared beneath her teeth. Zach added, "But they might catch a break and get here before the blizzard."

"Thanks." Georgie tapped her pockets. "I left my phone at the house."

"We can go back and get it," Zach said.

"No." Georgie opened her door. "We need to help."

Inside the dining hall, Hadley and Katie sat in chairs near the fireplace, their feet propped up on an empty bench. Both women clutched clipboards. Hadley's detailed inclement-weather procedures for the guest lodge and cabins. Katie's detailed the procedures for the ranch.

Katie pointed her pencil at Zach. "Ethan asked

if you could blanket the Ambassadors for the night and prep their stalls in case we lose power."

Zach nodded.

"Can you move the sand near the stable doors and spread more deicing salt outside, too?" Katie ran her finger down her clipboard. "And do the same outside the dining-hall doors."

"I can." Still Zach waited.

Katie lifted the top page on her clipboard. Her brow creased, and her mouth pinched into a thin line.

Dorothy scooted her chair closer to Katie and touched her arm. "It's not our first blizzard."

"It's the first one I'm not out there preparing for." Katie set her hand on her stomach and grimaced. "I should be out there. I have the list. I know what needs to be done."

"They all know what to do and what you expect." A gentle confidence wove through Dorothy's voice.

"It doesn't make it any easier to sit here." Katie frowned.

"Then don't sit," Dorothy said. "Help Georgie and Zach get ready to go outside."

Katie lowered her clipboard and studied them. Her frown deepened. "Georgie, you're going to need more than that out there. Temperatures are plummeting and the winds are kicking up."

"Use the stuff on the tree." Hadley threw her

hands over her head. "If ever there was a good reason to dismantle our Christmas tree, it's this. Zach, grab the hat near the top for Georgie and the red plaid scarf. It's the thickest one on the tree."

"And she needs these, too." Rosie slipped off her chair, unfolded her hands and revealed a pair of hand warmers.

"You need to keep those, Rosie." Georgie kissed the little girl's forehead. "I appreciate it, but I'll be fine."

Zach wasn't sure how much longer he'd be fine. Fine not holding her hand. Fine not sharing another kiss. Fine knowing soon Georgie wouldn't be beside him suggesting dessert before dinner, humming Christmas carols or simply settling him.

He'd have to find his fine again. The fine he'd believed he was before he ever met Georgiana Harrison.

Removing the items from Hadley and Ty's tree, he turned to Georgie and wrapped the scarf around her, tucking the ends inside her jacket. He tapped her hands away when she tried to help, intent on bundling her up to his satisfaction. After all, he still had a few days to pretend she was his. "There's snow and then there's the storm outside."

"It's cold on another level." Hadley hugged herself as if suddenly chilled.

"We have more hand warmers in the kitchen." Katie blew out a long breath. "I stashed a pack in the pantry behind the flour last week. The kids like to put warmers in every single pair of boots, and every jacket and pocket. Even in their clothes that no longer fit."

Dorothy went into the kitchen, then returned with coffee in one hand, hand warmers in the other. "I'll start brewing another pot of coffee and begin preparing dinner."

"It's going to be a long night," Katie said. "You might want to brew two pots."

Layered in the extra scarves they'd wrapped around their faces, hand warmers in their pockets and hair tucked inside their hats, Zach and Georgie ventured outside. He held on to her arm, and side by side they battled the wind and made it to the stables.

Inside, Georgie blew out a shivery breath and knocked snow from her boots. "Hadley wasn't kidding. I've never felt the wind dig right through my bones."

Zach turned on the stable lights. "Let's work quickly and get back to the warmth of the dining hall."

"I have no idea what to do." Georgie remained fixed near the doors, looking unsure about whether she'd rather face the snowstorm or the horses. "I also know nothing about horses other than I asked Santa for a pony when I was six because that's what Amanda and Lily wanted."

"There are no ponies here, only horses." Zach moved back to her side and took her gloved hand. "And I know a bit about horses. We'll work through the stalls one by one, starting with Elmer."

"Elmer." Georgie arched an eyebrow at him.

As if the older horse had been listening, Elmer set his head outside his stall. His ears pricked forward. Elmer nickered. Zach grinned. "There's my boy, now."

Georgie tugged on Zach's arm. "That's Elmer."

"He's reserved and seriously hard to impress." Zach pulled her toward the draft horse's stall. "And the definition of a gentle giant."

"And Elmer is one of your favorites," Georgie said.

"Maybe," Zach confessed.

The large horse was docile and subdued, as if he understood his size was intimidating enough. Even more, Cody would've adored the horse. His brother had always wanted their own ranch and pastures for their own horses. Ones Cody had insisted the brothers could train to be the best calf ropers around. Elmer wasn't cut out for calf roping, but that wouldn't have mattered to his brother.

Cody had often repeated Marshall's sayings to Zach, fully believing the longtime horse trainer's wise words were proverbs to live by. *Good people touch a place in your heart. Horses do the same.*

Zach reached for Elmer's stall door. "Let's introduce you."

Georgie introduced herself and proceeded to inform the giant of her equine inexperience and limited knowledge of horses. As expected, Elmer sidestepped her concern and nudged his massive head against her palm until she rubbed between his ears.

Georgie's smile grew. "I think he likes me."

Of course he did. Smart horse. "I like her, too, Elmer. But that's between you and me."

"I can hear you," Georgie teased. "Where's Elmer's blanket?"

"He's wearing it." Zach stepped around the pair. "He needs warm water and hay cubes."

"And a blanket." Georgie rubbed the horse. "Even big guys get cold."

"Elmer is already wearing his blanket. He's his own furnace." Zach opened the stall door. "Ms. Aggie and Misty Day prefer blankets, as does Lumber Jack. Shall we?"

Georgie designated herself the *company*

keeper—the one tasked with keeping each horse company in the holding stall while Zach removed the soiled bedding in the horse's stall. She stepped back into each stall to make sure he'd fluffed the clean bedding enough like a stern stable supervisor.

Other than his time with Cody, Zach had always preferred to work alone in the stables. Just him and the horses. Now Georgie was with him and his smile refused to fade. He was not supposed to discover more things he liked doing with Georgie.

The last stall cleaned, bedding appropriately fluffed and the Ambassadors prepared for the incoming storm, Zach high-fived Georgie. "If you hadn't stopped to confess to every horse that you didn't know what you were doing, we would've been finished sooner."

"I wanted to prepare them." Georgie bumped her shoulder against Zach.

He guessed she'd wanted to prepare herself. Talking to each horse gave her a chance to assess the animal and her surroundings first. Every horse seemed almost like a patient she'd wanted to get to know personally in order to best care for them.

The double doors swung open. A blast of cold air surged through the barn.

Grace tugged her scarf away from her mouth

and smiled. "Glad to see you two are still here. I could use some help with the foals."

Georgie and Zach hurried forward. Grace held the leads attached to three foals. "Ethan and Ty are fixing a shelter in one of the pastures. Ethan sent me ahead with the young ones."

Zach reached for the lead of a bay-colored colt. The colt looked about the same age that Rain Dancer had been when Zach and Cody first started training him. Zach glanced at Georgie. "You wanted to know what Rain Dancer looks like. He could've been this colt's sire."

"He's beautiful." Georgie accepted the lead of a gray filly. "Where to?"

"Let's keep them in stalls next to each other." Grace guided a brown-and-white paint foal into the first empty stall. "Who's Rain Dancer?"

"Zach's horse." Georgie disappeared into the middle stall with her filly and continued, "Zach's horse needs Ethan's help."

"I'm sure that can be arranged." Grace shuffled around the foal's stall. "Ethan hasn't ever turned away from an animal in need."

But Ethan would most likely turn away from Zach and Rain Dancer. Most definitely once the family learned about Georgie and Zach's deception. It hardly mattered that Zach considered his feelings for Georgie real now. He'd agreed to their scheme intending to deceive the Black-wells for his own gain. Zach stroked his hand over the bay colt, then removed the lead rope and prepared the stall. Too bad he hadn't been better prepared for Georgiana Harrison.

If Zach had tipped his hat over his eyes and fallen asleep on the airplane, he'd never have…

He shook his head and latched the colt's stall door.

The time for *ifs* had long since passed. He had to concentrate on the now. That meant an incoming blizzard, upholding his end of their deal and supporting Georgie's decision to move to London.

He ground his teeth together.

She no more belonged in a research lab in England than he belonged in a business suit in the city's financial district. He zipped his coat and yanked his gloves on, then checked to make sure Georgie had bundled herself back up. He'd walk her back to the dining hall and protect her from the wind gusts. Then he'd find a way to protect his heart from falling for her any further.

Zach escorted Georgie and Grace back to the dining hall, then headed out to scatter salt around the doors of the barn and dining hall.

Two hours later, Dorothy's beef stew and four loaves of homemade beer bread had been quickly devoured.

Their only remaining task was to enjoy Dorothy's chocolate gingerbread cake.

Zach stood now in front of the massive fireplace and sorted through the collection of wet scarves, gloves and hats. The saturated items he set closer to the fire to dry out before anyone had to go back outside.

"I'm not sure we'll be getting much sleep tonight with the wind and storm." Georgie handed him a coffee cup. "Figured caffeine won't hurt."

"Cheers." Zach tapped his cup against hers.

The blast of cold air and the booming voice shouting a hello from the dining-hall entrance muffled Zach's toast. The entire room quieted and turned toward the entrance.

Three men covered in snow and varying degrees of grins stood in the doorway.

"Dad." Georgie's whisper carried no farther than the steam in her cup. She started forward, then changed directions.

She stopped moving only when her arm connected with his. Zach swallowed a deep sip of his coffee and wished he'd thought to add something stronger than vanilla creamer.

The oldest gentleman, his grin clipped from one ear to the other, spread his arms wide. "Didn't think we'd make it home, but here we are."

"Elias Blackwell, I promised Georgie you

wouldn't be reckless." Dorothy wiped her hands on a kitchen towel. Her foot tapped on the wood floor. Her voice ricocheted off the vaulted ceiling. "What did you do?"

Zach rocked back. That was Georgie's grandfather and the man they all referred to as Big E? His cowboy hat was worn, yet had retained its shape, as if pride alone held it together. Or perhaps it was Big E's presence. He was a hard man to ignore, even buffered by two tall gentlemen.

"Wasn't gonna let a blizzard keep me from my family, especially during the holidays." Big E unzipped his coat, scattering snow around his boots.

"Well, get in here, get warm and get some dinner." Dorothy motioned to them. "Everything is still hot."

"I've got some introductions to do first." Big E cleared his throat and set his hand on the shoulder of the gentleman standing to his right. He was broad and built like a draft horse. His shoulders looked reliable, his face kind, despite the uncertainty narrowing his eyes. "Everyone already knows Rudy Harrison."

Georgie's dad had arrived. Georgie shifted beside Zach, bumping into him several times.

Big E motioned to the man waiting on his left. He was the tallest of the three men and lean. A salt-and-pepper beard covered his face and a watchful glint reflected in his gaze.

Big E pushed his shoulders back, and pride infused his words. "This here is Thomas Blackwell, my son and the girls' biological father."

CHAPTER EIGHTEEN

GEORGIE'S MIND SWIRLED and tumbled, tossing every rational thought around like the winds rearranging the snowdrifts outside.

She gaped at the three men in the dining-hall entrance. One she'd loved her whole life. One she'd only just learned was her family. And one she'd never considered she'd ever meet. Or ever want to.

Her dad. Her grandfather. And the man who had abandoned her pregnant mother and four young daughters and never returned. The coffee cooled to acid in her stomach.

What had Big E been thinking? To bring Thomas Blackwell here. Georgie blinked. Thomas was a Blackwell. He had every right to be on Blackwell land. Every right to get to know his family, too.

And Georgie had every right not to get to know him. But she had questions. Wanted answers.

The trio removed their jackets, set them on the hooks on the wall and moved into the room.

In her direction. Georgie wound her arm around Zach's waist and bunched his flannel shirt in her fist.

She needed more time. Time to process. Time to think.

She was the only Harrison sister present. Had her sisters known what her dad and Big E were up to? *No.* The storm hadn't been planned. Lily and Fee should've been there for dinner. Peyton and Amanda should've arrived earlier that afternoon. Thanks to a snowstorm, they'd get there the following day. Georgie shouldn't have been the only Harrison getting ambushed by her two fathers and one cunning grandfather.

She tightened her hold on Zach. Grateful he hadn't left her completely alone.

Her father reached her first. Concern smoothed across his face.

"Dad." A tremor worked through her, trapping her in place.

She'd always hated surprises. Disliked the commotion and disruption. But the anxiety coiling around her spine shredded her control. Her dad had always appreciated her need for preparation. But she'd reduced their communication to brief texts and even more rapid phone calls, preferring to concentrate on work, not her family.

Family first. She'd put her goals first. All to

honor her mother's memory. And she had to face the consequences now.

Zach introduced himself and shook her dad's hand. Zach's hold never loosened on Georgie, as if he understood her knees would buckle without him.

Big E took off his cowboy hat and shook Zach's hand, then greeted Georgie. Her grandfather held his hat, instead of reaching for her.

Zach and Big E parted and introduced Thomas Blackwell. Her biological father never stepped into her space. She assumed he too understood the precarious grip Georgie maintained on the situation.

"Georgie, we need to talk," her dad said. "Given the weather and the phone reception, we decided to wait until we arrived."

Georgie nodded, as if her dad had simply explained why they'd missed dinner. As if her father couldn't have mentioned their plans during any one of his hourly updates. "Peyton, Amanda, Lily and Fee don't know you located Thomas either?"

Her dad shook his head.

Big E settled his hat back on his head. "Some things are best said in person."

Or not at all.

Thomas cleared his throat. "I'd like to..."

She wanted to block him out. Outbursts

solved nothing. Logic and reason always centered her. Only she couldn't hold on to one coherent thought longer than a second.

"Georgie!" The panic in Katie's shout echoed around the pine rafters. "I think I'm going to need a doctor."

Doctor. That one word lodged inside Georgie and thrust the chaos of meeting her biological father aside. Shoved what would be Thomas's awkward explanations for abandoning his family and his much-too-late apologies to the far corner. To the deal-with-later-or-perhaps-not-ever category. Georgie latched on to her new focus, released Zach and rushed to Katie.

Chance knocked over two chairs to reach his wife's side and shouted, "Someone call 911."

Katie groaned through her clenched teeth. Her eyes squeezed shut. Pain pinched her entire face, drawing out the color.

"Breathe out during the contraction." Georgie squeezed Katie's arm and looked at Chance. Fear had set into his features. She scrambled to recall her training. Tips from attending physicians. She hadn't trained on the labor and delivery ward.

Zach stepped into her view and her world seemed to right itself. Georgie gathered her wits about her. "Chance, time her contractions." She paused, waited for Chance to blink and focus on her voice. On her instructions. "We need the time from the end of one to the beginning of the next. And the duration of each contraction."

Chance reached into his pocket, fumbled and dropped his phone. Tyler moved to his brother's side and accepted Georgie's dad's wristwatch. The one Georgie and her sisters had given him last year on his birthday—a simple, traditional watch with a second hand, a readable clock face and nothing extra, just the way he liked it.

Ty's hand dropped onto his brother's shoulder. "We'll time it together."

Chance focused on his wife. "Another is starting."

Georgie guided Katie through another round of breathing. Grace gathered Rosie and Eli by the fire. The others watched Georgie patiently, as if awaiting her direction. Georgie frowned. "Why isn't anyone dialing 911? She's in labor."

"Roads are closed, darling." Big E scratched his cheek. "No one else is getting in or out tonight."

Panic plunged over Georgie like a landslide. Katie needed a hospital. Her doctor. Nurses trained to guide her through the delivery process.

Katie clung to Chance's hand. Her head fell back on the chair. "This cannot be happening now."

"I think it is." Chance kissed his wife's forehead, then lifted his alarmed gaze to the room. "What are we supposed to do now?"

Big E clapped his hands together. "Blackwell Ranch hasn't seen a baby born on its land since my brother's birth too many full moons ago."

Katie lurched forward, buckled over and fisted her hand on the armrest.

Ty started another count. Chance monitored Katie.

Katie hissed, sucking her breath through her gritted teeth. The contraction ended and Katie rediscovered her voice. Her heated words vibrated around the room. "The ranch isn't going to see a baby born tonight, if someone doesn't tell me what to do. Now."

No one spoke. No one offered a suggestion. The baby was coming. Georgie rounded on the group. "We need a room."

"You can use the animal barn," Ethan offered.

"I am not giving birth in the surgical animal clinic where heifers and mares have been opened up." Katie groaned and clutched her stomach. "I. Am. Not."

"The main house is closest," Chance said.

Dorothy latched her arm around Hadley's waist. "We'll drive up there now and prepare one of the guest rooms."

"I can't leave Mama K," Rosie cried.

Katie lost her voice again to another contraction. They were getting closer.

"We'll have a movie night and popcorn in Hadley's family room." Grace picked up Eli.

Georgie bent down until she was eye level with Rosie. She wiped Rosie's tears off her pale cheeks. "You'll be close the whole time this way. And if Mama K needs you, I'll come get you."

"Promise?" Rosie's voice was waterlogged.

"Absolutely." Georgie held out her little finger for a pinkie swear.

Satisfied, Rosie kissed Katie's cheek, then took Grace's hand. They followed Dorothy and Hadley outside to the ATVs.

Ethan listed off supplies he had in the surgical barn, from sterilized clamps, forceps and scalpels, to scrubs, masks and gloves.

Thomas nodded. "We'll need it all."

Chance accepted the watch from his brother. Ethan and Ty sprinted out the side door to Ethan's large-animal clinic. No questions asked. No doubt about Thomas Blackwell and his instructions.

Georgie gaped at Thomas. She hadn't invited him. He wasn't part of her *we*.

"I'm a trained naval medic." Thomas held his hands behind his back and regarded her, his voice and face serious. "And I've heard from your dad and grandfather about your medical degree and accomplishments."

And she heard his kind understanding in referring to Rudy as her dad.

"Thomas is more than that." Big E slapped his hand on Thomas's shoulder. "He rescued the Frye family from their overturned car that had caught on fire just last month."

Her dad offered his support. "Two young children and their parents are able to spend this Christmas together, thanks to Thomas."

"We can talk more later." Thomas fastened his perceptive gaze on Georgie. "Right now, we have a scared first-time mother and a baby wanting to make its arrival."

Big E nodded to Rudy. "We've got a snowplow to run."

"Now?" Georgie asked.

"Gotta clear the road for the ambulance to get in eventually," Big E said.

Chance tossed his phone at his grandfather. "Find our doctor and call her for us."

"I'll do that." Rudy took the phone from Big E. "Then we'll discuss how and when to drive the snowplow."

Chance helped Katie stand. Thomas moved in to assist the couple. Chance looked back at Georgie. "You and Zach are following behind us, right?"

"Yes." Zach took Georgie's hand.

Too soon, Georgie was staring at the white farmhouse, obscured through the ATV's windshield by the steadily falling snow and her doubt.

"Ready?" Zach asked.

"No." Georgie twisted her hands together. "Not at all."

The list of potential problems and possible medical emergencies filed through her like an overloaded computer printout. There were too many opportunities for error. Mistakes couldn't be corrected. Or forgiven.

"It's going to be fine." Zach set his hand on her knee.

"It's a baby, Zach." She squeezed his fingers, as if the pressure would make him understand. As if her own terror could be as easily squashed. "This isn't a bloody nose."

"It's Katie." Zach covered their hands with his other one, applied his own pressure and warmth.

Georgie lifted her gaze to his. How could he remain so calm? So very composed? No wonder his brother had wanted him to be there for his treatments. Georgie wanted Zach beside her, too. Now and later.

Zach kept his gaze fixed on hers. "Your cousin needs you, Georgie."

Georgie stiffened. She hadn't left any of her sisters alone when they'd been hurt. Apart from when her parents had made Georgie stay home instead of going to the hospital with Lily after her sister's big accident. That hadn't been Georgie's choice.

She had a choice now.

Katie would not be alone. Georgie wouldn't leave Katie with a stranger to deliver her first baby. Katie would have her family to help her welcome the next Blackwell.

"Can you get my phone from Dorothy's house? Call Dr. Alan Stafford." She opened the door and squinted into the wind. "He's listed in my contacts. Tell him what's happening. He'll know what to do."

"Who's Dr. Stafford?" Zach asked.

"Remember the apple cider vinegar? He was the attending doctor on the floor that day. He'll help us." Georgie slammed the ATV door, raced into the house and called out to Dorothy.

"Upstairs, dear." Dorothy's voice swirled down the staircase. "Second room on the right."

Georgie walked into the bedroom to find Chance and Katie in a standoff. Hadley and Dorothy quickly retreated to the kitchen. Thomas stood guard near a tall armoire.

"Georgie, tell my wife to lie down." Chance pointed to the queen-sized bed.

"Georgie, tell my husband to leave." Katie massaged her back and walked in a small circle.

"Chance, pull the comforter and blankets off the bed," Georgie ordered. "Ethan is coming with supplies."

"She needs to be lying down." Chance never budged.

Thomas started rolling up the thick comforter.

"Only the one in labor gets to make the rules," Georgie said. She earned a grateful smile from Katie. "We want to get the bed prepared so Katie can lie down when she chooses."

Chance's mouth flattened. He turned and helped Thomas, then piled the pillows against the headboard for Katie to lean against. "Now she can lie down."

Katie glowered and continued her slow, circular walk.

Thomas grabbed Chance's arm and tugged him toward the door. "I hear Ethan downstairs. Let's get the supplies."

Katie lifted her head. "Is it so wrong that I want to stand?"

"Nothing is wrong," Georgie assured her. "You do what's comfortable."

Katie took both of Georgie's hands. "You're not leaving me, right?"

"We're in this together," Georgie promised.

Tears rushed into Katie's eyes and leaked from the corners. "I'm going to have a baby."

Katie's joy and wonder squeezed around Georgie's heart. And she was going to deliver her first baby. Her cousin's child. "Let's get ready to meet your child."

Georgie twisted her hair up into a bun, then helped Katie change into the loose nightgown and robe Hadley had left on the dresser. Chance and Thomas returned with Ethan, and they covered the bed in padding and sheets from the clinic. Georgie changed into the scrubs they'd brought and washed her hands in the bathroom sink.

Zach appeared in the bedroom doorway, holding Georgie's phone. "Dr. Stafford is on the line for you."

Georgie took the phone, squeezed Zach's hand on her way into the hallway and greeted Dr. Stafford. Five minutes later, she returned the phone to Zach and walked back into the guest room.

Katie still stood. Chance gripped the bedpost. Ethan and Thomas waited.

Chance stared at Georgie. "We can't get Katie's doctor on the phone. Now what?"

"Now we wait." Georgie rubbed Katie's back for her. "And we let Katie tell us what she needs."

"Georgie, we'll be right out here in the hallway," Thomas said. Zach and Ethan joined him.

After midnight, Katie's water broke, and the

contractions came faster and stronger. She finally agreed to get into the bed. Chance called
out the time. Zach relayed the information to
Dr. Stafford on the phone. Georgie never left
Katie's side. Hours shifted into minutes. Minutes into seconds.

Georgie followed Dr. Stafford's instructions
to determine how far along Katie was.

Only one hiccup derailed Georgie's concen-
tration.

Zach appeared in the doorway. His gaze was
wide and his voice dull. "Hadley is now in labor,
too."

Katie dropped her head onto the pillow and
moaned. "What time is it?"

"Almost three in the morning," Chance said.

"Hadley and I are going to deliver on the
same day." Katie grabbed both of her husband's
hands and panted. "It's amazing."

Perhaps for the new mothers and cousins
who'd share a birthday. But Georgie had never
delivered one baby, let alone two. How were
Thomas and she supposed to deliver two babies?
Thankfully, Thomas never flinched at the news.

"Let's concentrate on you, Katie, and welcoming your new Blackwell baby." Georgie
slipped on a new pair of surgical gloves.

Thomas said, "I'll check on Hadley and the
timing of her contractions and be right back."

"Right." Georgie examined Katie again and shoved every emotion surging through her out of her mental space. Georgie couldn't fail. She forced confidence and calm into her words. "Katie, it's time to really push."

After seven pushes and an assortment of prayers and curses from the mother, the baby's head appeared. Then one shoulder and the other. Georgie lifted the infant forward and the precious baby girl fell into her hands. Thomas handed her a clean cloth. She wiped the cloth over the newborn's face, earned the tiniest of cries for her reward. She laid the newborn on Katie's stomach, giving mom, dad and baby time to bond.

The rest of the delivery proceeded without incident. Thomas and Ethan prepared the umbilical cord to be cut and talked Chance through the process.

An hour later, the bedding had been changed and both Katie and the baby were clean and resting together. Chance sat beside them, watching over his family. A sleepy Rosie had also been welcomed in to greet her new sister before Ethan carried her off to bed.

Dr. Stafford had been thanked and advised there could be another call regarding Hadley. He'd gladly agreed to take it.

Thomas, Zach and Georgie headed into the

master bedroom. Once again, Georgie walked into a husband-and-wife face-off.

"Georgie, tell my wife she should rest and save her energy for delivering our child," Ty said.

"Georgie, tell my husband to make himself useful someplace else," Hadley said.

Thomas and Zach retreated toward the door. Georgie shook her head and composed herself. "Here's what we're going to do."

CHAPTER NINETEEN

"GO AWAY."

Zach ignored Georgie's command and continued into the sunroom. He took her hands and pulled her out of Dorothy's rocking chair. Then sat and tugged her onto his lap.

"You're supposed to go away when someone tells you to." She shifted and curled against his chest. Her cheeks were damp; her voice was hoarse.

"I don't feel like it." He wrapped his arms around her. Finally, the tension in his body receded.

The stress, strain and worry of the past hours weakened its vise grip around him. And he breathed long and deep for what felt like the first time since dinner the previous night. He'd never have guessed a blizzard would only be a backdrop to the drama that had played out indoors.

He rubbed Georgie's back. Amazed all over again at how she'd maintained her poise and confidence the entire night. Never once had she cracked or lost control. Not when she'd met her biological father. Not even when she'd delivered her first baby.

"I don't feel like letting you see me like this." She mumbled into his shirt, which was already damp from her tears.

"Like what?" Raw. Honest. Emotional.

"Weak."

He kissed the top of her head. "You are anything but weak."

"You don't believe that." She sniffed. "I don't believe it. Look at me."

He recognized her need to argue. Now that he had her in his embrace, he was content and willing to let her have her way. "I suppose you want to tell me what I believe."

Her head wobbled against his chest. "You believe I'm stubborn."

He didn't disagree. "That's not a fault. It means you are more decisive than other people."

"You also think I'm controlling." She scrubbed her palm across her cheek. Sniffed again.

"That's not a fault either." He handed her a tissue from the box on the side table. "It just means you are not afraid to act and get things done." He admired her strength, courage and so much more about her.

"I was terrified tonight," she countered. "Terrified." She stretched out the one word into three long phrases.

"But you didn't back away." If anything, she'd become more involved. More connected to Katie, then Hadley, assisting the new mothers every moment. Her generosity and compassion humbled him. To be loved by someone like her would be a true gift.

"I'm cold and closed off," she challenged.

Not with me. Not ever with me. "You don't put your emotions on the stage for the world to see." He touched her chin, lifted her gaze to his. Wanted her to see all he felt for her. All he couldn't put into words. "That doesn't mean you don't feel. Can't feel. It doesn't mean you refuse to feel."

He searched her face. So many of her emotions leaked out in the tears trailing down her cheeks. Wavered in the tremble of her lips. Shivered in the scratch of her voice.

"I don't want to feel like this." She bunched his flannel shirt in her fists. Anger and defeat in her words. "I don't want to feel all of this all at once. It's too much. I want to feel nothing."

How many times had he prayed for the very same thing? Wished for a numbness to consume him over the years. He ached for her. "I can't take it away for you."

"Why not?" She pushed her fists into his chest.

"Because this is how you know you're living." *Always drive through the storm, son. The sun will greet you on the other side every time.* Zach often wondered if his father had ever found his own sun. Looking at Georgie, Zach could believe he'd found his. If only...

"My mom would say this is how we get to those best moments." She sniffed and dabbed a tissue against each eye. The tiniest of smiles wavered. "I brought a new life into the world last night."

The wonder in her voice stirred through him. "You did. How was it?"

"Besides terrifying?" She straightened her fingers and flattened her palms on his chest. "It was extraordinary. Exhilarating. Beyond words, really."

He'd been the same just watching her work all night: beyond words. He tucked a strand of hair behind her cheek. "What's wrong?"

"I haven't heard about Hadley." She checked the time on the fitness band on her wrist.

An ambulance had arrived for Hadley and Ty shortly after sunrise, while Hadley was still in labor. Thanks to the early morning snowplow skills of Big E and Rudy, the road on the Blackwell property and beyond had been cleared for the EMTs. Katie's doctor was on her way to the ranch to check on Katie and her daughter, Holly. Zach glanced at the clock on the wall. "It hasn't been two hours since they left for the hospital. I'm sure we'll hear soon."

"Are you always like this?" she asked.

"Like what?"

"Positive and calm," she said.

Only with her. "That's kind of you to say that about me."

"I'm serious," she pressed.

"We survived a blizzard, delivered a healthy baby, kept the baby's mom safe, coached another new mom and met your biological father all in one night." He nodded. "That's quite a successful night. We should be positive."

She dropped her forehead back onto his chest. "My biological father is here."

Zach had one dad he hadn't seen enough of. Now Georgie had two fathers. And from his brief conversations with them, both were good men. He wasn't certain Georgie wanted to hear that just yet. "What's the plan?"

"I don't have one." She rose up to stare at him. "I should have one. Peyton and Amanda will be here this afternoon. Lily and Fee, too."

The tension returned to her tone. He rubbed her back. "You have to talk to him."

"I know and I will." She settled against him

and yawned. "But not right now. Can it just be us right now? For a little while longer."

It could be us forever, if you wanted it. If you chose me, not your career. Selfish. His mother had been right about him all along. Zach pressed his head back against the rocking chair and closed his eyes. He rubbed Georgie's back until her breath evened out and she finally surrendered to sleep.

He carried her upstairs, set her on the bed, covered her and kissed her forehead. She never stirred. Never woke. He stretched out on the floor and stacked his hands behind his head.

Sleep eluded him. That was the fate of the greedy who always wanted more.

He could want more from Georgie. With Georgie.

But he would never ask. Never ask her to choose.

He squeezed his eyes shut and willed sleep to claim him, too. If he slept, he wouldn't have to face the truth. Face his enormous mistake.

He'd fallen in love with Georgie.

He shouldn't have forgotten what it was like to not be alone. He'd forgotten his loneliness. Now loneliness would return and this time with a vengeance.

CHAPTER TWENTY

GEORGIE PULLED HER damp hair into a ponytail and headed downstairs, restored by her nap and shower. Voices and laughter rolled from the sunporch. Her smile widened. *Zach.*

She'd woken up alone, but she'd fallen asleep on Zach's lap. In the safety of his arms. Zach had been her rock last night. Knowing he had been within reach, would catch her if she stumbled, had kept her steady and buoyed.

Then she'd broken apart in his embrace earlier. It wasn't weakness that pulsed inside her now. Surprisingly, she felt empowered and energized. All thanks to Zach.

"I hope we didn't wake you, dear." Dorothy came into the kitchen from the sunporch. "Your dad and I have been sharing stories about your grandfather."

My dad. "Is Zach with you?"

"It's just Rudy and me. Zach left about an hour ago." Dorothy pulled a coffee mug from the cabinet and filled it. "He wanted to get the final parts to finish the bench."

Georgie smoothed her fingers over her hair and eyed the sunporch. Her dad waited. They hadn't shared a real conversation in months. Her continuous commitment to her work had only disappointed and frustrated him. His unrelenting determination to find her a date and possible husband had only dismayed and exasperated her. Until she'd reduced their conversations to the weather and his eating habits. Her dad had a weakness for hot doughnuts and dipped ice cream cones.

She skipped her gaze to Dorothy. "I don't know what to say."

Dorothy set a cup of coffee in her hand and pressed a light kiss on her cheek. "Just tell him what's in your heart."

Zach had given her the same advice yesterday.

But her heart was confused. Her heart was a traitor and not to be trusted.

Her heart had made a connection to her biological father last night. They'd worked side by side throughout the night. Thomas had assessed, anticipated, then acted. His approach was a mirror of Georgie's. He'd been handing Georgie what she had needed before she'd even asked. Thomas had been reserved, composed and perceptive, offering encouragement to Chance and

Katie, and continuous support to Georgie. She was grateful Thomas had been there.

And she felt like she'd betrayed her dad. The man who'd raised her and loved her. The man who'd understood her goals before she had put them into words. Rudy Harrison had given Georgie her first stethoscope, microscope and doctor's kit with her very own lab coat.

Georgie clutched the coffee mug and walked into the sunroom. "Dad."

He turned from the window. Fatigue extended the lines fanning from the edges of his eyes. His hair had transitioned to pure silver. The short cut only enhanced his distinguished look. He opened his arms. "There's my girl."

Georgie set the mug on the table and hurried toward him. So much had changed. But not Rudy Harrison's bear hug of an embrace that had always comforted and protected. And Georgie found the right words. "I love you, Dad."

"I love you, too." He squeezed her and pulled away. "And I'm so very proud of you."

Georgie released him, reached for her coffee and sipped, soaking her guilt. He wouldn't be proud of her deceit. Perhaps not even of her career move. Not to mention her disloyalty. How could she like Thomas Blackwell after one night?

"It's remarkable what you did for your cousins last night." Approval carved into his words. The pride that always held his chin high and his shoulders straight expanded into the smile he aimed at her. "My girl delivered a baby last night. It's extraordinary."

"It's an experience I'm not sure I'll ever be able to repeat," she said.

"I imagine there will be many extraordinary experiences in patient care," he said.

Georgie sank onto the couch. "What do you mean?"

"You brought a baby into the world." He sat on the other end of the couch. "And from what I've heard, helped your other cousins with their medical issues."

"That was nothing." Georgie sipped from her coffee cup. If her dad heard about Iris and Estelle's idea for Georgie's own medical practice in town, he'd have her moved in and the sign repainted before the end of the year. "I haven't changed my mind about my research work."

Her dad wiped a hand over his mouth. "I just assumed…"

"I've been helping family." And enjoying herself in the process. But she liked her work in the lab, too. "You always told us to put family first."

"Yes, I have." He leaned into the couch. "You know that's all I've been trying to do. I'm sorry if it hasn't always seemed like that."

She was sorry, as well. Sorry she wasn't the doctor he wanted her to be. "I know. And I appreciate you watching out for us."

"That's a father's job," he said. "It's also a father's job to help guide his daughters to what he thinks is best for them."

"My work is important to me," she said.

"I'm not talking about your career." He leaned toward her. "I'm talking about Zach. This new man in your life."

Zach. The temporary man in her life. Georgie sipped more coffee. The caffeine only jolted another surge of guilt through her. "What about him?"

"I like him." Her dad nodded as if that settled everything.

Except nothing was settled. Not inside Georgie. "You just met him and barely spent more than five minutes together."

"But I saw how he was with you all night," he argued. "And I talked to him this morning. He's taking me to the Once Was Barn later."

Zach had been attentive, considerate and protective. He'd been everything she could've asked for in a fake boyfriend. He'd been everything she could've wanted in a real partner. If she'd wanted a relationship. She couldn't simply set her own goals and career aside for a man she'd only just met. She couldn't simply follow her heart. She'd never followed her heart. "He's a good guy."

"That's all I ever wanted for you," her dad said.

"Someone to take care of me," she said.

He straightened and considered her. "You don't need anyone to take care of you, Georgie. You need someone to challenge you."

Was that what drew her to Zach? He never acted as though he was intimidated by her degree. Instead, he'd pushed her to use what she'd learned to help her family. He hadn't let her retreat and observe. Not once. "You know that I'm happy on my own, don't you?"

"I do." Her dad sighed. "I also know that having a partner and strong foundation allows you to stretch further than you ever thought possible."

"Did Mom do that for you?" she asked.

"Every single day," he admitted. "She made me a better man. A better person."

"And a better father."

"That, too." His smile barely creased his mouth. "I was never quite sure what I was doing, but I tried. I hope you think I was a good father."

She leaned across the sofa and hugged him. "You were the best dad I could've asked for."

"That's all I needed to hear." He took her

hands and looked her in the eyes. "You need to talk to Thomas."

"Can I wait for Peyton and Amanda to arrive this afternoon?" she asked.

Her dad shook his head. "You'll retreat to the corner, let your sisters take control and only join in if you sense someone needs your help."

How well he knew her. "There's nothing wrong with helping."

Her dad tensed his grip on her hands. His voice serious. "There's also nothing wrong with listening to the man who gave me the gift of raising five daughters as my own."

Not a burden, but a gift. Thomas Blackwell had also given Georgie a gift: the ability to call Rudy Harrison her dad. "I'll talk to him for you, Dad."

"You and Thomas are more alike than you know." He released her hands and rose. "I think I'm going to head to the dining hall. Dorothy mentioned brisket and warm apple pie for lunch."

"Keep it to one piece," Georgie ordered. "There's going to be more good food tonight at the Ugly Sweater Bash."

Her dad tugged a knit hat over his ears, pretended he hadn't heard and disappeared outside. Georgie's phone buzzed on the kitchen island. Tyler's name flashed on her incoming-call screen.

Twenty minutes later, Georgie hung up, set her hands flat on the kitchen counter and inhaled around her surge of unease. A knock came from the back door. She called out, "Come in. It's open."

The door opened and closed. Footsteps tapped across the mudroom into the kitchen. "Is this a bad time?"

Georgie turned and found Thomas Blackwell standing on the other side of the island. He regarded her with the same hazel eyes she saw in her own reflection every morning.

"I saw Rudy in the dining hall," he said. "He told me to come up to the house. Now was a good time to see you."

"It's fine." Georgie motioned to the coffee maker. "Would you like something to drink?"

"I'm okay." He rubbed his hand over his chin. "Are you sure you are?"

He'd trimmed his full beard to a close shave and stood several inches taller than her dad. He was handsome, but it was the keen insight in his warm gaze that made him approachable. Relatable. "I just spoke to Tyler. They're taking Hadley in for an unplanned C-section now. The baby is in distress."

"Hadley and Tyler are exactly where they

need to be," he said. "They'll get the care and treatment they need at the hospital."

Georgie exhaled, but her breath still stuttered. "I know. I just keep thinking what would've happened if they'd been trapped here." With Georgie—an inexperienced doctor.

"You would've found them the help they needed." Certainty claimed his words.

"How can you know that?"

His grin came and disappeared just as quickly. "It's what I would've done."

"You think you know me?" She couldn't clip the curt tone from her voice. Or the hurt.

"I wouldn't presume to know anything about you." He held his hands behind his back, in the relaxed military stance her dad often slipped into. "We've only just met."

"But you claim to know I would've helped them and saved the baby." His calm demeanor was like tinder on her frustration and sudden anger.

"It's what we do. You're a doctor." He regarded her. His face was expressionless, his gaze intent. "I'm a retired medic. When someone needs help, we answer that call."

Resentment pulsed, shaking her core. She sat on a stool at the island. "Except Mom was pregnant, with four young daughters, and she needed help. Yet you never answered that call. You walked away."

"I was deployed overseas and had recently re-upped when I learned your mom was pregnant." He never flinched. Never moved. "I had a duty to serve my country."

"You'd also vowed to love our mom until death do you part," she charged. Vows were supposed to mean something. Vows were supposed to be sacred. Not something easily discarded like yesterday's leftovers.

"I never stopped loving your mom." His voice thickened. A sheen covered his eyes. His jaw flexed. "If you hear only one thing I tell you today, hear this. I never stopped loving your mom or you."

"But you abandoned us." She slapped her palm on the island, caught sight of her mother's bracelet dangling on her wrist. Tears pooled in her eyes. She wanted to cry for the mother she'd lost. For the father she'd never known. Her voice cracked. "That's not love. You have to know that's not love."

She wasn't an authority on love. But she understood that much.

He paced toward the kitchen sink, paused and stared out the window. His shoulders remained set. But his chin dipped once toward his chest, as if he'd been given silent orders and agreed just as silently to follow them. He turned back to face her. "Your mom sent the divorce papers to me while I was overseas."

"Why would she do that?" Georgie curved her fingers over her mother's bracelet, as if protecting herself and her mother from his allegations.

"She hadn't wanted me to continue serving." His gaze slipped away from her and fixed on a spot past Georgie's shoulder. "I thought serving was the only way I could survive and protect my family."

"You make it sound like you wanted to protect us from yourself." She watched his jaw tense and relax, his gaze narrow, then his cheeks soften. And she knew the truth: that was exactly what he'd been doing.

"I served in active combat as a medic." His voice lowered as if weighted down by his confession. "I was good at my job and with my men. Very good. Work kept the memories and nightmares in their place. As long as I worked, I was untouchable. The past couldn't get to me."

Georgie crossed her arms over her chest, blocking out a sudden chill.

"I came home on leave," he continued. "Came to see you."

"We never saw you," she whispered.

"By then your mother was dating Rudy. She was in a better place. You all were." His gaze connected with hers. Quiet and sincere in its intensity. "That's when I walked away."

But not to abandon his family. To give them a different future. One he thought would be better. "What did you do?"

"Re-upped again." He shrugged one shoulder. One corner of his mouth tipped into the smallest smile. "And fortunately, my commanding officer saw what your mother had seen all along. I needed help and couldn't fix myself on my own."

"How are you now?" she asked.

"I go to a therapy group once a week." Pride framed his grin. "I lead the group."

"Why did you never find us?" she asked. "Never try to see us again?"

"I thought about it. So many times, I've played it out in my head." He rolled his shoulders back. "But every version ended in hurting your mother. Hurting you all. I'd already done enough of that."

"What now?"

"That's up to you and your sisters," he said.

"Well, my dad says you and I are a lot alike."
Georgie released her wrist and her mother's brace-

let. Something inside her shifted and opened. "I'd like to find out if he's right."

Thomas smiled. His first real smile since she'd met him. "I'd really like that, too."

CHAPTER TWENTY-ONE

"SIMON, PUT THAT DOWN." Georgie watched Fee's boyfriend until he put the barrel-shaped glass jar back on the table beside the other two. Georgie and Dorothy had filled the extra-large jars for one of their Ugly Sweater Bash games. One contained an assortment of colored bells. Another was filled with round ornaments. And the one Simon had picked up held green-, red- and silver-wrapped chocolate candies. The game was simple. Guess the number inside each one and win.

"He should be disqualified." Amanda jabbed her elbow into Simon's side, setting the pair of Santa's boots attached to Simon's ugly sweater swaying. Her laughter lifted her eyebrows. "The sign clearly states no touching."

"But you picked up the ornament jar earlier." Fee's snow-globe sweater—a clear plastic bag stuffed with cotton balls and wrapped over her green sweater—prevented her from pointing to Simon and Blake, Amanda's boyfriend. Still, she gleefully outed her sister. "We all watched you, Amanda."

"It doesn't matter what you guys do. Carry it around the dining hall if you must." Blake wrote on a piece of paper and held it up over his head. "I guessed correctly on all three. You all are going to lose."

Blake's declaration resulted in several hands reaching for his piece of paper and demands to reveal his guesses.

Georgie shook her head at her family. *Family.* She touched her mother's bracelet, saw her mom's smile in Fee's radiant grin. Heard her mom's laugh in Amanda's joy. She sighed, starting to understand Iris's and Estelle's full hearts.

A rogue bell rolled against her boot. Georgie bent and held the bell up. "Anyone lose this?"

Rosie, Poppy, Abbey and Gen giggled. The young Blackwell cousins stood together behind Matteo's son, Gino. The group gathered at the bell-toss game.

Gino lifted his hand. "Sorry. That was mine."

"Can I try?" Georgie stepped up to the line they'd taped on the floor.

"Adults have to toss from back here." Rosie tugged on her, nudging her back to the second line.

"How many chances do I get?" Georgie looked at the kids. They shuffled their feet and avoided looking at each other. Georgie straightened. "What's going on?"

The others urged Rosie forward, who said, "Pops and Grandma Dot declared we can have as many tries as we want."

"What about me?" Georgie asked.

"Three." Gino tapped his foot against a handwritten rules sign. "That's what it says."

"Who do I need to speak to about this?" Georgie whispered, attempting to look offended.

The kids pointed at the massive fireplace. Alice Gardner and Conner's mom, Karen, sat in the rocking chairs near it, each one cradling one of Jon and Lydia's sleeping twin boys. Dorothy and Pops sat nearby. A crate of wrapped prizes for the bell-toss competitors was on the floor between their chairs.

"Don't try to change the rules now." Pops shook his finger at Georgie. He wore a knit cap rather than his usual cowboy hat. The end of a bandage was visible beneath it. Pops had already promised he'd be talking to Georgie when he first arrived. "Kids, make sure Georgie doesn't step over the line."

The cousins took Pops's orders to heart and ordered Georgie to step back on her second toss. Georgie played four rounds, then declared defeat and claimed the kids were clearly the experts at the bell toss.

"I lost already." Peyton unwrapped a candy cane and aimed it at the table next to her.

Chance dealt from a deck of cards to Lydia, Jon, Ben, Rachel and Matteo. Five candy canes rested in the center of their table. No one spoke. Gazes remained fixed on their individual hands.

"You didn't win one hand?" Georgie murmured.

"Not one single round." Peyton bit off a chunk of candy cane and crunched down on the hard candy. "This group is ruthless."

Ben frowned across the table at them. "Peyton, can you chew a little quieter?"

"We really need to concentrate." Matteo lifted his head. His grin refused to remain hidden.

Peyton faux huffed and raised her voice. "Ruthless. I'm telling you."

Rachel reached into the center of the table and grabbed a candy cane. The others quickly followed. Rachel laughed and raised the candy in triumph. "You just have to have really good reflexes."

Georgie snapped off a piece of Peyton's candy cane. Once again, her chest felt full. Her smile stretched.

Peyton yanked her hand away. "Hey. Not you, too."

"You'll get them next time." Georgie laughed,

hugged her sister and made her way to the table where spiked hot apple cider was being served.

Two glasses in hand, she wove around Conner's friends, entertaining Lily with an amusing childhood story about her groom. Their joint laughter interrupted the retelling, causing the story to stop and start in spurts.

Georgie wedged herself between Thomas and Zach, handing one cider to Zach. Rudy and Big E faced them. The Harrison beach-themed tree stood between Thomas and Rudy like an honored guest.

Last week, she'd arrived at Blackwell as a stranger. Tonight, friends and family surrounded her. Joy and delight infused the hall, elevating the celebration into one that would be remembered in detail decades from now. Her smile refused to dim. She edged into Zach's side. His arm settled around her back, drawing her even closer, exactly where she wanted to be.

Grateful and content on a ranch in Montana, beside a cowboy, accepted by family. Such an outcome hadn't been included in her original scheme. Yet she wanted nothing to change.

Lily and Conner, linked arm in arm, joined them. Fee and Simon followed. Again, Georgie's smile expanded like her mom's used to during their annual Harrison holiday party. Her mom had greeted and hugged every arriving guest as if they'd been the only ones she'd been waiting for. *Come in. Come in and enjoy. We're thrilled you came.*

And Georgie was thrilled, too. For her sisters and the love they'd found. She sipped her cider and curved her arm around Zach's waist. One more time, she let her gaze track over the crowd, collecting the moment like her mom had reminded her to do.

"Zach, ever have a ride like that?" Rudy asked.

Her dad's question drew her into the conversation. She hadn't paid attention to Big E's story, wasn't certain what ride her father referenced.

Zach laughed. "More times than I can count."

"But you've succeeded, too, and that's the difference between you and me, son." Respect bolstered Big E's words. "Even garnered all-around winner last month at the Legacy Pro Rodeo Days. No small feat."

"Is that the rodeo where you two met?" Fee rested her head on Simon's shoulder. "Where was that again?"

Zach's arm tensed around Georgie's waist. "Kingston."

At the very same time, Georgie blurted, "Kingstown."

Then she cringed. She'd heard the first part

of Zach's town and reached for the only name she recognized in North Carolina.

"There isn't a rodeo in Kingstown—at least, not the size of Legacy Pro." Thomas smoothed his hand over his chin. "I've driven through that town many times. It could use a rodeo to bolster the local economy."

Georgie stared into her cider cup, ignoring her sisters' probing gazes.

"They met on an airplane." Big E swept both hands back and forth as if clearing smoke from the air. "Never mind all that. When is Ethan heading to Colorado? Zach can't earn another all-around title without his horse."

Georgie coughed as if she'd inhaled a mouthful of smoke. *Airplane?* How had her grandfather...?

"Colorado?" Ethan handed Eli and the toy train the pair had been playing with over to Grace. "Big E, what are you talking about?"

"How else are you going to treat Rain Dancer?" Big E set his hands on his hips. "Man can't compete without his horse."

Ethan confronted Zach. His gaze narrowed. Accusation was clear in his tone. "You're that Zach Evans."

Zach released Georgie and lifted his hand, palm out. "I didn't know about Butterscotch until I arrived."

The entire room quieted, as if Zach had cursed. Or worse, had broken a law. More specifically, a Blackwell family rule. Georgie's contentment dissolved. Her smile wavered and weakened.

"Did Big E tell you to come here?" Ethan's voice darkened. Anger rolled across his face. "Promise he'd take care of everything for you and your horse?"

Zach never backed down. "I just met Big E."

"I paid for Zach's ticket and seated him beside Georgie on the airplane." Big E stepped into the fray. No remorse. No apology. Then he aimed his wry grin at Georgie. "You're welcome, my dear."

Georgie stammered. "Excuse me?"

"Big E said you're welcome." Suspicion and disapproval clouded Lily's gaze.

"I got that," Georgie ground out. Peyton and Amanda moved into Georgie's view, standing behind Lily and Fee, uniting the rest of the Harrison sisters against her. "I want to know about the seating part."

"You sent your flight information to Rudy. I booked Zach's flight." Big E shrugged. "You ended up in the same row."

"I'm confused." Fee raised her hand as if she was in a classroom asking about an algebra problem. "Did you meet at the rodeo or on the plane?"

"The plane." Zach's voice and frown sank into grimness.

"As in, the plane you were on one week ago," Lily clarified. Censure coated her tone.

Was Lily upset that Georgie had lied to her, or annoyed that Georgie brought home a stranger? Did it matter? Dismay was already pulling Amanda's mouth into a thin line. Disappointment stole the usual light from Fee's gaze. Only Peyton held back, her face expressionless. She'd want all the facts and then she'd render her judgment. Still, her older sister offered no encouragement. And just like that, Georgie's joy vanished. And the truth demanded its retribution.

"Yes. Fine." Georgie flung her hands into the air. "I met Zach on the plane. Colin never showed up. I needed a date and here we are."

"This is some place to be." That from Blake.

Georgie glared at Amanda's boyfriend. As if Blake should talk. He'd been engaged to another woman, planning his wedding at Blackwell, before he'd finally realized what they'd suspected all along. He was in love with Amanda and had been for years.

Lily drew Georgie's focus away from Blake.

"You brought a stranger to be your date to my wedding?"

And I then lied to you, convincing you he was my boyfriend. Letting her sisters down always made her edgy, tense and miserable.

"I don't want to hear it, Lily," Georgie lashed out. "You rode across country in an RV with Conner. He was a stranger to you, too. Do not lecture me."

Lily's eyebrows lifted. Fee caught her gasp in her hand over her mouth. Amanda straightened, her eyes wide. Peyton nodded. The tiniest of grins arched across her mouth, then disappeared. Georgie never yelled. Outbursts had never been her thing. She'd definitely shocked her sisters. Were they mad at her deceit or only that they hadn't been clued in from the start?

"What was your angle, Zach?" Ethan asked. "You knew Big E wasn't here to champion your cause, so you decided to use Georgie instead."

"Something like that." Zach nodded. His words were too cold and too calculating.

It was nothing like that. Georgie flinched. "No. It was…"

Zach cut her off. "The fake date was my idea. I talked her into it on the plane."

"You certainly fooled us all." Chance crossed his arms over his chest and eyed Zach. "Making yourself quite indispensable around the ranch."

"And at Brewster's." Ethan's eyebrows pulled together. "Was that the plan? Work for the family, garner their praise and trust. Then I'd have to help you."

Zach crossed his arms over his chest and remained silent.

Georgie wanted to shove him. Yell at Zach to tell them all that Ethan was completely wrong. Besides, she'd used Zach as much as he'd supposedly used her. But she'd failed on her end of their deal. She hadn't helped him save Rain Dancer.

"You wasted your time." Ethan wiped the back of his hand across his mouth. "There is no treatment. It failed on Butterscotch."

"Now. Hold on. You have to try again," Big E said. "You can't give up, Ethan."

"I don't have to do anything for the man who used my cousin," Ethan countered.

"We don't turn our back on family." The stiff set of Big E's shoulders matched his inflexible tone.

"He's not family." Ethan stared Zach down. "What is Georgie to you, Zach?"

"You said it," Zach replied. "My way in."

My way in. Perhaps at the beginning. But what about now? After all they'd shared. He'd kissed her, tenderly and passionately. Surely not to save his horse. He'd had to earn the trust of her family for that task. He'd never told her about Butterscotch. Even her grandfather had played a part in putting them together. Had she really been nothing more than a means to an end for Zach? His horse couldn't be all he cared about. *Rain Dancer is my family.*

"Excuse me." Zach turned and headed for the door. He never looked back.

Everyone faces a choice at some point and proves their true loyalty. Georgie swayed as if she'd been rammed in the stomach by one of Zach's bucking broncs. Lily reached for her. Fee stepped forward. Georgie's gaze was fixed on Zach's retreating back. She stumbled forward, righted herself and raced after Zach, the guy she...

ZACH TOSSED HIS suitcase on the bed in Dorothy's guest room and crammed his clothes inside. If only he could cram his churning emotions inside, too.

Wade had given Zach the plane ticket to Falcon Creek. Told Zach to head to the Blackwell ranch and made Zach believe Ethan would help him, even after Ethan had refused Zach's inquiries. Wade had never mentioned he'd spoken to Big E or even that he knew the Blackwell family. Zach would have time for those details after he returned to Colorado.

But Wade hadn't counted on Georgie Harrison. Or Big E's absence from the ranch.

Zach hadn't counted on discovering his heart—the one he'd purposely misplaced after he lost Cody.

"What are you doing?" Georgie's voice, rigid and unyielding, cuffed the back of his knees.

The right thing. Finally. He smashed the last of his T-shirts into the suitcase, and kept his back to Georgie and his resolve in place. Georgie deserved someone who could give her the world, not someone who wandered around the country.

"Why did you do that?" She walked past him and yanked his flannel shirts from the hangers in the closet. "Why did you tell them it was all your idea?"

"The deal is off." He tugged one shirt from her grip and tossed it into his suitcase. "You don't belong in London."

"One week together and you claim to know where I belong?" She folded the shirt she still held, then rolled it tight. Irritation and anger curled around her words. "You're always chasing the rodeo and the next ride, too afraid you might find someplace you want to belong."

"Don't talk to me about being afraid." He straightened and faced her. "You're hiding inside a lab, avoiding life because you're terrified to let people down. Your mom is gone, Georgie. You can't let her down anymore."

"Everything I'm doing is to honor my mom's memory." She twisted his shirt in her hands. "Is that how you honor your brother? Avoid your grief. Live only for the next eight-second ride. What happens when the rides stop? What will you have then? Would Cody be proud or disappointed?"

Zach spun away and yanked the zipper on his suitcase closed. His brother's voice wasn't as easy to shut out. *Promise me, Zach. No regrets.* He'd regret losing Georgie. He'd never regret doing the right thing. At least after he left, she'd have her family, and that was all he could give her. "The broncs haven't stopped bucking, and my brother would tell me to keep on riding."

"My mom wanted me to spread my wings and fly." Sadness carved an edge into her small grin. "That's exactly what I intend to do with or without your endorsement."

"You can spread your wings right here," he said. "Surrounded by family that loves you."

"You've fallen for my family," she said. "This is exactly where you've always wanted to belong, not me."

"I won't deny I dreamed of a family like yours when I was a kid." He swung his suitcase onto the floor but missed knocking back the past.

So many nights, he'd counted the stars out-side their bedroom window and imagined. So many times, he'd raked leaves, cleaned gutters and mowed lawns, then stolen glimpses inside houses. Saw the board games. The presents piled underneath Christmas trees. Heard the laughter and the calls to come to dinner—it was ready and on the table. Then he'd stopped look-ing. He'd stopped wishing.

Until he'd met Georgie. But lessons forged in childhood ran deep. *You boys ruined my life. Look at what I've become. Look around. This is the best you'll ever have. The best you'll ever deserve.* "I know now I belong on the road."

"Why?" She charged forward into his space. "So you can keep running and never build a future?"

She wanted him to build a future. But never offered a future with her. Frustration fisted around his throat, roughening his voice. "Is that what you're doing in London? Building a future?"

"You sound like my dad."

"Thank you."

"It wasn't a compliment."

He took it as one all the same. He reached down, tugged the handle out from his suitcase.

"This is it, then. You're just leaving." She crossed her arms over her chest, still clutching his shirt in her fist. "You break your word and walk away."

He wanted to walk to her. Run to her. He wanted her to reach for him. Hold on just as tightly as she did to his shirt. Hold on as if she never wanted to let go. Wishes and dreams were for kids, not cowboys. Especially not ones like him, with nothing more to offer than a sick horse and battered heart. "Yeah. I am."

"You're doing what you think is right for me." Resentment sliced a bitter sharpness through her words. "Not what you promised. You can't do that."

He curled his fingers around the suitcase handle, leveled his gaze on her and gave her words he'd never spoken to another person. "I can because I love you."

She sucked in her breath, held it and launched her own challenge. "Then ask me to stay."

Georgie wanted proof of his love, as if walking away wasn't enough. *I had dreams. I did. Married your father and ended up trapped here in a town time forgot. Look what love gets you, boys.* Better for Georgie to hate him now, not resent him later. "I'm not making that decision for you."

"Because you love me." Her words landed between them like a curse.

"Exactly."

"So, that's it? You won't fight for us and you won't support my decision to move to London." She tossed his shirt at him and scowled. "This isn't love."

He let the shirt drop to the floor beside his heart. "It's my kind of love."

"Then keep it." Anger and hurt washed over her face. She tipped her chin and locked her gaze on him. "I don't want it."

"You mean you don't want me." That truth he'd learned years earlier. The reminder wasn't required. He rolled his suitcase over the pieces of his broken heart and walked out.

CHAPTER TWENTY-TWO

SOMETIME AFTER MIDNIGHT and well before the
first rays of sun had slipped around the window
shutters in Dorothy's guest room, Georgie had
come to a conclusion.

Zach loved her family—the Blackwell side—
not her.

The Blackwells represented everything he'd
ever wanted in a family as a child.

Georgie gripped the steering wheel of the
silver truck she'd borrowed from Dorothy, and
concentrated on the road leading into town and
the facts.

The facts were indisputable.

First, they were kindhearted, close-knit and
protective. Zach had only ever been the protec-
tor, always looking out for his younger brother.
And he'd been alone. He was not alone among
the Blackwells.

Second, the Blackwells owned working
ranches and lived their values, respecting the
land and the livestock. Years ago, Zach had discovered his place on a working ranch, thanks to

his ex-girlfriend. Even on the Blackwell ranch, he'd been working most mornings in the stables and helping where he could, as if compelled to be outdoors on the land.

She drove past Jem Salon, Silver Stake Saloon and the crowded bakery. She hadn't been in Falcon Creek long, but she knew the locations of all the local businesses—ones she wanted to visit and ones she already wanted to return to. But she was only passing through Falcon Creek.

She returned to her facts, almost finished convincing herself that her conclusions about Zach were correct.

Third, and most vital, the Blackwells understood Zach's connection to his horse and his lifestyle better than Georgie ever could. She'd grown up in the suburbs, had never ridden a horse—although she wouldn't mind learning—and struggled to understand the call to get thrown from a bucking bronc.

Zach and Georgie were much too different. Beyond the outer appearances—cowboy hat and boots versus a lab coat and face mask—Georgie and Zach wanted different things.

Never mind that she'd been her happiest having Zach beside her the past week. Never mind that she'd laughed more in the past week than she had in months. Never mind that she liked the Blackwells, the land and the town.

An unexpected peace had settled through her since her arrival. That was only a result of Georgie needing time off. A brief break from her work. She would most likely have found the same calm at the beach among strangers. She pulled into an open parking space at Brewster's. The front wheels bumped against the curb. Doubt bumped inside Georgie.

Zach and she might be too different. But she doubted anyone would love him as fiercely as she did. If she did love him.

That had been her second conclusion that morning. She did not love Zach. She liked Zach. She was attracted to Zach. Her feelings were the initial stages of her relationship guideline. All correct and proper emotions for their friendship to grow into something stronger. Perhaps if she weren't moving to London. Or if he'd stayed and fought. Perhaps they might have progressed to the next level.

But she was moving. He had left. She wouldn't be sad, and she wouldn't let her heart hurt. He loved her extended family, not her. She liked—didn't love—him.

Her breath caught in her throat.

Georgie hurried inside Brewster's, escaping the bite of the cold wind and the twinge in her chest.

She located Ethan in the feed section. He had

a handwritten list in one hand and clutched the handle of a rolling flatbed cart with the other. She skipped the small talk and launched into the reason she'd tracked her cousin down. "Ethan, you can't walk away from Rain Dancer."

"I can't help the horse." Ethan dropped two bags of alfalfa pellets on the cart.

"You won't help," she countered. "But you and I both know it's not going to let you rest."

"What isn't?"

"The what-if," she said. "You're always going to wonder about Rain Dancer. Always wonder if you could have helped. If you could have made a difference."

"Is that so." He checked his list, then the items on his cart.

"Yes." She stood in front of the stack of alfalfa feed bags and forced him to look at her. "I'm always going to ask *what if?* over my mom. What if I'd gone to her doctor's appointments? Read her blood work. Lived closer. Would I have seen the warning signs?" Could she have saved her mom?

"I'm sorry about your mother." Sympathy soothed the edge from his voice.

"I'm sorry about your mother's horse." She might not have bonded with a pet, but she understood loss. Understood the sorrow that stuck inside like knotted stitches, catching and pulling when least expected. "But you have another chance."

A second chance. What she wouldn't give to have one with her mom. She pressed her hand against her stomach, pushing back that familiar tangle of grief.

"And if I fail again?" He shook his head as if discarding her suggestion. "Zach's horse is his family. His career."

"Everyone else has walked away." Georgie would be walking away soon, too. That ache in her chest pinched into her ribs. She had to give Zach something. He'd be completely alone. She hated that fact. "Zach has nowhere else to go."

"You're telling me that I'm his last hope." Ethan folded his list and stuffed it into his pocket.

"Hope is a powerful thing." Every patient, every family member of a sick loved one relied on hope. Hope the medicine would work. Hope the doctors found the right treatment. Hope the surgeons removed every last cancer cell. Hope the damage wouldn't be permanent. Hope that tomorrow would be brighter, better, pain free.

"It is." Ethan lifted his face to the ceiling, then leveled his serious gaze at her. "You might consider giving it to patients, too, instead of keeping it to yourself."

"I'll take that into consideration." The only

hope Georgie cared about right now was Zach's. She gripped her hands together. "So, you'll see Rain Dancer."

"I'll talk to Zach. Review the vet records."

Georgie grinned and hugged her cousin, quick and easy.

"No promises," Ethan warned. "No guarantees either."

But it was more than Zach had had yesterday. Georgie walked beside Ethan down the aisle. "Zach isn't a bad guy."

"He's more than that to you or you wouldn't be here right now." Ethan slowed again in front of the pig feed.

"What changed your mind?" she asked.

"You and my wife." Ethan smiled. A small laugh escaped. "Grace reminded me of the things we do for love and the lengths we go to to avoid love."

She wasn't avoiding love. This was just something she had to do for Zach, her friend. Georgie thanked Ethan and rushed toward the exit before her cousin could ask her what she was avoiding.

"What'd you find in the feed section?" Pops hollered. "A giant rat?"

"Georgie, you're running like your pants caught fire. Come here, child." Big E pointed to the empty rocking chair beside him and Pops.

"You best sit and tell us what Ethan has done now."

"Ethan. Nothing." Georgie inhaled, forcing her racing heart to slow, and sank into the rocker. "Ethan agreed to treat Zach's horse."

"Assess," Ethan called out from behind the checkout counter.

"Treat." Georgie studied the chessboard on the table and hid her grin. "We all know Ethan is going to treat Rain Dancer. He just doesn't want to admit it yet."

"Lot of that going around these days," Big E said.

"No one will admit Georgie is the one who caused this." Pops tapped his forehead, near a large square bandage, and grimaced at her. "Can't wear my favorite hat now. Always win when I wear that hat, too."

Georgie picked up Pops's white knight and placed it in attacking range of Big E's queen. "Family looks out for family."

Pops eyed the board and released a smile. He dipped his chin at Georgie. "This doesn't make up for my oversized bandage, but it's a start."

Georgie relaxed into the rocker. Helping Pops had been the right thing to do and they both knew it. Zach had told her he was doing the right thing, too. How could walking away ever be right? She rubbed her chest. She'd be walking away soon enough herself. "I have it on good authority that family comes first."

Both Pops and Big E leaned back in their chairs and regarded her.

Big E tilted his head toward the game board, encouraging her to take his turn. "Then, as family, we're allowed to look out for you in the same manner."

Her grandfather's looking out surely included matchmaking. He'd helped complete her sister's online dating profile and spent weeks in an RV with her dad, who'd taken on the matchmaker mantle. Georgie moved Big E's queen to safety and blurted, "I just helped Zach with his horse. That doesn't mean we have a future together."

"I only put you and Zach together on an airplane." Big E removed his hat and hung it on the back of his chair, as if settling into the conversation. "The rest was and is up to you two."

"Really?" She let her disbelief stretch through her tone.

"I don't have none of those Cupid's arrows." Big E patted the pockets of his plaid flannel shirt as if to prove his point. "Neither does Pops."

Still, Georgie had heard rumors about Big E's antics with his grandsons. She wouldn't put it past the wily gentleman to have Cupid on speed dial.

Pops slapped his knee. "Certainly would have come in handy with some of these young couples."

"They do seem to struggle." Weariness sank into Big E's tone.

"Too many ways to talk now." Pops tapped a silent beat on his leg.

Big E touched the corner of his eye and looked at Georgie. "Used to be when you wanted to say something, you looked a person in the eye and said it."

Zach had looked her in the eye and claimed he loved her. He'd looked slightly ill at ease and none too pleased over the admission. Butterflies hadn't flapped inside her chest. Her feet hadn't been swept off the ground.

Love was better left alone. Not shared. It was far from perfect.

"Got the words wrong plenty, too." One side of Pops's mouth ticked upward. "But eventually you got the words right."

"There's nothing wrong with technology," Georgie argued. She'd be relying on it to stay in touch with her sisters. It wouldn't be the same, but she'd already accepted that well before she met Zach and the Blackwells. She'd adjust to the distance, the same as she'd adjust to Zach not being in her life. She cleared her throat. "Technology keeps us connected over long distances."

Big E set his rocking chair in motion casually, as if he always spent his days sitting around at Brewster's. "Speaking of distance, Dr. Cummings's offices are exactly one block away from here."

Her grandfather's voice, easygoing and mild, slammed inside Georgie like a dozen of those arrows neither of the men possessed. Not Big E, too. Zach hadn't understood her need to honor her mother's memory. Would her grandfather?

Pops pointed his thumb at the front entrance. "Out the door, then turn right, and you'll run into Dr. Cummings's sign."

"You talked to Estelle and Iris." How could such lovely older ladies cause so much of a commotion? One of the pair should consider running for Falcon Creek mayor, given their ability to change the town's business landscape with only one suggestion and a piece of paper. She had to get Iris to give her the paper or ask her to tear it up.

"Didn't have to talk to Iris or Estelle." Pops set his hand on his bishop, then paused, considered the board. "Although it's always a pleasure to see them."

Georgie liked the women, too. Wanted to be more angry about their interference. But frustration filled her. She wasn't the doctor her dad wanted her to be, and now she'd suddenly let down Iris and Estelle, too.

"Folks been asking us about you all morning," Big E offered.

Georgie opened and closed her mouth. She simply wanted to honor her mother's memory the best way she knew how. Why was it that, to do that, she felt like she was letting so many people down?

Big E set his elbow on his knee and leaned toward her. "I just want to know what your mom would want you to do."

"My mom." Georgie curled her fingers around the armrests. That was simple. "She'd want me to do what made me happy." All her mom ever wanted for her girls was for them to be happy.

Georgie was happy inside a lab. But she'd been happy caring for Rachel and Eli. Challenged and energized delivering Katie's baby. Yet it was the aftermath—seeing Rachel eating again, talking magic dragons with Eli and meeting baby Holly, knowing she'd made a difference, that she'd touched their lives—that had fulfilled her in a way she couldn't quite explain. Took her beyond happy.

Honoring her mother's memory meant touching as many lives as possible. In the biggest way possible. Her research work would allow her to make that kind of impact.

Fly, Georgie. Spread your wings and never be scared to look down and see how far you've gone.

"All good mothers want their kids to be happy." Big E leaned closer and locked his gaze on hers. "I'm talking for you specifically. What would your mother advise you to do?"

"Moms know their kids the best," Pops said. "My mom warned me I'd be calling her for her skillet corn bread and brisket within a week of leaving home. Promised there was no better cooking than a home-cooked meal."

"When did you call her?" Big E rubbed his hand through his gray hair.

"Second night, I called for her recipe. Had no kitchen in my truck, mind you." Pops leaned his head back against his chair. "But I had my pride."

"Nothing to apologize for." Big E glanced at Georgie.

Pride was not sending her to London, was it? Like Ethan, she was terrified of failing a patient. But she wasn't hiding inside her lab the way Zach had accused her.

"Mom served brisket and corn bread when I returned home eight months later." Pops rubbed his stomach. "Best thing I'd ever eaten."

Alice swooped in, carrying two cups of coffee. "Dad, not the brisket story again."

"There's a lesson in every story," Pops argued.

"That your favorite food is brisket and corn bread." Alice set the cups and some napkins on a small side table.

"My mother knew I'd be miserable away from the ranching life even before I did." Pops picked up his coffee cup and sipped. "That's the lesson."

"I think Georgie has had enough lessons for one day." Alice touched Georgie's arm and smiled. "Come on with me, Georgie."

Georgie stood.

Alice wrapped her arm around Georgie's waist and squeezed the same way her mother had after Georgie had spent all night cramming for an exam. Or after Georgie had skipped a pep rally to study on a Friday night. Or after she'd stayed too late at the library and missed family dinner again. Her mom had always wrapped Georgie in her love and strength.

"I've got peppermint brownies in the back," Alice whispered. "Warm brownies cure everything from minor arguments to bad moods to heartache."

Her mom had always had chocolate chip cookies at the ready and a strong shoulder like

Alice Gardner's. Georgie leaned into Alice, grateful for the woman's support and the moment to remember her mom.

Never forget to come home, Georgie. Home is what gives you the courage to fly.

CHAPTER TWENTY-THREE

ZACH CLOSED HIS hotel-room door and headed to the lobby of the Falcon's Nest Hotel. He hadn't slept more than an hour, and even that had been fragmented into ten-minute naps. He could have stayed in his car, but the below-zero windchill and heavy snowfall had forced him into the hotel for the night.

Georgie's accusations had forced him awake. *Would Cody be proud or disappointed in me? Am I too afraid to belong someplace? Will I ever have the courage to stop running?*

He'd punched the pillows. Stuffed them over his face. Turned on the TV. Opened the curtains to the pitch-black skies. All to block Georgie's voice. All to avoid everything he hadn't wanted to face.

After midnight, his grief had rolled into the room like a boulder. Inescapable and inevitable.

For the first time since he'd buried his brother, he acknowledged his grief rather than turning away. Rather than running. He mourned the loss of his brother taken too soon. His horse's declining health. And his childhood—the one his mother's addictions had stolen from his brother and him.

He'd watched the sun rise and accepted that he'd always be raw inside from his brother's passing. Some wounds never quite healed. But that wasn't a reason not to laugh or remember Cody and the good moments. That wasn't a reason not to live.

He supposed he had Georgie to thank for his new perspective. Would she be pleased or challenge him to do even more? He shook his head, vowing to stop thinking about her once he left Falcon Creek.

He stepped up to the reception desk of the Falcon's Nest Hotel and handed the manager his key. The manager gave him a printed room receipt and a message from Brewster's to stop in before he left town. Assuming Frank had received the special vitamin blend Zach had ordered for Rain Dancer, he headed to the supply store. One stop and he'd be on the road, free of Falcon Creek.

If only he felt like cheering and speeding out of town. Rather, he welcomed the delay as if content to linger.

The store was surprisingly empty; even Pops wasn't in his usual rocking chair. Although, it was Christmas Eve and families were most likely home preparing for Santa's arrival and family gatherings.

Zach stepped up to the checkout counter and rang the bell labeled Press for Service.

Ethan walked through the warehouse door, stepped behind the counter and pushed a piece of paper toward him, his expression neutral. When he spoke, his tone was detached. "Just need your signature on this."

Zach took his cue from Ethan and a pen from the holder. Nothing more needed to be said. He glanced at the paper. Confusion crowded his words. "This is a medical release waiver."

Ethan tapped his finger against the paper. His voice mild. "I can't review Rain Dancer's medical records without your consent and your signature."

Apparently, there was much more to discuss. Hope chased through Zach, kicking up his heartbeat. He dropped the pen and eyed Ethan. "I don't understand."

"Welcome to my practice." Ethan held out his hand. His gaze thoughtful. "You should know this comes with conditions."

Ethan Blackwell wanted to treat Rain Dancer. He hadn't lost yet. Zach set his hand in Ethan's. "I'll accept the terms."

"I haven't explained them." Ethan grinned. Nothing could be worse than walking away from Georgie last night. Zach dared Ethan to try. "What are the conditions?"

"I can't guarantee we change Rain Dancer's fate." Ethan ran his hand over his mouth. "Extend his life, perhaps."

"I don't want him to suffer." Zach had watched his brother suffer for too long.

"I agree." Ethan nodded. "We'll discuss that when the time comes."

Zach exhaled.

Ethan smiled. "Now for the conditions. You train both my colt, Storm Chaser, and my filly, Butterfly Blue, for the rodeo."

Zach flattened his hands on the counter and stared at Ethan. "You're serious."

"Very." Ethan waved to an assortment of family photos filling the wall behind the checkout counter. "I have nieces, nephews and a son who will want to ride one day. If Rosie wants to barrel race, she'll need the best. If Eli wants to be a calf roper, he'll need the best, too."

"You think I can deliver the best," Zach said.

"Absolutely." Ethan watched him. "I spoke to Wade McKee this morning. He told me you trained Rain Dancer."

"With my brother." Zach's voice caught. That wound inside him pulsed.

"Then consider this a legacy you're building for your brother, Butterscotch and Rain

Dancer," Ethan said. "A gift for the next generation."

Would Cody be proud or disappointed? Finally, Zach had an answer. The grief inside him settled. "I'd be honored." More than he could put into words.

"Then it's settled, except for that signature." Ethan nudged the paper closer to Zach.

Zach picked up the pen and signed the medical waiver. "What changed your mind?"

"There are women in my life and yours that like to set us straight when we are wrong." Ethan picked up the paper and slid it into a folder.

"I need to thank them." Zach wasn't sure he could ever thank them enough.

"And love them." Ethan locked his gaze on Zach.

Love. Zach rubbed the back of his neck. Nothing calmed the stab in his chest.

Big E held the break-room door open for Pops to walk through. Pops shuffled over to the counter, a coffee cup in one hand, a plate of brownies in the other.

"Trust me. It gets easier when you stop trying to dodge the truth." Ethan's tone was full of sympathy.

"Georgie doesn't want my kind of love." Zach returned the pen to its holder and avoided looking at the men. "Her words. Not mine."

"She wouldn't have been in here fighting for Rain Dancer if she didn't want your love," Ethan argued.

"She just doesn't know what she wants." Pops set the plate of brownies in front of Zach. "Alice claims chocolate cures anything. I claim it just tastes good."

"You have to show Georgie." Big E picked up a brownie and waved it at Zach.

Zach wiped his palms over his face. "How am I supposed to do that?"

"A grand gesture," Big E announced.

Was that a ring? A ticket to London? Her favorite candy? "What if it isn't grand enough?"

"It's not a grand gesture you need." Ethan bit into a brownie and chewed. "You have to show her what your love means."

"That is exactly what a grand gesture is." Big E frowned at Ethan and tugged the brownie plate away from his grandson.

Pops's head bobbed up and down. "Big E is right. Gotta have one of those."

"Gotta have what?" Grace nudged open the warehouse door. Alice followed her into the store.

Both women carried boxes marked Flannel Sheet Sets and stared the men down, as if considering dropping the boxes and stealing the brownies.

"A grand gesture." Big E finished his brownie and wiped his hands together as if there was nothing left to discuss.

Grace and Alice deposited their boxes on the floor. Then they each crossed their arms over their chests.

"Every great love story has one." Pops slid the brownie plate away from the women as if he didn't trust them not to take it.

"Whose love story are we discussing?" Alice asked.

The men all pointed at Zach.

Alice raised an eyebrow at that. "What have they told you?"

"Don't listen to any of it." Grace shook her head. "None of it."

"Nothing wrong with a grand gesture." Big E tapped the cowboy hat on his head as if punctuating his claim.

Pops touched his own head and the knit hat, then frowned. "Nothing at all."

"For goodness' sake." Alice huffed. "Zach, do you love her?"

Zach rocked back on his boot heels and locked his knees. For the second time that day, he stopped running. Stopped avoiding and accepted the truth. He loved Georgiana Harrison. "Yes, ma'am. I do love her." With everything he had.

"Then that's all you have to tell her." Alice's voice softened and soothed.

"He already did." Big E scratched his chin and shook his head. "Georgie told him to keep his love."

"Then show her," Grace urged.

"Grand gesture," Pops muttered and nudged his elbow into Zach's side.

"He already showed her," Ethan argued. The Blackwell twin had suddenly turned into Zach's champion. "Zach took the blame last night for everything. For all of it. Only a man in love would do that."

"I told her I love her and wouldn't stop her from going to London." Zach pressed his teeth together, stopping himself from quoting the line about setting something free if you love it.

The women's faces had become more closed off. Even more skeptical.

"But did you support her?" Alice asked. Her casual tone hit its mark with more force than a well-aimed, hard-packed snowball.

Zach folded his arms over his chest as if blocking her next shot. "It's the wrong decision."

Ethan's chin dipped. He gave a small head shake.

"But it is wrong." Georgie should have been caring for patients. Calming their nerves and offering sensible solutions. He'd watched her. Been awed by her. She could touch patients' lives and their families' lives in so many ways. The same as she'd changed him. "Pops. Big E. You guys agree with me, don't you?"

"It's not about right or wrong," Grace said.

"It's about understanding and compromise," Alice said. "Finding what works for *we*, not just yourself."

Zach knew he didn't want to work without Georgie. He wanted a life with Georgie. A messy, complicated, wonderful life spent beside the woman he loved. He wanted roots and family. He wanted to become a husband and father his brother would've been proud of. "She wanted me to fight."

"She wanted you to fight for what you could be together," Alice corrected.

"I got it." A lightness lifted his shoulders as if a weight had been removed. Or perhaps that boulder from last night. He hadn't asked Georgie to choose simply because he hadn't wanted to choose either. Such a scared fool he was. Georgie had been right. He wasn't scared now. Far from it. "Georgie and I make a really good team."

"Don't tell us," Big E shouted. "Get out of here and tell my granddaughter."

"Yes, sir." Zach pulled out his car keys. "I need to head to Bozeman first."

"Bozeman." Ethan gaped at him.

"That's the wrong way, son," Pops said.

"I'm finally headed in the right direction." Zach shook their hands. "Thanks to all of you."

"I just put the two of you together on a plane." Big E held on to Zach's hand and gripped his shoulder with his other. "You two messed up the love part all on your own."

"That's what I'm going to fix," Zach promised.

"Make it a quick trip." Big E held on to Zach's hand and his gaze. "I want my whole family together on Christmas. You understand?"

Family. One that included him. Now he wanted his own family with Georgie. London. North Carolina. Montana. The where didn't matter. Only who he was with mattered. "Yes, sir."

Big E smiled and released him.

Zach rushed toward the front entrance. For the first time, envisioning a future he wanted to take part in.

Pops asked, "What's in Bozeman, anyway?"

"My grand gesture."

CHAPTER TWENTY-FOUR

"THAT'S THE LAST PIN." Dorothy stepped back and wiped her hand over her brow. "Peyton, you can change and bring your dress to me in my bedroom."

"Grandma Dot, what can we do?" Lily unzipped the back of Peyton's bridesmaid's gown. "You've helped us so much."

"You can sit and take some time together as sisters." Dorothy picked up her sewing kit and touched Lily's arm, stopping her argument. "There won't be much time in the coming days. Sit and be together. Take this time for yourselves."

Lily hugged Dorothy and glanced around the family room. "Anyone want a glass of wine?"

Each Harrison sister raised her hand. Georgie stepped beside Peyton. "I'll help Peyton out of her dress. I know how to do it to avoid the pins."

"We'll get the wine and snacks," Lily said. Amanda and Fee followed Lily into the kitchen.

Georgie helped Peyton, gave the gown to Dorothy and escaped upstairs to find the jewelry box. Zach's flannel shirt lay on her pillow where she'd left it. She hadn't worn it, only rested her head on the soft fabric last night, wanting to feel closer to him.

She picked up the jewelry box and headed downstairs before her sisters came looking for her. One of them would surely notice Zach's shirt and have questions. Questions she didn't want to answer.

Amanda carried wineglasses into the family room. Fee placed a tray of fruit, cheese and nuts on the sofa table. Peyton returned, dressed in warm winter clothes, and picked up the wine bottle from the kitchen counter.

Lily added poinsettia napkins to the table. "We have red velvet cupcakes from Maple Bear Bakery for dessert, if you need something sweet."

Georgie set the jewelry box on a side table out of view and stepped in front of Dorothy's Christmas tree. "Before we have wine and get swept up in a cupcake sugar rush, I wanted to apologize."

Lily sat on the couch, Fee beside her. Peyton stopped filling wineglasses. Amanda leaned against the side of the couch.

Georgie inhaled and took Dorothy's and Zach's advice. She spoke from her heart. "I'm sorry I lied about Zach being my boyfriend. I hate that I disappointed you guys."

Peyton pressed a wineglass into Georgie's hand. "Apology accepted."

"There's more." Georgie touched her forehead. Her voice cracked. "I lost my suitcase and Mom's charm bracelet was inside. The bracelet I was supposed to give Lily for her something old."

"The airline lost your suitcase. Not you." Amanda walked over and touched Georgie's arm. "It's not your fault."

"You guys have to be mad at me." Georgie sipped her wine and set the glass on the table. "How can you not be mad? It's the something old."

"You will get your suitcase back," Fee promised.

"And if I don't?" Georgie paced across the carpet. "Then I lost Mom's bracelet."

"I never really liked that charm bracelet anyway." Lily picked up her stemless wineglass and took a large sip. "What? It has, like, fifty charms on it and it would've only gotten in the way."

Peyton laughed first. Amanda and Fee followed. Lily grinned at Georgie, then released her own bubbly laughter. Georgie joined, although her own joy dimmed faster than her sisters'. She reached for her wineglass and continued, "I'm still sorry about the bracelet. I'm really sorry I failed Mom."

The sisters sobered. Fee gaped at her.

Amanda studied her. "You're serious?"

"I wasn't there," Georgie said. "I should've been there. Maybe I could've done something." Saved their mother. Saved her sisters from the pain.

"None of us were there." Peyton closed the distance between them. "We don't blame you."

Amanda, Fee and Lily closed the circle around her.

Fee took her hand. "There's nothing to forgive, Georgie."

Lily brushed Georgie's hair over her shoulder like their mother used to do. Lily looked her in the eyes. "There is someone who needs forgiveness, and it's you. Georgie, you need to forgive yourself."

Georgie squeezed Fee's fingers. Opened and closed her mouth. Her voice lacked strength. "I wasn't there."

"And if you had been, you would've been asleep or at work," Fee said.

"I'm always at work," Georgie whispered.

"That's a conversation for later." Amanda slipped her arm around Georgie's waist. "Right now, it's about letting go."

Peyton wrapped one arm around Lily, the other around Fee. The sisters linked arms until their circle was unbroken. Peyton said, "We lost Mom. Our love for each other—that's how we remember her and her love for us."

"It's unbreakable," Fee said.

"Unshakable," Amanda added, repeating the words their mother had often recited.

"Unstoppable." Lily looked at Georgie.

Georgie's gaze slid around the circle. In the safety of her sisters' arms, she let go and opened herself to what had always been right in front of her. Her sisters' love and support. *Girls, remember you are family. That means your love for each other is unbreakable, unshakable, unstoppable and...* "Always unconditional."

The sisters held on. One minute or ten. It didn't matter to Georgie.

Amanda wiped her cheek. "Okay. Lily is getting married tomorrow and we can't have puffy, red eyes for the pictures."

Tissues handed out, the sisters refilled their wineglasses and settled around the Christmas tree. As kids, they'd sit around their Christmas tree and make up adventure stories about their favorite ornaments.

Fee switched on the tree lights and picked up a present farthest from the branches. "Georgie, this one is for you. It's from Zach."

Georgie lowered her wineglass, willed her hand to stop shaking. "He left me a present?"

"You should open it." Lily touched the colorful ribbon attached to the top.

The very same ribbon she'd attached to his ugly sweater. That shouldn't be making her smile. "I'll open it tomorrow."

Peyton stacked cheese onto a cracker. "It's Christmas Eve. Close enough. Open it."

Georgie handed her glass to Fee and accepted the gift. She'd been telling her sisters she was fine that Zach had left. More than fine—it had all been fake anyway. He'd probably gifted her his ugly sweater back. She hadn't seen it in the bedroom and doubted he'd have packed it. He hadn't seemed inclined to want any memories of his time at the Blackwell ranch with her.

The ribbon curled around her fingers. All she seemed to have were memories. Ones that kept replaying, as if she'd set them on repeat. Georgie shook herself. "Let's see what it is."

Wrapping paper torn, she lifted the lid off a box and gasped at the wind chime nestled inside the tissue paper. A chill skimmed over her. Her fingers trembled.

She opened the note inside. *This won't break on your flight to London.*

But her heart would. Her heart broke now.

That chill sank deep, as if to shatter her completely.

Fiona lifted the wind chime from the box.

Lily touched the cylinders, tapping them together. "It's beautiful. I've never seen anything quite like it."

Georgie had never met anyone quite like Zach.

"Is that handmade?" Amanda leaned closer, touched the curved wooden top.

Georgie nodded and lost her voice in a full body shiver.

"I didn't know you liked wind chimes so much." Amanda's soft voice sounded confused.

"I've never had any before." Tears filled Georgie's eyes. Impossible to blink away. "I didn't know what it would mean."

"Look. He carved your initials with a heart around them on here." Fee turned over one of the wooden pipes, pointing to the heart. "That's sweet."

And devastating. So very devastating. Zach had spent time hand-carving a wind chime for her. She'd spent time tossing his love back in his face. Convincing herself he was only a friend. No one worth crying over. More tears pooled, blurring her vision. What had she done? "I don't think I want to go to London."

"London," Amanda said. "You're going to London?"

"When?" Peyton looked around the room, as if trying to determine which Harrison sister knew and hadn't told her.

"What do you want, Georgie?" Lily pressed several tissues into Georgie's hand.

"Zach." Her misery released her tears, spilling them onto her cheeks, dampening her sweater and her voice. "I want Zach."

"We can call him," Peyton suggested.

"It's too soon." Georgie flattened the curly ribbon in her fist.

"It's the afternoon." Amanda searched in Georgie's purse for her phone. "He's awake, I'm sure. It's the working ranch way of life. No one sleeps in here, and no one takes naps ever."

Zach had invited her to nap beside him. She'd fled from the room. Now she just wanted him next to her. Georgie dropped her face into her hands. What was she thinking? "It's too soon to be in love."

The movement around her stopped. Georgie peered at her sisters—each one seemingly frozen in place. Amanda with Georgie's purse. Peyton with her hand poised over the grapes. Lily's hand stalled on Georgie's shoulder.

"Did you say 'in love'?" Fee scooted into Georgie's other side.

"Yes." Lily squeezed Georgie's shoulder again. "She did. Quite clearly, too."

Nothing was clear. Georgie traced her finger over the heart engraving on the wind chime. Who got upset over a wind chime? "I'm crying. I hurt all over. It cannot be love. It's probably the flu."

Peyton and Amanda knelt on the rug across from her.

Amanda set her hand on Georgie's knee. "Do you feel like you're drowning without water? Like your lungs have been misplaced and you need to keep on gulping air?"

Georgie nodded. More tears dripped free.

"Are your hands and feet cold while the rest of you is numb?" Fee passed her the tissue box.

"Do you feel like a part of you is missing?" Lily asked. "A part you can't live without?"

She felt all that and so much more. Georgie rested her head on Lily's shoulder. "Make it stop."

"We can't." Peyton raised her wineglass and toasted Georgie. "You're in love. Welcome to the dark side."

"Peyton," Fee scolded.

"What?" Peyton swirled her wine around in her glass. "Georgie doesn't want us to sugarcoat it. Love isn't rainbows and sunshine all the time."

"But sometimes it is." A wistful smile spread over Fee's face, as if she was skipping through a field of wildflowers.

"It's also complicated," Peyton countered.

"Challenging," Amanda added.

"Painful." Peyton tapped her glass against Amanda's.

"Frustrating." Amanda toasted Peyton back.

"That's enough, you guys." Lily's voice dipped into a scold. "We get it."

"Then why fall?" Georgie cradled the tissue box and yanked several out. Her sisters hadn't quite sold her on the virtues of love.

"Because despite all that, it's the best feeling in the world." Peyton dropped back onto the thick carpet, as if she intended to make snow angels and sing love's praises.

"And love is the most empowering feeling." Lily's voice lifted into lyrical.

"The most amazing feeling." Amanda sighed.

"When do I get to the best parts?" Georgie asked.

Peyton sat up, took Georgie's hands and looked her in the eyes. "When you finally accept it. When you finally embrace it and let love embrace you."

Georgie stared at their joined hands. Silenced her logic. Quieted her reason. And focused on her heart. More tears leaked down her cheeks.

A laugh swelled inside her. She'd have thought it impossible to feel joy and pain together. She had thought love was impossible. Until Zach...

"I think I'm in love."

Peyton squeezed her hands. "You can't think it."

"You have to know." Amanda set her palm on her chest. "In here."

"I'm in love!" Georgie shouted and released her laughter. Her sisters cheered.

"Now we find Zach." Fiona clapped. "So you can tell him."

"Wait." Georgie touched Fee's arm, stopping her from standing. "Can we just be here together a little while longer? Just us, like we haven't been in way too long."

The Harrison sisters wrapped their arms around each other. Laughed and cried over time lost. Their mom. Shared memories. Shared even more secrets and future dreams. Discovered peace and joy in what they'd gained. Their bond stronger than it'd ever been.

Their afternoon together ended only long enough for the sisters to change for Christmas Eve dinner. Georgie slipped on a sweater dress she'd borrowed from Lily. The sleeves were too long, the length closer to her ankles than her knees. Georgie didn't care. She beamed from the inside out and wanted to share her joy with everyone around her. Her sisters hadn't been wrong.

And for the first time ever, Georgie chose love.

CHAPTER TWENTY-FIVE

"I GOT THE address from Grandpa E." Georgie rushed inside the bridal room attached to the bridal barn. Her steps were small due to her fitted bridesmaid dress. Her excitement leaped out of her in cartwheels. "And Grandpa E told me I can use his motor home."

"Grandpa E." Peyton opened a satin pouch.

"Big E, you mean." Amanda attached Lily's wedding veil and straightened the tulle.

"Yes, Big E." Georgie bounced in her heeled boots. "But we agreed on Grandpa E."

And Grandpa E and she had agreed she'd wait until after Christmas Day to head to Colorado to find Zach. They'd also agreed she'd reconsider speaking with Dr. Cummings. She'd warned both Grandpa E and her dad that she wasn't making any decisions without Zach.

"Grandpa E, I like," Lily said. "Driving that motor home to Colorado… Not a good idea."

"I don't think I like that either." Fee bent down and helped Lily into her bridal boots. "Have you been inside that thing?"

"It'll be an adventure." Georgie slipped on the teardrop emerald earrings her mother had given Georgie after she'd been accepted into medical school. The sisters had agreed to wear their favorite pairs of earrings from their mom to complete their bridesmaids' attire.

"You don't like adventures." Lily watched her in the full-length mirror. "How many times did you lecture me about my adventures and possible injuries?"

"That was different." Georgie touched the earring and smiled, liking that their mom was woven through the entire day in small meaningful details. "I'll have a map and a plan."

And an entire family behind her. She'd wanted so badly to move away from her family and yet she'd been discovering she was at her most invincible surrounded by them.

"I had all of that on our adventure excursions at my old business, and while we were growing up, too," Lily reminded her. "And you still lectured me."

"It's going to be fine," Georgie said. More than fine. She had a foolproof strategy now. She was in love and love conquered all. "Now, you're getting married. Enough about me. I have something for you."

Her sisters crowded around the table where Georgie had set the jewelry box.

Lily reached out her hand. "Is that for me?"

"I was supposed to give it to you yesterday, but I fell in love and got distracted." Georgie opened the frosted glass door. "I found it in the Once Was Barn. Zach and I figured it belonged to one of Grandpa E's sisters."

Fee opened and closed a drawer. "It's stunning."

"Zach restored it." Pride expanded Georgie's smile.

"We know all about his talents," Amanda teased. "You wouldn't stop telling us last night at dinner."

"I want you to like him as much as I do."

Her sisters let out a collective "We know."

Georgie laughed and waved her hand. "Back to Lily. There's more. I have Lily's something old."

"Your suitcase actually arrived on Christmas Day?" Doubt rolled through Peyton's voice.

"No, but this is so much better." Georgie opened the bottom drawer of the jewelry box and lifted out a gold locket on a gold chain. Delight colored her words. "This belonged to Mom."

Lily gasped and reached out to cradle the locket against her palm. "Where did you get it?"

"Thomas." Her second father had given Georgie the locket after dinner the previous night.

They'd sat together near the massive fireplace in the dining hall and talked while the young cousins opened gifts from each other. Her sisters had floated in and out of their conversation, easily and naturally, as if Thomas had always been in their lives. Acceptance wasn't immediate. There were more discussions, deeper and more emotional, to come, but the Harrison sisters were on their way to discovering the power of having two fathers in their lives who'd both loved their mother.

Georgie unclasped the hook. Fee and Peyton adjusted Lily's veil so Georgie could put the necklace on her. "Mom gave it to Thomas on his first overseas tour. He has kept it with him ever since."

"He wanted me to wear it?" Lily stepped up to the mirror.

Georgie peered over her shoulder and smiled. "Thomas wants you to have it."

"It's like Mom is walking down the aisle with me now." Lily pressed her hand over the locket. "It's perfect."

"So are you." Georgie handed her sister her cascading bouquet of red roses, pine and eucalyptus greenery, and baby's breath. "And it's a perfect day to get married. Ready?"

THE MINISTER HELD his hands over Lily and Conner's bowed heads and recited a quiet prayer.

Georgie swept her gaze over the wedding barn, taking advantage of her optimal bridesmaid position at the side of the wedding arch.

Glass globe vases hung from the ceiling. An LED candle inside each one illuminated the wedding barn in a soft glow. Glittery silver and white tulle had been draped from one log beam to the next. Large mistletoe bouquets had been put up around the space, inviting guests to share a kiss. White covers and silver sashes had been placed over the guests' chairs. Candles and roses floated in shimmery water in tall cylinder vases on the tables. Holly-berry garland extended the length of the aisle. No detail, from the rose and pine-cone arrangements surrounding the couple to the thick curtain of lights adorning the archway from ceiling to floor, had been forgotten.

Georgie had known the wedding would be beautiful. She hadn't expected the barn to be transformed into a perfect setting for a timeless Christmas romance.

She shifted slightly, peeking into the reception area. More floating candles and roses waited on the white-linen-covered tables. More tulle and silver sashes. And even more romance. She'd never considered the appeal of a winter wedding until now.

"Stop fidgeting." Fee tapped Georgie's elbow.

"Sorry," Georgie mumbled. "I wanted a peek."

"Planning your wedding." Fee giggled.

"Maybe." She smashed her lips together.

Fee's eyebrows lifted.

Georgie had to stop jumping ahead. The first step was driving to Colorado and finding Zach. And there were multiple steps between finding Zach and walking down an aisle to marry him. A sigh built from her toes, swept through her. The kind that made her want to catch the bride's bouquet and celebrate love.

She ran her fingertips over her baby's-breath bouquet. The eucalyptus had been given a silver shimmer. The silver-and-white winter theme was truly lovely. But a deep winter blue would add another level of drama. Or even a royal purple. And a horse-drawn sleigh. Zach would surely approve a sleigh.

Perhaps that was all they needed. A sleigh. A minister. And family. Nothing more extravagant than a couple committing their lives to each other. Another sigh curved inside her.

"He's here." Fee nudged Georgie hard.

Georgie blinked. "Who?"

"Zach," Fee murmured. "In the corner."

Georgie lifted her head. Her pulse slowed as if time stalled. Her gaze landed on Zach as if she'd always known he'd been standing in that exact spot. He wore a dark suit, no cowboy hat and a warm smile. Her cowboy looked devastatingly handsome, as if he'd just stepped out of her wedding wish.

His focus fastened on her, made her pulse kick into a race and a blush heat her from the inside out. She wanted nothing more than to get to him. To finally speak from her heart.

She rocked forward in her boots, as if ready for a race to begin. She only needed the starting bell to be sounded. Then she'd be off. She bumped into Amanda.

"Stop it," Amanda whispered. "We're getting to the 'does anyone object' part. They'll think you do."

Georgie lifted her bouquet to cover her face. "Zach is here."

Amanda's gaze lifted to the crowd. Her smile broadened. "Yes, he is."

Georgie took Amanda's hand. "How much longer?"

Peyton eyed them, disapproval in the narrowed glance she aimed their way. Amanda leaned toward Peyton and whispered. Peyton's eyes widened. Her smile shifted into radiant, her head tipped toward Grandpa E, Rudy and Thomas seated in the front row.

Her dad turned first, glancing over his shoulder, followed by her grandfather, then Thomas. Grandpa E faced forward and gave Georgie two thumbs up. Thomas nodded, his grin kind and gentle. Her dad brushed his fingers against the corner of his eye. His smile was tender, proud and steeped in the affection he'd always shown his daughters.

Fee leaned in. Her voice as wispy and delicate as the baby's-breath bouquets they each held. "I love *love*."

"I love you guys," Georgie whispered. And she loved Christmas. And she loved Zach.

Finally, the minister announced, "I now pronounce you husband and wife. You may kiss your bride."

It was past time Georgie kissed the man she loved, too. She joined the cheers and hollers for the new Mr. and Mrs. Conner Hannah. Waited her turn to leave the ceremony area. Grandma Dot and Big E followed Lily and Conner. Jon escorted Karen, Conner's mom. Her dad and her second father stepped in behind them. Finally, Tyler held his arm out for Peyton. Amanda linked her arm with Ben's.

And it was Georgie's turn. She curved her

arm around Ethan's and squeezed. "Zach is here."

Ethan laughed. "He made it back."

"Where was he?" Georgie glanced at Ethan.

He leaned toward her, as if to tell her a really good secret. "You'll have to ask him."

Georgie couldn't wait a second longer. "Just tell me."

Ethan stared straight ahead and ignored her. His grin never faded, despite her best badgering efforts. At the end of the aisle, Ethan hugged her. "You didn't really think we were going to let you drive off in Big E's motor home, did you?"

Georgie embraced her cousin. Her extended family wasn't stifling or interfering like she'd first assumed. They were generous and caring, making her even more grateful to be able to call them her family.

Ethan released her and gave a last piece of advice. "Don't leave any what-ifs on the table."

Georgie turned, wove around several guests and made her way to Zach. Tall arrangements of roses and more tulle draped from the rafters framed him. The candlelight from the hanging glass globes added a soft, inviting glow to the shadows, as if the space had been created just for Georgie and Zach. A private moment in a crowded barn.

Georgie closed the distance, until it was only herself and Zach. One leap away from each other. Her footsteps slowed. Her heartbeat chased around her chest.

"I have something for you." Zach reached into his suit jacket pockets. He lifted his hands and revealed a ceramic penguin in each palm. One penguin wore a white knit scarf and hat, the other a red knit scarf and hat.

Georgie caught her laugh in her bouquet. "You went to the antiques mall?"

"They're the last items on our scavenger hunt list." He raised the salt and pepper shakers. "Light and dark duo. We have to win."

"I thought it wasn't always about winning." Georgie took one step closer.

"This is about winning the heart of the woman I love." Zach returned the penguins to his pockets and closed the distance. Only the baby's-breath bouquet separated them. "I had to go all in for love."

Georgie set her hand on his chest, over his heart. "What does 'all in' mean?"

"After Cody passed, all I had left was my horse, my gear and the rodeo, as well as a few dreams Cody and I talked about over the years." He reached up, curved his fingers around hers and held their hands in place. "Then I met you. And I realized the real dream, the one Cody meant all along, was giving my heart to a woman like you and building our life together."

"I want that, too." Georgie wrapped her arm and the bouquet up and around his shoulder. Then stepped fully into his embrace. Right where she wanted to be. Right where she belonged. "I want to build our life together."

"I know it's complicated." His arm tightened around her waist. His words rushed together. "But I love you. And if we want it badly enough, we can work it out. If we…"

She placed her fingers over his mouth. This man—this cowboy—was hers. And she wasn't letting go. "Zach, I love you."

He inhaled and exhaled. His fingers flexed on her back. "I never knew." His words started and stopped. "There's so much inside those three words. So much inside me now. Because of you."

She leaned in. He met her halfway. Their lips connected. The moment stretched. Unhurried and captivating. Deliberate and absorbing. Giving and taking. A joining of hearts. A belief that now anything was possible.

The kiss slowed and ended. But not the connection.

Zach set his forehead against hers. "Wherever you are is where I belong."

"I understand what Pops meant now." Georgie set her hand against Zach's cheek. "Zach, you're my home."

Together, they fell into another kiss.

"You two need to stop stealing all the kisses under the mistletoe." Peyton's voice interrupted their moment.

Georgie pulled away, curved into Zach's side and faced her sister and Matteo.

Matteo pointed at the large mistletoe bouquet fastened to a beam above their heads. "Save some of the mistletoe magic for the rest of us."

"Just one more." Georgie laughed and pressed her lips against Zach's cheek.

"Okay." Peyton cleared her throat and raised her voice. "We need to take wedding pictures now. And you don't want to make the bride mad on her big day. I'll tell Lily we're late because you and Zach wouldn't leave the mistletoe alone."

"Fine." Georgie released Zach and tried to look downtrodden but failed. Her smile wouldn't weaken. "I'm going to take pictures."

Matteo shook hands with Zach and grinned. "Do you think Peyton and I could have a minute?"

"Sure thing." Zach wrapped his arm around Georgie's waist.

"Now she's going to be late," Georgie teased.

Zach guided Georgie away from her sister,

Matteo and the mistletoe. He tucked her hair behind her ear. "Save the first dance for me?"

"It was always yours. And the last dance, too."

EPILOGUE

"MERRY CHRISTMAS, RUDY." Big E tapped his etched-crystal whiskey glass against Rudy's. "We did good. Real good."

Rudy nodded and drank his cocktail. "Never would've guessed five months ago that we would end up here at the Blackwell ranch celebrating Lily's marriage."

"The heart is full." Big E gazed out over the couples crowding the dance floor for one of those fast-paced pop songs. His great-grands twirled and swayed, holding on to their parents' hands, heads thrown back, gleeful smiles aimed to the roof. So much laughter the vaulted ceiling should be raised. So much joy the wedding barn should burst.

"Susan would've loved this." Rudy swirled the whiskey in his glass. His tone was pensive.

"She's here." Big E lifted his glass and pointed. "In the hug just now between Lily and Georgie. And Peyton and Fee's joined hands as they sway across the dance floor. And look, there in Amanda's head resting on Blake's shoulder."

"Susan and I used to sit the same way on the back porch." A small laugh escaped. Rudy added, "Usually when the girls were asleep, and the house was finally quiet."

"I always wanted the peace. Wanted the silence." Big E slanted his gaze toward Rudy and chuckled. "Then the boys would fall asleep and I'd wander around the house, restless and plotting our activities for the next day."

"Do you miss it, Elias?" Rudy asked, his tone earnest. "Do you miss the days when the boys lived at home and you didn't have to share them?"

"I've got the great-grands to fill the quiet now." Big E searched until his gaze landed on Dorothy. She spoke to Thomas on the edge of the dance floor. "And the love of my life to share the nights with. Man can't ask for much more than that."

"Grandkids." Rudy finished his whiskey. "Hadn't considered them."

"I'd imagine you'll have one or more on the way soon," Big E said.

"Only Lily has gotten married." Rudy frowned.

Big E set his hand on Rudy's shoulder. "You seem to be forgetting that twins and triplets run deep in our family lines. The girls are bound to have a pair or two along the way."

"Kids will need help with twins." Rudy grinned. "Not easy raising children these days."

"You'll want to have a place in California," Big E said and shifted to look at Rudy. Such a good and honorable man. One Big E counted himself fortunate to call family. "And you'll always have a home here on the ranch."

"Thank you, Elias." Rudy tipped his head toward the dance floor. "Shall we wager if we have another wedding or a baby announcement first on the Harrison side?"

If Big E guessed right, the engagement news would be dropping between New Year's Eve and Valentine's Day. And that baby announcement... He watched Conner pull Lily in for a slow dance. That'd be coming along soon enough. "Family, Rudy, is the biggest blessing I know."

"Sure is." Rudy rose and picked up his glass. "I'm going to head over to the dance floor myself. I think your other half is coming to get you, too."

Big E laughed and watched Dorothy make her way to his side, pausing only to press a kiss on Rudy's cheek. She slipped into the chair beside him and slipped her hand into his. He squeezed her fingers. "Want to take a turn across the

dance floor? Show 'em how a couple is supposed to dance."

Dorothy chuckled. "I've requested a two-step.
We'll show them how soon enough."

"Good thing I polished my boots." Big E
straightened.

"What's wrong?" Dorothy followed his gaze.

On the edge of the dance floor, Amanda
walked over to Thomas and held out her hand.
Thomas grinned, set his hand in hers, and the
pair stepped onto the dance floor. Rudy took a
slice of cake to Karen and settled into a chair
beside Conner's mom, closer to their kids. As
for Big E's grandsons and granddaughters, they
filed onto the dance floor surrounding Lily and
Conner.

"Nothing." Big E raised Dorothy's hand and
kissed the back of her wrist. "Everything is finally right."

* * * * *